IN LOVE AND HONOR

A Novel of a Navy Nurse

IN LOVE AND HONOR

A Novel of a Navy Nurse

ANNE O'CONNELL

CUSTOM BOOKS
SAN DIEGO, CA

IN LOVE AND HONOR

Copyright © 1990 by Anne O'Connell

All rights reserved. No part of this publication, may be reproduced or transmitted in any form or by any means, electronic or mechanical, including photocopy, recording, or any information storage and retrieval system now known or to be invented, without permission in writing from the publisher, except by a reviewer who wishes to quote brief passages in connection with a review written to inclusion in a magazine, newspaper, or broadcast.

IBSN 0-9627274-1-5

published by:

CUSTOM BOOKS
PO BOX 24056
SAN DIEGO, CA 92124

Design by BEST BETS

First Printing September, 1990
Second Printing November, 1990

Printed in the USA

DISCLAIMER

With the exception of public buildings, figures and known celebrities, all characters in this novel are fictional. Any resemblance to people living or dead is purely coincidental.

ACKNOWLEDGEMENT

Each Tuesday morning for three years, a group gathered in my living room, where we shared our love of creative writing. Week by week, this story grew among these wonderful people.

I would like to thank the regulars, Vicky Ciccone, Carol Hemingway, Jean Jones, Martha Kelley, Vaughan Lyons, Kay Sterling, and the others, Bev Clay-McNamara and Fran Geis, who dropped in now and then. It was not only our words that we shared, it was also our hearts.

I also wish to thank Karen Kenyon, my first writing instructor who fired up in me the love and beauty of putting words on paper, one after another.

DEDICATION

This novel is dedicated to the nurses, doctors, corpsmen, chaplains and, of course, the patients, who were at the Yokosuka Naval Hospital during the Vietnam war. They all made me a better nurse and twenty-five years later, have helped me to become a writer.

Even in our sleep, pain, which cannot forget, falls drop by drop upon the heart until in our despair, against our will, comes the awful grace of God.

AESCHYLUS

Any man who may be asked what he did to make his life worthwhile can respond with a good deal of pride and satisfaction, "I served in the United States Navy."

JOHN F. KENNEDY
UNITED STATES NAVAL ACADEMY 1963

TABLE OF CONTENTS

BOOK ONE   CAROLINE   PAGE 1

BOOK TWO   JOHN   PAGE 160

BOOK THREE   SUSAN   PAGE 260

PROLOGUE

Washington, DC
August, 1988

    Susan strolled slowly down the long black polished granite wall drifting in and out between the reflection of her image and thousands of names etched into the wall before her. Her eyes searched and searched but within her was a void, the same emptiness she had lived with for years. Fighting back tears, she looked up at Doug, her husband, shaking her head back and forth.
    "I'm so disappointed, darling, I felt that if I could just come and stand here, his name would jump out at me and I would feel something inside that would let me know."
    "I'm sorry, honey, I know this is a big letdown for you. Why don't we take a break from all these names and walk over to the Lincoln Memorial. The exercise will do us good."
    Taking her hand, he led her across the road. They passed the three fighting men and he felt as if their eyes held the secret that his wife so desperately sought. Must be the heat.
    "Susan, I just had a thought. Do you think it is possible that instead of knowing which name up there is your father's, you could think of yourself as the daughter of all of them and carry each one away in your heart?"
    Susan would think about it. Right now her heart was pounding just a few inches above the infant in her womb, the infant whose grandfather's name was enshrined somewhere up on that wall.

BOOK ONE

CAROLINE

1

Yokosuka, Japan
February, 1967

"Can I give you a hand, Lieutenant?", asked the tall, handsome marine Captain.

Looking up, Carrie glanced at a man with a bandage on his neck, dark circles under his steel blue eyes, dressed in jungle fatigues. His soft smile sent a warm feeling through her at this ungodly hour of night duty at four a.m.

Now, five months later, sitting in the first class compartment of the rapidly moving train, Carrie knew she would never forget that face nor the man she met that busy night in the hospital.

This is the first time I've ever been to Tokyo alone she thought. At seven o'clock on this cold rainy Saturday morning in February, the Yokosuka train station had practically been empty and though that's exactly as she had hoped it would be, it only added to her sense of desperation and loneliness. For, Caroline Craig, the tall, pretty, blond Navy nurse, was, on this chilly morning, on her way to a Japanese hospital in Tokyo to have what she called a termination. She was so despondent and ashamed, she could not even bring herself to say the other ugly word.

Finding her way to the hospital was no problem for three months earlier, she had accompanied her friend, Annie, to Tokyo for the same procedure. Filled with shame and pangs of conscience, she had resisted when Annie, in tears, had asked her to go. Her staunch

Catholic upbringing told her that having an abortion was just about the worst sin anyone could commit and as far a Carrie was concerned, it was almost as bad to go with someone else.

"But, Carrie, you're the only one who knows, the only one I can trust." She could hear Annie's pleas echoing in her ears that morning. It had been a horrible experience she would never forget. The language barrier, the strange ways of the Japanese staff and hospital, the pain and the lonely scary night they spent in a Tokyo hotel afterwards, each with their own thoughts unable to talk and express them to each other; Annie with her broken heart and Carrie with her guilty conscience. Later on, she talked her feelings over with Tom Paige, the Catholic chaplain.

"You were being a friend, Carrie. That doesn't mean you approved of what she was doing. She was desperate and you were being kind. Don't be so hard on yourself."

Now, three months later, here she was, alone, Annie having already returned to the States on orders, her secret safe in the Orient with Carrie.

How did I ever let this happen to me, she asked herself as the train passed through the historic town of Kamakura on the way? Me, Carrie, Miss Goody Two Shoes, the one who never caused any problems, always did the right thing. She never missed Mass, always was on time and was pretty much the classic picture of the Catholic school girl of the 50's, mixed with a heavy dose of John F. Kennedy "ask not" patriotism of the early 1960's.

She looked down and touched the front of her dress and tears came to her eyes. Oh baby, please forgive me but I have to do it, there's just no other way for us, not with the family we come from. What could I do with you?

Her nearly two years as a Navy nurse were better than she ever dreamed they would be when she accepted her commission. Bored to death with her job in the small community hospital back home in New England, she had volunteered to go to Vietnam. There was something in her that craved adventure and she had always been a junkie for the romance of war, first getting hooked by watching old World War II movies. Instead, she was ordered here to Japan. The hospital received casualties from Vietnam and even though the work was grinding, she found caring for the brutally injured marines challenging and rewarding. She loved the friends she made, the social life was great, and then there had come along Pete, dear sweet Pete.

A month ago, she was both elated and surprised when she finally received orders to Vietnam. The paper work was complete and she was all set to leave next week, but first she had to get through today.

She didn't tell a soul. She felt so ashamed, guilty and confused. The pregnancy meant that she would be discharged from the Navy. I just can't go home and return to that old life, she reasoned, besides my family will never accept this. Going against everything she believed in she decided to end the pregnancy and go to Vietnam. She didn't pretend to think it was right, only a choice that she felt forced to make.

Now, as the train neared the end of the ride to Tokyo, she was awashed in fear and guilt. What if something went wrong during the procedure? No one even knows I'm here. The enormity of her impending sin was so onerous, she didn't feel that she even had the right to pray. She tried to say a prayer but felt unworthy of trying to talk to God.

At last the train pulled into Shimbashi station. She reached up, retrieved her overnight case and left the train. Walking outside the station, she got into the first taxi in line and handed the driver a note with the words of Kanto Women's Hospital written in Japanese. She had stopped in the Officers' club last night and asked Reiko, the hostess to print it out for her saying she wanted to visit a friend. Resting her head against the back of the seat, her eyes again welled with tears as she thought about where she was going and why. Her thoughts again drifted back to September and the night when she first met Pete.

Yokosuka, Japan
September 8, 1966

Ward 2B, the Officers' Ward was busy. Friday was their surgery day and the night corpsman had two patients to get ready for the operating room. It was now four-thirty. They'd have to work fast to finish on time this morning.

As busy as she was, Carrie was aware of the chemistry that quickly passed between her and the handsome marine. Shortly after she'd heard the roar of the helicopter pass over the hospital, the corpsman from the Officers' Ward called over to where she was busy with an orthopedic patient to tell her that they had received three admissions.

Standing next to the marine was Dr. Jim Randall, who had come up to the ward from the emergency room with the three patients.

"What's the story?" asked Carrie.

"One has malaria, Captain Pachulis, here, has shrapnel in his neck and the third guy's pretty sick. He has multiple abdominal wounds, a high fever and everything is infected and oozing puss. I called the surgeon on call and Dr. Pellagrino is coming in and taking him to the operating room just as soon as you guys can get his fever down. The marine with malaria has a fever too, and I guess the Captain here, just hitched a free ride on the chopper to avoid the three hour bus trip down from Yakota Air Base. Can't blame you, Captain, especially at this hour."

"Yes Sir, you are absolutely right. I was telling the Lieutenant I'd be glad to help out as I'm sure I'll never get to sleep now."

After a half hour, Carrie checked Lt. Shield's temperature. It had fallen to 101, and the operating room crew arrived to take him to surgery.

Entering the nurses's station, she could see that Bishop seemed to be caught up. "Will you be ready for report, Bishop?"

"Yes Ma'am, when you called from ER, I got busy with my paper work and by the time the three patients got here, I was all set. Captain Pachulis helped me, too."

"You're a good man. Bishop, you can think on your feet."

Breakfast after night duty was always fun. As the sun came up, Carrie got her second wind and by the time she got to the officers' mess, she was giddy.

"I heard the chopper. Who got the admissions?", asked Annie as she sat down across from Carrie.

Annie Mae Bowman was as close to a stereotype of a southern belle as Carrie had ever known. Tall with strawberry blond hair, her slow speaking southern drawl was a perfect match for her quiet passive manner. She had been one of Carrie's dearest friends and often had Carrie in gales of laughter, telling her about the terrible things she had been taught about Catholics by her grandmother. Her tour of duty was nearly up and she was hoping for orders to Jacksonville, Florida so she could be back close to her family in Auburn, Alabama.

"I did," said Carrie. "They were all officers so they went to 2B. One was pretty sick, he's in the OR now and will probably go to Intensive Care after surgery. Am I glad this week of nights is over. Oh!, Annie, look what I got in the mail."

Annie opened the memo.

>From: CDR Greta Neuhiser, NC,USN
>To: LT Caroline Craig, NC,USN
>Subject: Appointment
>
>1. Please stop by my office tomorrow morning after breakfast.
>
>Respectfully,
>
>Greta Neuhiser, CDR,NC,USN

"What do you think it's all about?"

"I don't know. Killer is back in the states so it can't be too bad. The beauty shop doesn't open till nine thirty anyway. Why don't you go back to your room after breakfast and I'll come by after I see Greta." Killer was the less than flattering nickname the nurses had given CDR Catherine Mullaney, the Chief Nurse.

Looking up, Carrie greeted Jim Randall just taking the seat beside her.

"What a night," said Jim. "I treated everything from casualties from Vietnam to casualties from the barrooms. I wish if sailors and marines were going to fight, they wouldn't do it on nights I had the duty."

"Well, you can celebrate with us at the "Hail and Farewell" party tonight; you're going, aren't you?"

"Wouldn't miss it, besides, it's the farewell for Paul Gutierrez and I would never miss honoring him after the years training he's given me."

Paul Gutierrez was from the dental department. With Jim's specialty, ear, nose and throat, they often worked together on patient's complicated facial injuries.

"I'm going to miss him. You know Carrie, when I came here I would never have believed how close I would become to some of the folks, yourself included."

"I know what you mean. There's a deeper level of caring here. I think it's because we've had to face so many intense situations together and have had to rely on one another."

"Speaking of intense, something's up. I've got a memo to stop by the nursing office."

"Oh?" asked Jim.

"Those blue notes are always scary but Killer is in the States so even if it's bad news, the blow will be somewhat softened by Greta."

Rising, Carrie put her hand on Jim's shoulder. "Wish me luck. Get some sleep and I'll see you at the party tonight."

The early morning had been such a madhouse that Carrie did not have time to sift it all out until she was under the hairdryer.

Yokosuka in the morning was a explosion of color and frenetic activity. The streets were jammed with cars and taxis as thousands of Japanese hurried to work. The grinding sound of chain linked safety metal doors serving as security for the hundreds of shops added to the din.

ICU. She couldn't believe it. She felt both honored and terrified.

When she entered the nursing office after breakfast, Greta got right to the point.

"Caroline", she said, "Miss Mullaney apologizes for not asking you herself. As you know, Peggy Moore has orders to Great Lakes and will be rotating back in about a month. We would like you to think about being the new charge nurse of the Intensive Care Unit."

"I'm just overwhelmed," said Carrie, "but also honored. I'll do my best to learn all I can while Peggy is still here." She couldn't believe it. She didn't think Miss Mullaney even liked her. It wasn't anything she could put her finger on, just a cold feeling she had every time the Chief Nurse came on the ward to make rounds.

"I think when you have time to think it over, you'll feel quite good about it. Now get out of here and I'll see you tonight at the club."

The bell went off on the hairdryer bringing Carrie back to the sound of Fumiko asking her to move over to the chair in front of the mirror. As she finished combing and shaping Carrie's blond streaked hair, it looked beautiful. Carrie's thoughts went back to Captain Pachulis and she smiled. It was not unusual for the nurses to date the officer patients. Maybe he'll be at the club tonight, she thought. She knew he would have base liberty and usually the club was the first place the patients headed. She thought back over all the different guys she had dated since coming to Japan. There were so many that after awhile, the faces blended together. It sure would be nice to be in love again, she thought as the memory of the picture of his broad smile with the perfect white teeth stayed in her mind.

Annie Mae was finished also, just as Fumiko was spraying Carrie's hair.

"Ready?", she asked.

"All set", replied Carrie. "I'm beat. I can't wait to fall into bed."

"Carrie", Annie paused, "I really need to talk. Can I come to your room for just a few minutes? I promise I won't take long but this won't wait."

"Well, sure, Annie, of course."

Passing by the Marine guard at the main gate, Carrie showed her ID and drove up the short hill to the BOQ. She opened her room and invited Annie to sit on the sofa while she got out of her clothes and into her nightgown. "I can't stand these clothes on more minute. Now, Annie, what's up?"

"Carrie, do you remember at breakfast when Jim said he was going to miss Paul Gutierrez? Well, I'm afraid he's not the only one." Annie burst into tears, tears that seemed like they had been stored up for a month.

Carrie looked puzzled but continued to just listen. Annie was so pretty with her strawberry blond hair and ivory skin, now covered in tears.

"You and Paul?" asked Carrie dumbfounded. Through sobs, Annie nodded.

"Remember last May when Joanne decided to leave early and go to Bremerton to look for a house and check out schools for the kids?"

"I guess I do," said Carrie, "but I didn't pay much attention because quite a few other wives did the same thing."

"After she left for the states, Paul gave up the house and moved into the BOQ. It started so innocently. One night I couldn't get one of the speakers of my stereo components to work right. I saw him walk by my door and I hailed him and asked if he knew anything about fixing the speaker. He came in and had it connected in no time and then I fixed him a drink. Carrie, we sat up that night talking until three-thirty and when he finally left, I could feel butterflies dancing in my stomach. The next night he came by with a sheepish grin and asked if I had any speakers that needed fixing. We both laughed and I invited him in. After that one thing led to another and I've been with him almost every night since the beginning of June. I really love him and now he's leaving next week. I know that will be the end of it but that's not all. Carrie,......I'm pregnant."

"Oh Annie, no, Are you sure? I had no idea. Does anyone?"

"The only other person that even knows about Paul and me is Father Paige and even he doesn't know I'm pregnant. I'm not Catholic but he's such a great guy, I knew he would help me if he could."

She lit a cigarette.

"No one knows I'm pregnant, not even Paul. I was so distraught that I had to tell someone, that's when I went to see Tom Paige. He was great and so understanding. Instead of trying to make me feel guilty, he tried to point out how if I kept seeing Paul, I was the one who would lose and get hurt, but he told me that he was always available for listening and to come and see him anytime. I guess there are others that must have seen us at places but, you know, Joanne and I knew each other quite well, so I think people think Paul and I were just friends.

"Carrie, the real reason I came by is to tell you that on Monday, I'm going to Tokyo to have an abortion. I know from our conversations that you think that is terrible and actually, so do I, but I've thought it over and I have to do it. Would you please go with me? You're the only one I trust to take good care of me and not tell anyone."

An abortion, Oh God! Carrie looked down in her lap. Why me? Why does she have to ask me? Can't she ask one of the nurses that doesn't feel so strongly about it?

"Will you go with me Carrie? We're both off and we can stay there in a hotel till evening and then take the train back here for duty on Tuesday."

Carrie thought of trying to talk Annie out of it but she knew she made up her mind.

"Isn't there anyone else you can ask?"

"No, there's no one else I trust like you, please Carrie?"

Filled with conflict, Carrie finally agreed to go with her friend.

"Okay, I'll go, but I wish I didn't have to. How do you know where to go?"

"Last year a friend of mine who is an Army nurse at Camp Zama went with a friend and I remembered all the information. Little did I know."

"How come you haven't told Paul?"

Annie looked down.

"I guess I don't want to face what he would say. He says he loves me but I know he'll never leave Joanne. It's really all my fault."

"Oh no it isn't, it's never just one person's fault and don't you forget it. You're just too darn nice, Annie. I've always said that, you're just a doormat."

Annie started to cry.

"I'm sorry, I shouldn't be so hard on you. I guess I'm just tired of the way some nurses have been used over here." She got up, walked across the room and put her arms around her sobbing friend.

"Don't worry, you can count on me. We'll get you taken care of and no one will ever know."

"This is off the subject, but last night, you know those three admissions I got? Well, one of them was absolutely gorgeous and a real nice guy, too, a Marine Captain. I'm hoping he'll be at the club tonight. You know how sometimes you can feel a spark? It was like it was there right away between us even though we were both really busy trying to take care of the mess on 2B."

"I think I saw him in the passageway when they came in," said Annie.

"Did he have sandy hair?"

"Yeah."

"You're right, he was good looking."

"Why don't you try and get some sleep now. Are you still going tonight?"

"Sure. It'll help make the weekend pass quickly and even though you probably think it's crazy, I still want to spend every minute I can with Paul."

"I don't think you're crazy. I'm just sorry that it has to hurt so badly for you."

Carrie bid goodnight to her friend, took her phone off the hook and crawled into bed smiling at the thought that when she awakened this afternoon, she would not have to go to work. She had finally finished her week of nights.

The band was playing a medley of Johnny Mathis hits. The Hail and Farewell party was a success but was starting to break up as people went into the dining room for dinner.

"Hi, Lieutenant. Wow! You look beautiful."

Carrie's pulse quickened when she turned and saw Captain Pachulis standing off to the side by the cocktail lounge, looking at her with a wink and a broad smile.

"Thank you, Captain, I see you've changed your clothes, too."

"Yes, I picked these up at the exchange today but I have to say your transformation is quite spectacular."

Carrie blushed and suddenly found herself at a loss for words. She hoped he would be here and now that he was, she was overcome with self-consciousness.

"Can I buy you a drink, and please, call me Pete."

"Thanks Pete, I'm Caroline, Carrie. I think I've had enough at the Hail and Farewell. What I really need is something to eat."

"How about joining me for dinner? I have a reservation in just ten minutes."

"I'd love to," replied Carrie trying hard to contain her excitement. She could not believe her good fortune at running into him alone.

Looking around, Pete shook his head and said, "I just can't believe it. Seven days ago I was in the middle of a lousy, dirty jungle with gunfire all around me and tonight I'm in a ballroom surrounded by men and women having the time of their life. It just doesn't make sense."

"Where were you in Vietnam?" asked Carrie.

"Up in I Corps, outside of DaNang. I was a company commander. Had some great guys working for me and then one night on patrol, I caught the fragments from a grenade explosion in my back and neck. They removed the large piece of shrapnel from my back at the Battalion Aid Station, but the small fragment in my neck is so deep that they wanted to send me where there is both a neurosurgeon and vascular surgeon. It has to come out so by sending me here, the surgeons can thoroughly evaluate it before surgery. How long have you been here?"

"Just over a year and I love it."

Soon after they were seated at their table, the band began to play Barbra Streisand's hit song, "People". As the romantic strains filled the air, Pete looked at Carrie and offered her his hand. Carrie placed her hand in his and they both rose and walked to the dance floor.

Pete was six foot two. With his blue eyes and sandy hair cut in a close Marine crew cut, he stood straight and strong. When he took Carrie in his arms, his lead was so subtle that Carrie felt like she was floating through space.

The familiar lyrics of "People" and "Chances Are" sounded lovely in spite of the accent of the Japanese vocalist. Everyone on the dance floor looked like they were glued together. Romantic music did that to you overseas. It was other songs like, "I Left My Heart In San Francisco", and "California, Here I Come", that sent the crowd wild. They seemed to make every drop of American blood surge through the dance floor.

"I thought you looked pretty at four thirty this morning, but now I see that I didn't know what pretty was."

"Oh, thanks, Pete. It's such a relief to be off nights and thanks again for your help this morning. In typical fashion, all hell broke loose at once and you were a welcomed and needed extra pair of hands."

"My pleasure. You looked like you had everything under control though. I have a lot of respect for you nurses."

They continued to dance and Carrie felt like she was in heaven.

"How about you, do you like being a Marine Officer?"

"Yeah, I do, I like it a lot. I especially love the leadership role of being a company commander. A company commander in a war zone is probably the ideal assignment for a Marine Captain. It offers the opportunity to carry out in action all the principles and training you've been rehearsing for years. It's quite a dual role. From above you carry out the tactical instruction of the Battalion Commander while you hold a paternalistic position over your Lieutenants and troops."

"I bet you're good at it," said Carrie and she looked up at Pete with a smile. She felt his hold on her tighten a little.

"I try to be fair and treat people like I want to be treated, the old Golden Rule." The music stopped and Pete walked Carrie back to the table.

During dinner, the conversation never stopped.

"Where are you from, Pete?"

"I'm from a little town outside Syracuse, New York. How about you?"

"I'm practically a neighbor, at least from the same quadrant of the country. I'm from a little town in Southern Massachusetts."

"Whatever possessed you to join the Navy?", asked Pete.

"I wish I had a dollar for every person that had asked me that question in the last two years. Actually, I just found myself in a situation where all my good friends married early and I was in a real social rut. At first, I thought I'd try the Peace Corps and I did take their exams but than I opted for the Navy. I've never regretted it.

"What about you Pete? How did you end up in the Marine Corps?"

"By a very crooked road", said Pete. "I was the class valedictorian from our small Catholic boys high school, and I won a one year scholarship to Fairfield University, a Jesuit college in Connecticut. I did real well in school but there was no money for a second year so I decided to join the Marine Corps. That way I could go back to Fairfield on the GI Bill when I got out. After I finished boot camp, I was sent to an advanced Marines school and while I was there, they selected me to go OCS on the basis of my short but good record and the fact that I'd had one year of college. So here I am, twelve years later, a Marine Corps Captain still with only one year of college but I've promised myself that when I get back to the States this time, I'm going to start taking courses and one way or the other I'm going to get my college degree."

The band started to play again.

"How about another dance?"

"Sure," said Carrie. The music was slow and mellow. The lights were dim, and Carrie glided around the floor with Pete as if she had been dancing with him for years. There was an inner strength about him that Carrie felt she could almost touch, a goodness, a wholesomeness. She had never felt such an instant attraction for anyone. The chemistry between them was electrifying and somehow, she knew he felt it, too.

The band began to play, "The Shadow of Your Smile", and she looked up at Pete. He looked down at her, winked and said, "You have a beautiful smile." Just the words caused her to grin more and Pete squeezed her and said, "See what I mean?"

The band finally played the traditional, "Good Night Ladies". Pete took Carrie's hand and said, "Come on, I'll walk you to your quarters."

When they got to Carrie's room, she unlocked her door and then turned to Pete and said, "Thanks for walking me home, and thanks for the dinner and great dancing. I really enjoyed talking with you."

"The pleasure was mine," said Pete. There was an awkward moment and Carrie did not know what to do. Again, she felt terribly selfconscious. She cast her eyes downward and as she did, Pete put his finger under her chin, lifted her head and gave her a quick but tender kiss on the lips.

"It was a lovely night for me, Carrie," and he turned and left.

When Carrie walked to the mirror over her sink, she touched her lips and looked in to see herself looking back with a broad grin on her face. She felt drunk but she'd only had two drinks all night. There was something so different about Pete. Maybe it was his take charge attitude or just his impeccable manners. He wasn't like any of the guys she had dated the past year. Suddenly, she was overcome by her feelings. Dear Lord, she begged as she crawled into bed, please let him be a bachelor.

2

Yokosuka, Japan
September 10, 1966

On Saturday, Carrie, Annie and Paula Ferrara, another nurse, went shopping in Yokohama. They had all purchased woodblock prints and wanted to leave them with the frame man there. It was good for all of them to be together and Carrie's main concern was not to let anything slip about her plans to go with Annie to Tokyo on Monday. Not that she didn't love Paula just as much, probably a little more. They had met on the ship coming to Japan and had become instant friends. Short, dark eyed and full of spunk, Paula was everything that Carrie wasn't.

"You're so straight laced, Carrie. That's your problem."

"No, I'm not," argued Carrie. "You were taught the same rules I was."

Paula, educated in the same 50's parochial schools as Carrie, practiced a different Catholicism. She went to church when she felt like it and slept with whom she wished.

"But, you took it all to heart while I thought a lot of it was a pile of bunk."

Carrie didn't know what her problem was but she knew that all around her the rules were changing and her conscience was just standing still mired in rules drilled into it in the fourth grade from the Baltimore Catechism.

"With you, everything is black or white, right or wrong or mortal or venial. Don't you ever make any decisions for yourself?"

Carrie knew that Paula was right. Her free spirit was just what she needed to help her try and make some changes in her life, but, oh, it was so hard after living such a life of rigid rules to make the changes that she saw Paula do so effortlessly.

The three of them stopped for lunch in the Silk Hotel and when Carrie finally returned to her BOQ room at three, her phone was ringing.

"Hi, Carrie, this is Pete."

Oh, thank God, thought Carrie.

"Thanks for a wonderful time last night. I was wondering if you would like to have dinner with me again tonight."

Rats, thought Carrie.

"I'd love to Pete, but I've already accepted an invitation to dinner with the pediatrician and his wife at their home."

"My loss", said Pete. There was an awkward pause.

"How about church tomorrow? Would you like to go with me and then we can go to brunch at the club?"

"Sounds wonderful. Why don't we plan on ten-thirty mass."

"Fine. I'll come by for you at ten."

Carrie hung up the phone and cradled it to her chest. Just the sound of Pete's voice made her tingle. She knew she was falling and falling fast.

By the time Carrie finished Betsy's delicious beef stroganoff, she'd had two martinis and two glasses of wine. If I don't get to the bathroom, I'm going to burst, she thought.

Making her way down the hall to the bathroom, Carrie felt giddy and a little wobbly. As she walked into the bathroom, she saw Jim Spino and Evan Siegal talking in Betsy's den.

"I'm about to burst," she laughed, only to hear Evan respond, "You got it here, you might as well leave it here."

"Spoken like a true urologist," said Carrie laughing and holding her belly.

Carrie loved Evan. He was a big, brusk, earthy guy who looked like a garage mechanic but just a gentle as velvet with his patients. She wished she could say the same for Jim. She would never, 'til her dying day, figure out why he went into medicine because he certainly didn't seem to have much respect for people. He was a wiry little guy with kinky salt and pepper hair and was the perfect caricature of the man with "the short man's complex".

Suddenly, from the den, Carrie heard Evan say, "You've got to be kidding me, I don't believe it!"

"Yes, Sir, the lucky bastard, he's been screwing her all summer. Just goes to show you that those southern belles aren't just talk."

"How do you know?" asked Evan.

"Paul told me himself."

Carrie listened as Jim continued.

"He said she really has the hots for him but, he's just having a great old summer reliving his bachelor days. With Joanne in the states looking for a house, he has his freedom. When he gets on that plane next week, it's going to be 'Good-bye Annie'. Some guys get all the breaks. I wish my old lady would go off someplace for two months. Paul Gutierrez is as smooth as silk and apparently Annie just fell for the whole line."

"Well, I'll be damned," said Evan, "goes to show you, you just never know who's sleeping with who."

Carrie was furious. She could have sat there and wept for Annie. Not only was that sleaze of a Jim broadcasting gossip but when she remembered Annie's pain in her room yesterday morning, she seethed. I only hope that Annie never finds out. As long as it's nearly time for him to leave, she might as well live the dream 'til the end.

When she opened the bathroom door, Jim and Evan looked as white as sheets. They knew she had to have heard. Disgusted, she knew if she said anything, she'd regret it later, so she just rejoined the group in the living room. We women are so stupid, she thought. We fall for it every time no matter how many times we are warned. Just let those guys cross the international date line and their wedding rings melt away with their vows. Geographical bachelorhood was a contagious disease in the orient. The more she thought about it, the madder she became. That creep, she fumed. A geographical bachelor is one thing but a geographical bachelor with a big mouth is a slime.

The group played charades which was fun but Carrie couldn't get what she overheard in the bathroom out of her mind and when she looked over at Sally Spino, she thought, "What a jerk you're married to."

Saying her prayers before getting into bed, Carrie's thoughts were split. She thought about the conversation she'd overheard at Betsy's and then, her date with Pete for church and brunch tomorrow. She thanked God for her day, and said an extra prayer for Annie.

The ten-thirty Mass was crowded. Word got around fast. Poor Father McSweeney was a nice old pious priest, but he was slow as molasses and his boring sermons were interminably long. He usually celebrated the eight o'clock Mass at the base chapel which people avoided like the plague leaving Father Paige to say the mass at ten-thirty in the hospital.

Tom Paige was a strikingly handsome man. His square jaw was covered by a natural five o'clock shadow that only highlighted his clear blue Irish eyes. He had the build of a fullback but his personality was as gentle as an understanding grandmother. It's not that he overlooked the bad in people, he just didn't see it to begin with. Everyone on the base adored him and his Mass was always jammed.

Carrie felt radiant sitting with Pete. Just being next to him gave her a feeling of strength and joy. She smiled to herself as she thought back to a line from one of her favorite books. "Seventeenth Summer", by Maureen Daly. She read it when she was in the eighth grade and remembered when the heroine went to church with her boyfriend, she said that there was something terribly romantic about going to church with a boy.

She couldn't keep her eyes off Pete. He was attentive and reverent and sang the hymns with all his heart. The gospel was the story of the Good Samaritan and Carrie heard the message that it was the good that we did and not necessarily the little wrongs that interested God. In his sermon, Father Paige elaborated on Christ's message by pointing out that even though the staff got tired at times, it was the little and tedious acts of kindness that were precious to the patients and to the Lord.

When it came time for Communion, Pete and Carrie both walked up the aisle to receive and then returned to their seats and bowed their heads in prayer. Suddenly, Carrie could not remember the prayer she always said after Communion. Her mind and heart were both racing. She knew she was overcome with emotion. Her head down, she prayed, "Dear Lord, please help this to work."

Leaving church, there were lots of people to greet and many of them were heading toward the club for brunch.

"How was last night?" Carrie asked Paula.

"Great, we had fun. I'm meeting Yale Bradshaw at the club. Do you remember him from the last time the Kittyhawk was in, the night we met all those crazy pilots in the club?"

"How could I ever forget? I remember I got zapped on the head with a paper airplane just as we saw some drunk pilot divebomb himself on a cocktail table. They were something else, sitting there waving their arms around pretending to be flying their phantom jets through the cocktail lounge."

"Well, anyway, he's back but there was no way I could drag him to church. He teased me saying that if his family thought he was in a Catholic church, they'd cut him out of the will. Between you and me, I think he just wanted to sleep in."

Carrie introduced Paula to Pete. Remembering she hadn't told Paula about Pete she did not miss the puzzled look on her friend's face as if to say, "Where did you get this one, where on earth did he come from all of a sudden?"

"Why don't we eat together?" suggested Pete.

"Sure, thanks, I'll walk over with you if you don't mind. Yale should be there by now. He said he'd meet me in the lobby at eleven thirty."

Pete spoke up. "You know, I'd like to ask Father Paige to join us. We had a nice visit when he made rounds in the hospital yesterday to make up his Communion list for today. I liked him and I bet he'd enjoy going to brunch."

While Pete went back to the sacristy to ask Father Paige to join them, Paula poked Carrie in the ribs asking, "Okay, squirrel, where have you been hiding that one?"

Carrie giggled. "I knew you were dying to ask me. I haven't been hiding him anywhere, I just met him on Friday."

"On Friday", said Paula, "I spent all yesterday afternoon with you and you never said a word."

"I know, you're right, but he sought of crept up on me and I'm a little confused about the whole thing. I just decided to keep it to myself for a few days."

"Keep it to yourself? Lady, when you parade into Mass on Sunday with a guy, that's like flashing a neon sign around here that says, "SERIOUS SERIOUS!"

"Hi Father", said Paula, as Pete appeared with Father Paige, "glad you can join us. Thanks for the boost in the sermon. I needed that. I sometimes forget that the million little chicken details I have to do around here may be music to the Lord's ears." Father Paige gave Paula a hug and another to Carrie.

The walk over to the Officers' Club was a short one and the girls walked ahead chatting about the dinner party at the Gleasons' while Pete and Father Paige followed. The dining room in the club looked bright and fresh. Each table had a starched white table cloth and fresh flowers. Carrie was amazed that it could look so warm and welcoming after what must have been a wild Saturday there. Reiko, Carrie's favorite hostess, found them a table right away and asked if anyone wanted drinks. By now, Yale had joined them and Paula and the men ordered French seventy fives, a concoction of champaign and brandy but Carrie, still hung over from her evening at the Gleasons', begged off, settling for a club soda with lime juice.

With two carriers in port, the room filled up quickly and the noise level rose as people started table hopping.

The table slipped into the usual overseas conversation of "who do you know that I know?"

"Are you related to Gardner Bradshaw?" asked Father Paige.

"As a matter of fact I am, Sir, he's my older brother. How on earth do you know Gardner?"

"He was in my class at Princeton. I knew him quite well as we were both majoring in Business Administration."

"Wait a minute, Sir. You were at Princeton with Gardner and now you're a priest? I have to admit, I'm a bit confused."

"I fool a lot of people. I came to the priesthood by a circuitous route. I was an enlisted grunt in the Korean War and when I was discharged, I went to Princeton to study Business to prepare me to enter our family's business. In the middle of my senior year, I could no longer ignore the call to the priesthood that I had first heard in Korea but had managed to squelch. Ask your brother about me, he'll remember because he use to stay up nights trying to talk me out of it."

"More drinks?" asked Reiko. The group looked at each other and decided they'd all wait awhile.

"Anyway, I graduated from Princeton, and entered the seminary to study for the priesthood. I was ordained four years later in 1961. I wanted to be commissioned in the Chaplain Corps right away but there is a requirement that all priests serve in their home diocese for three years. You see I'm a little older than your junior chaplain."

"That's quite a story. Father," said Yale. "You're right, wait till I tell Gardner."

"What do you do Yale?"

"I'm a jet jockey on the Kittyhawk. We're on our way down to Vietnam. I hope you'll say one for all of us Father."

"You can count on it."

"What's everybody doing today?" asked Paula. There was an awkward silence and Pete said, "I was going to ask Carrie if she would show me some of the sights. How about it Caroline?"

"Sure, it's a beautiful day to go to Kamakura. We could either drive or take the train. The station in Kamakura is a stone's throw from the big Buddha. Anyone else want to go?"

"I'm beat", said Father Paige, "but thanks. I'm going to take a nap and catch up on some letter writing. Yale, could I please have your brother's address? I'd like to surprise him with a letter in the next few weeks."

"Sure Father. Maybe you'll even drop me a line. Mail is so important when we're down there on the line."

Yale took one of his calling cards out of his wallet, printed Gardner's address and his, and handed it to Father Paige.

"Carrie, I'd like to take Paula over to the Kittyhawk and show her around so I think we'll take a raincheck."

The group stood up at the same time looking around and waving to other friends in the club. Yale extended his hand to both Pete and Father Paige and thanked them for their company.

Pete and Carrie ran down the platform in the Yokosuka station just in time to jump on board the first class car to Kamakura. The first class cars had light green stripes painted on them and were worth the few extra yen that they cost. Kamakura was the fourth stop on the Yokosuka train to Tokyo so the ride was short.

"I always enjoy coming to Kamakura," said Carrie. "I enjoy the shops, the history, the solemnity of the Buddha and it's not so far away that the trip is tiring."

The main attraction of Kamakura was an immense bronze statue of "Daibutsu", or Buddha, that was over 700 years old. Eleven meters in height, it was originally enclosed in a wooden building that was swept away in a tidal wave in 1495. Kamakura was also the first seat of the Japanese military government. As they left the train station, Pete and Carrie stopped at a pedestrian crossing and waited for the light to cross the street. Pete took Carrie's hand and when he cupped her palm in his, she felt a glow radiate up her arm. They walked along the cobblestone street and she remarked about the plastic replicas of entrees that the Japanese restaurants displayed in the windows. It you wanted something to eat, you need only take the waiter to the window and show him your choice. Bowls of soup with all sorts of articles of food floating in them, replicas of shrimp tempura and tea cakes were all lined up for patrons to select.

As they approached the Buddha, they stopped by a low wall on the first plaza-like level to appreciate the vista of the Buddha from afar. There was a quiet serenity in the air and Carrie wondered if this was the Japanese equivalent of a Catholic going to the Vatican. While they were sitting there, two giggling teenage girls approached them and shyly asked, "May we have English lesson please?"

Pete looked puzzled.

"Sure", said Carrie. "Pete, that means they want you to talk with them in English so they can have some practice. They are studying English in school and they love to talk with Americans when they have the chance."

Pete thought this was great and he started asking the girls their names, their boyfriends' names and when they were getting married. The Japanese girls were beside themselves with laughter and Carrie was in awe of Pete and the instant rapport he'd created with the teenagers. They took several photos and then walked up to the great Buddha. Carrie was struck by the reverence the Japanese showed their God and was intrigued by small handclapping rituals and candle lighting. "I guess its no different than holy water and making the Sign of the Cross", she thought to herself. It was the first experience she'd had in a non-Christian faith environment but she recognized the air of adoration present in the Japanese just as it was in her own church. Nearing five o'clock, they started to walk back to the train station. The day had been magical for her, first church, then brunch and now this lovely afternoon.

When the taxi dropped them back at Carrie's quarters, they both made a mad dash for the bathroom. Japanese public facilities left much to be desired.

Back in her room was a doorway in which she had hung mahogany beads. She had fixed the room up with a shag carpet and drapes and had tossed several Japanese pillows about giving it a casual by homey atmosphere. Her greatest treasure, next to her stereo, was an old refrigerator, procured by a friend in supply, that she kept in her bedroom.

"Here, why don't you look through my record albums and put on some music while I fix us gin and tonics."

"Do you want classical or pop?" asked Pete.

"Your choice." said Carrie. In a few minutes, the room was filled with the soft sounds of Tchaikovsky's Sixth Symphony, "The Pathetique".

"One of my favorites," said Carrie. "It's supposed to be sad but I think it's haunting and beautiful." She got her cigarettes and their drinks and sat down on the sofa next to Pete. The room was starting to darken and the only noise was that of the music and the low hum of the air conditioner. They both sat quietly sipping their drinks and smoking. Carrie made small talk about the various paintings and objects in her room and Pete said how great it was just to be in someplace that resembled a real living room after barracks, bunkers, hooches and tents.

"It's quite easy to become uncivilized after awhile. This may be just a BBQ room to you, but to me, it looks like a palace."

Carrie finished her drink and cigarette at the same time. She didn't really want another one but she could feel an uneasiness building up within her.

"I think I'll light the candles," she said. As she reached for her cigarette lighter, Pete said, "Come here," and pulled her to him, his right arm around her back.

She was stretched awkwardly, so she pulled her legs up on to the sofa, kicked off her shoes and nestled her head in his chest. The room was very still. Pete leaned forward, put out his cigarette with his left hand and lifting Carrie's face kissed her gently and lovingly for a long time, his arms holding her tight to him. Carrie responded, releasing all the unspoken tension that had built up between them all day. She felt it flow from her to him and she responded by moving her body against his, lost in his embrace. They held each other tenderly, closely, kissing like two children edging their toes into the cold ocean a little bit at a time. She felt at home in Pete's strong muscular arms and she knew never think of the "Pathetique" the same way again. As the caressed and kissed each other, the sexual tension between them grew 'til Pete sat up suddenly and said, "Let's take a cigarette break."

Carrie laughed. "I think that's probably a good idea," she said. "These cigarettes have kept me out of a lot of trouble. How about something to eat or another drink?"

"I'm not really hungry. Do you have any cheese and crackers?"

"I do. I think that's about right for me too." Carrie went into the bedroom half of her suite and fixed slices of cheese, and crackers adding sliced apples to the plate.

"Ah, that'll keep body and soul together," said Pete, reaching for a cracker.

"Speaking of soul, Pete, I have to ask you................."

"Come here, Carrie," he said, pulling her to him again. "Sshh", he said, kissing her lightly. She looked him in the eyes but then cast her eyes downward overcome by the intimacy of the moment.

"I know, I know," he said, and they held each other in an embrace that said it all.

After a long pause, Carrie found the courage to ask the question that had plagued her since she first felt the attraction to him.

"You're married, aren't you?"

"Yes, yes I am."

There was a long pause and then Carrie said, "I don't know what to say."

She was crushed. She thought she had been in love before and there was no way she could love Pete in just two days but she did know that she was crazy about him. She felt as if she had known him for years. A lot of the nurses dated married guys, always starting out innocently. Many of them were patients in the hospital who were recuperating in the quarters before returning to Vietnam. With lots of time on their hands, they often invited a nurse to dinner just for female company. The group, as a whole, accepted this, something they never would have tolerated at home where girls who dated married men were considered homewreckers or scorned by friends. But, over here, it was different. Many times, what started out innocently, soon became a true love affair and no one demeaned a nurse who fell in love with a married man. In fact, it was not unusual to start hearing their names paired just like any other couple. "How could I have been so smug and so judgmental myself", she asked herself when she thought of some of the attitudes she'd harbored towards some of the other nurses. "Just because I was taught those rules doesn't mean everyone was, nor does it necessarily mean that we all interpret them the same way". She knew now that it did not look the same from the inside looking out.

"Carrie, I wasn't trying to hide anything, and we haven't done anything wrong. The subject hadn't come up and there didn't seem to be an appropriate time for me to tell you without making it seem like a formal announcement. I don't know whether you are aware of it or not but you are a very special young lady."

Carrie blushed with shyness. It was still difficult for her to think of herself as pretty or special but she knew that Pete meant it and his saying it just made him more precious in her eyes.

"Of course, there are some things I'm curious about but I don't know if I have a right to know or even if I want to know them."

"Well, why don't I help you out a little with some of the basics. I've been married ten years and my wife's name is Rita. We have two children, Diane is eight and

Nick is six. Right now they are living at Camp Pendleton because that's where I was before I left for Vietnam. "

He took another sip of his drink and sighed.

"On Friday morning, when I met you, besides the nurses in DaNang and on the air-evac flight, you were the first American woman I had seen in seven months. I am not a philanderer or womanizer but I was so hungry just to sit and talk with a woman. Little did I know that I had struck a real treasure. Today was a fantastic day for me and the more I am with you, the more I realize just how unique and special you are."

"I have never been out with either a married man or divorced man. This is a first for me and is something I said I would never do," said Carrie.

"You can make that two. I am quite happy in my marriage and have never found any reason to jeopardize what I have at home."

The words stung Carrie's heart.

"We've only known each other two days and they have been wonderful days. Why don't we just lighten up on this conversation and enjoy the rest of the evening," said Pete.

"Good idea. Oh!, I forgot to tell you that I am starting a new job tomorrow. I am going to be the charge nurse of the Intensive Care Unit."

"You mean you won't be on 2B so I can harass you."

"No", laughed Carrie, " as a matter of fact, I'm pretty scared. ICU is an entirely different kind of nursing but they are being patient with me and are giving me a good orientation before I have to take over on my own."

At ten o'clock, Carrie decided it was time to end the day. It had been a busy and full one but she knew she wanted to have a full night's sleep in preparation for ICU. As they said goodnight, Pete held her close and kissed her with a renewed passion after an hour's light talk and banter.

"Good luck tomorrow, Florence Nightingale."

"Thanks, and thanks for a special day."

Sleep did not come quickly for Carrie. She was someone who found it hard to wait for decisions with her black and white mentality, and she knew whether or not she continued to see Pete was up to her. From watching the other couples, she knew there was not a lot for the recuperating patients to do which contributed to so many single girl-married men romances. Pete had touched places in her that she did not even know existed. He made her feel adored and beautiful and without acting possessive, conveyed the feeling that she belonged to him, that he would take care of her. The last image before her eyes as she fell asleep was his final wink and beautiful smile as he walked out of her door.

On Saturday night while Carrie was at the dinner party at the Gleasons', Pete stayed in his hospital room and wrote to both his wife, and his parents. He and Rita had shared their lives through the mail during their seven month separation. This was their second separation, the last being a year long tour in Okinawa six years ago. He missed her a lot but not as badly as when he first got to Vietnam. Those first two weeks were brutal as the reality of fear set in as he wondered if he would ever see Rita and the children again. But, after awhile, he became so engrossed in his work, both with the battalion and leading his company, that he was able to adopt a philosophy of living in the present and placing his life in the hands of God. He met Rita in high school and they dated a few times. It was not even she that he took to the senior prom. They had common backgrounds and she was studying to be a social worker. When he came home after boot camp graduation from Paris Island, he met her at the drugstore when he went into the village to get the evening paper and some cigarettes.

"How great to see you", he remembered greeting her. He was genuinely happy to see her and stood talking for a half an hour before he got the nerve to ask her for a date. They saw each other every night for the remaining three weeks of his leave and became engaged the night before he left for duty with a Battalion in the Mediterranean. Seven months later, when he returned, they were married and Diane was born ten months after that. By then, he'd been selected for OCS, so he packed up his wife and baby and headed for Quantico, Virginia. He remembered thinking he was the luckiest man in the world. He was a Marine Corps Officer, with a beautiful wife and baby girl, both of whom he adored.

After OCS, he received orders to Camp Pendleton in California where they enjoyed two years as a young married couple, visiting places in the West that previously were only known to them as places in geography books. In 1960, Pete received orders to Okinawa and after he left, they discovered that his wife was pregnant again. His son, Nick, was born halfway through his tour there delaying his first glimpse of him until the child was nearly six months old. He smiled as he thought of his family and was grateful for the blessings of his life. In his letter, he reassured Rita that he was fine and that the upcoming surgery was more precautionary than emergency. Sending all his love to his wife and family, he finished his letter to Rita. He was tired and didn't really feel like writing his folks but with Rita in California, they really appreciated getting their own letters. With his Dad's chronic heart disease, he didn't want to cause them any undue worry.

Just as he was finishing his letter to his folks, Father Paige came by and they'd had a nice visit. They mostly talked about Father Paige's old Marine Corps days in Korea and lied about how good they both were at golf. When Father Paige left, Pete took another shower, a luxury he was enjoying after the filth of Vietnam, and went to bed early around ten. Part of his head was still in Vietnam and he was tired but as he shut off the lights, his last thought was not of his wife, but of the girl he was escorting to Sunday Mass the next day.

3

Carrie loved the Intensive Care Unit. The challenge of caring for the injured marines caused her to reach far into herself for nursing skills she scarcely knew she possessed. The patients were such nice young men, boys really, with terribly complicated wounds. To relieve some of the tension, as in most cases, the staff had created their own irreverent vocabulary and subculture.

One of their tenets was that a patient couldn't come to ICU unless he missing at least one limb and had four tubes. Nearly all the patients in ICU had severe abdominal wounds complicated by adhesions and infections. Peggy Moore suggested and Carrie agreed that the best way for her to learn the unit was to spend the first week assigned to patient care.

When she walked into the first room with the wash basin and clean linens to start the daily care of her patient, he looked familiar to her. Oh my God, she said to herself, it's Lieutenant Shields, the officer from 2B that I sent to surgery early Friday morning.

Lieutenant Shields was acutely ill. Not only did he have a diaphragmatic abscess as they suspected but when they explored his abdomen, they found a small leak in his bowel and he now had acute peritonitis. Dr. Pellagrino performed a temporary colostomy and now the Lieutenant was a mass of tubes and drains. If there was no further complications, it looked as if his body was starting to repair itself but, nonetheless, the road to recovery for Lieutenant Shields would be a long one.

"Nurse, can I have something for pain?", the soft barely audible voice asked.

"Hi Lieutenant remember me? I'm Miss Craig from the Emergency Room the night you arrived," she said as she reached for his hand. Like a frightened child he grabbed it with all his strength and a tear dropped on his cheek.

"Miss Craig, yes, I do remember you. That seems like three months ago, not three nights. I'm sorry I'm such a baby but as soon as anyone is nice to me here, I seem to cry."

"Your injury and surgery have robbed you of your defenses for awhile. Don't be embarrassed. How are you feeling?"

"Not too good. I can't move a muscle without everything feeling like it's being ripped in two."

"Let me fix you your pain shot. I'll be right back."

Carrie left the room and went to the narcotic locker. She could not believe how terrible Lieutenant Shields looked. He was so pale, drawn and listless. Every patient battled so many enemies in this war. There was the Viet Cong, then the injury, on top of that, they had to battle infection. It seemed to be the infection and the secondary effects of injury that really got the patients in trouble. She returned to his room and gave him his injection.

"I'm going to hurry and bathe you and shave you. It'll take about twenty minutes for this to take effect and if I speed it up, I can finish just as the pain relief comes and you can have a nap for a few hours."

During the last year when she was exhausted at work, she developed a little prayer to help her get through her day. In it she asked the Lord to give her strength and thanked Him that she was the one giving the care not the one lying in the bed.

Each day the first week, she cared for a different patient and by Friday, out of sheer necessity, she pretty well knew where everything was on ICU. She was grateful that she'd had a full year on the open wards where she had learned the daily life of the ground troop along with their lingo, slang and foibles. On ICU, sometimes, knowing that information helped her to introduce levity with the sick patients. She would often tell the ones who were on liquids only that as soon as they could eat, she would be sure to see that they got a good cold can of ham and limas. Of all the C ration choices in the field, that seemed to be the one the Marines disliked the most.

"How do you know about ham and limas?", they'd ask her in shock and she'd tease them telling them she knew everything.

On her third day in ICU, Miss Mullaney returned from her father's funeral and made rounds. Carrie expressed her sympathy and Miss Mullaney apologized for not asking Carrie about ICU before she left.

"I see you fit right in here, Caroline. I knew you would."

She really isn't a bad egg, thought Carrie. I bet inside that starched uniform, there's an old broken heart that has never healed. If she would just smile once in awhile, she wouldn't be so intimidating. With her gray hair pulled back tightly in a bun and her wire frame glasses, she was so stern looking.

Each day when Carrie returned to her room, Pete called to see how her day was and without any formal plans they began to drift into a pattern. He ate dinner in the hospital dining room, and then walked over to her quarters. Carrie usually ate her main meal in the Officers Mess at lunch unless she planned to go to the club for dinner. She had a bowl of soup or chili or some cheese and would usually be reading the Stars and Stripes when Pete arrived around seven.

"Pete, is it my imagination or is this casualty list getting longer every night? Look, tonight, there are twenty "killed in action", and thirty "missing in action". You know, even though I work with these guys everyday, it is still hard for me to believe that I am taking care of war casualties. When I joined the Navy two years ago, I had romantic images of World War II movies, but I never dreamed for one minute that I would be involved in a war."

"Oh, you're involved in a war alright. I can attest to that," said Pete, "that's if you consider guns, bombs and people getting killed and injured, war. I'll tell you something else my fair friend, it's not going to be over for a long time, either."

"I know you probably think I'm crazy, but I'd love to get orders to the Naval Hospital in DaNang."

Pete fixed himself a gin and tonic and came and sat next to Carrie on the sofa. Kissing her gently, he told her that he could understand her attraction to the excitement, but to take it from him, she was 100% better off where she was.

"How's ICU going?"

"Busy. It's always busy up there. The guys are so sick but the corpsman staff is terrific. You know the Navy takes nineteen and twenty year old guys off the streets and tries to make nurses out of them. I have to tell you, in the case of ICU, they've done a great job. They were all pretty upset today. It seems the word is starting to pass that a corpsman draft is coming in."

"A draft, what's that?" asked Pete.

"They need corpsmen in Vietnam so desperately, that what they do is take twenty or thirty corpsmen from places like ours where they've had excellent experience and send them down there. They then replace ours with brand new kids from corps school. It's hard on us. We have to continually train new guys, but at least we are sending our best to Vietnam. The rumor is that there is a list in personnel with twenty of the corpsmen's names on it. I wouldn't be surprised if they started doing the same thing with the nurses. If so, in spite of your warning, I hope that I'm the first name on the list."

"Are you a crossword puzzle fan?", asked Carrie.

"I am, and I missed them in Vietnam."

"There's a pretty good one in the stars and stripes. Let's do it together."

Across and down, Pete and Carrie worked their puzzle with frequent interruptions for hugs and kisses. Pretty soon, the puzzle was completed, the room was dark and they were leaning against each other in the corner of the sofa. The desire between them grew and they became so familiar and free with each others bodies. No longer strangers, they acted like a couple, exploring and learning more about each other day by day. Three weeks tomorrow night was when they first met which also meant that Doctor McLean would be back from leave. Chances were that Pete would have his surgery next week.

"How many hours do you think we've spent on this sofa?" Carrie teased asking Pete.

"Not enough."

On more than one night, they had drifted through the mahogany beads into the bedroom. Locked in each other's arms, they had lovingly entwined their hearts and bodies. With great conflict and control they had stopped short of completely surrendering to each other. She loved Pete deeply and now had less restraint about his making love to her but Pete could not bring himself to that final infidelity. He loved Rita and thought of her at home alone with the children. He had vowed his love and fidelity to her in marriage, and, now was in deep conflict with his love for Carrie. Not only did he feel that he loved her but gradually he had to admit to himself that they were closer and knew more about each other in three weeks than he and Rita knew in ten years. Nightly, he and Carrie struggled with their feelings. They didn't pretend to believe what they were doing was right, they only knew that Pete could do no more and live with himself. They were both sexually frustrated but survived by calling on what they both believed and had been taught by the church. In a way, Carrie found it humorous. "I finally decided Paula is right, that it is different when you are in love, and what do I get, a guy with more scruples than I?"

Night after night and on weekends, they were constantly together, living in their magical world. Carrie knew how long Pete's recuperation would take so she never dwelt on his leaving. She loved and lived with him each day like he was going to be there forever. She had never loved anyone the way she loved Pete. He made her feel like the most beautiful girl in the world.

After their first two weeks together, she brought him over to meet George and Betsy. When she got Betsy aside, she asked her what she thought.

"Carrie I've known you a long time and I think I know what you're looking for. There's not doubt this time that you've finally found it. My heart is breaking for you."

"Well, thank God, he's going to be here at least another month", replied Carrie, "who knows what will happen?"

Carrie was brought out of her reverie and back into her own room by the sound of Pete's voice asking,

"How would you like to spend some time somewhere besides your room?"

"What do you mean?"

"Tokyo."

Carrie couldn't believe her ears.

"Do you mean it?"

"Sure, I have a full weekend liberty and you have the weekend off. If we wait any longer, I'll be recuperating from my surgery and I'll be lucky to get over to your room."

Carrie pulled away to look at him.

"Oh, Pete, I'd love to go. It'll be like a ...."

"I know, like a honeymoon." said Pete. "Don't be afraid to say the word. We both know how we feel. Let's plan on leaving right after work on Friday and come back on Sunday. By then, I'm sure Doctor McLean will be looking for me to schedule me for the OR."

All day Friday at work, Carrie's mind was on the upcoming weekend. Two whole days and nights with Pete away from this base. She just couldn't believe it and was so afraid something would happen and they wouldn't be able to go.

The unit was busy on Friday, and she wanted to make sure she did everything to get it ready for people working the weekend.

Early in the morning, the senior corpsman checked all the supplies and drugs. The admission schedule was so unpredictable that the kindest thing they could do was have a couple of units all set up with everything in them but the patient.

Many of the patients were incontinent and to avoid the possibility of an infection from a urinary catheter, the staff made up a device using a condom, some paper tape and a drainage tube to collect the patient's urine and keep the bed dry. Checking the supplies, Carrie noticed that they were out of condoms. Lynch, her senior corpsman, called down to supply and was told they were also out of them but if he would come down they would issue a requisition for purchase at the Base Exchange. Lynch agreed to do the errand on his lunch break.

When he returned, he approached his charge nurse bent over, practically hysterical with laughter. It was his intention to purchase a large box from the store manager but found the only condoms in the exchange were the ones on display, three to a package. So, he took twenty packages to the cash register and placed them down for the cashier to ring up.

"Miss Craig, if you could have seen the faces on the people in the cashier's line looking at me with those twenty packages of condoms. They must think I'm planning quite a weekend!

"I'm sorry Lynch. You were a dear to get those. Look at it this way, your reputation has improved, mine would have been destroyed. Those people can laugh but they don't know how many wet beds these things have saved us," Carrie said giggling at the whole matter.

During the night, a patient, Mr. Phelps, had been admitted to the unit with a severe heart attack. He was both in congestive heart failure and pulmonary edema and was placed on the danger list. When ever anyone on the unit was in danger of death, Carrie tried to be sensitive to the youth of the corpsmen. She knew it was hard for them to care for dying patients. Mr. Phelps was only fifty-two and had retired in Japan after he married his second wife, a Japanese woman. While Carrie was checking his blood pressure, he asked her if he could see a priest.

"Are you Catholic, Miss Craig?" he asked.

"Yes, I am. I'll call Father Paige right now. Would you like me to tell him to bring you Holy Communion?"

"I can't receive. I'm married outside the church to my second wife, but I want to talk with him."

Mr. Phelps words stung Carrie. The guilt she felt about Pete had kept her away from receiving Communion and the feeling that passed between her and Mr. Phelps reinforced her belief that she didn't think she could ever leave the church and its sacraments, even for Pete. Carrie held Mr. Phelps' hand for a minute and then left to call Father Paige. She got him right away, and relayed the story. He said he would be right over. What a dilemma thought Carrie. According to the rules of the church, Mr. Phelps could be given absolution only, if he promised to live with his second wife as brother and sister. But, she thought, on a deathbed, I guess you'll promise anything.

Pretty soon, she heard the door to the unit open and Father Paige came into the nurses' station. She took the priest in and introduced him to Mr. Phelps, leaving the two to their private visit.

None of the rooms on ICU had doors on them so it was not difficult to hear conversations in the rooms. Carrie tried to busy herself and rattle the metal charts so she could hear only murmurs as the patient and priest talked with each other. Snatches of, "I didn't see them very often because they were in the states and I was here but I did send by ex-wife money to take care of them..........." snuck into her consciousness.

Carrie turned on the running water. She did not want to hear another man's confession, especially not today with the joy of her Tokyo trip ahead of her, but just then, the patient in the next room to Mr. Phelps called her and as she walked by the room with the priest and the dying man, she heard Father Paige ask,

"Did you do the best you could? That's all Our Lord asks."

The words struck Carrie like a thunderbolt. No lecture, no sermon, just the unconditional love and forgiveness of God spoken through his minister, Father Paige. If that was me, thought Carrie, I would have had to torture myself with questions and rules about the divorce, the remarriage and being away from the sacraments. But, wasn't that what I was supposed to believe, how I was supposed to live? The rules were very clear with little or no room for deviation. She felt confused but the echo of the sincerity of Father Paige's words rang in her heart, "Did you do the best you could?"

As she returned to the nurses' station and passed Mr. Phelps door, she saw Father Paige lift his right arm in the blessing of absolution. She was in awe of the holy and compassionate priest and filled with joy for the peace of Mr. Phelps. Father Paige came into the nurses station.

"Thanks for the call, Carrie. I usually get called when the patients are placed on the danger list, but, somehow, this one slipped through the cracks."

"I know your visit meant a lot to him, Father. I've been Catholic all my life but I have a lot of confusion with church rules. Maybe, I should come talk with you sometime. "

"I'm always available. Just give me a buzz and we can have a talk anytime you're ready. Do you have a nice weekend planned?"

Carrie wanted to die right on the spot.

"I'm going to Tokyo with a friend; can't wait to get away from this base for awhile."

"Well, you have a nice time up there. If you need a place to go to Mass on Sunday, there is a Franciscan chapel down by the American Embassy."

After the priest left the unit, Carrie felt terrible. Of all the people to ask her about her weekend, the Catholic chaplain. Thank God it was now two-thirty and the evening shift would soon arrive for report. The guilt stimulated by Father Paige's innocent question now propelled her to get out of work and off the base with Pete faster than ever.

Tokyo, Japan
October, 1966

The Sanno Hotel in Tokyo was one of those wartime crossroads, like the Hilton in Hong Kong. Although operated like a regular hotel, it was funded by the military. In addition to the rooms, there was an exchange where beautiful Oriental goods were sold and could be mailed back home, a slot machine room, a cocktail lounge and a dining room, with a band and dance floor. The Sanno also ran tours throughout the rest of Japan.

Because of its renown, Carrie and Pete decided not stay there, but opted to stay at the Hilton which was directly behind the Sanno, thus allowing them to use all the Sanno's facilities.

Their room was on the fifteenth floor and after the porter left, Pete took her in his arms and said, "Carrie, I want you to be comfortable. Just take a few minutes and walk around the room, open all the drawers. Look in the bathroom, out the window, everywhere. Your self consciousness is written all over your face. If we bring it out in the open, maybe we can dispense with it right now."

Carrie held him tight, whispering, "I don't know why I'm so nervous, it's not like I don't know you."

By now it was dark. It had been a long day and long train ride up from Yokosuka so they decided to have their dinner in the Hilton dining room. This is the happiest I've ever been, Carrie thought to herself. I don't want it to ever end. It just has to work out for us.

"A penny for your thoughts." Pete's words brought her back to their conversation.

"My thoughts are beautiful. Thank you for this superb idea. The Officers' Club is nice but being here with you is special because I have you all to myself."

Pete took her hand. "You'll never know how special. These three weeks have been like three months. I feel I know you so well, almost even better than................well, maybe that's not fair, but I do feel like I know a lot about you, who you are, how you think, what's important and what is not."

"Same here. What I feel about you, and us, is the fulfillment of what I've prayed about for years, someone who I could love that would really love me and take me with all my crazy quirks."

The look on Pete's face turned to sadness.

"I know, I know exactly what you are saying."

The intimacy between them was powerful and to break the impending feeling of sadness, Pete suggested a walk over to the Sanno for an after dinner drink and dance.

The cocktail lounge at the Sanno was jammed and as soon as they walked in they were greeted by waves from friends also up for the weekend. They each ordered a stinger and after a few sips headed for the dance floor.

"Anyone you see that you're uncomfortable about?" asked Carrie.

"No, only the people from Yokosuka and they have already seen us together so much that they'd have to be pretty stupid not to know we are here together."

The band played a medley of romantic Broadway show tunes and as they danced, they softly sang the words to each other. As the lyrics grew more tender, Pete clasp of Carrie became tighter until they were barely moving on the dance floor, just staying close together swaying gently to the music. Suddenly, the band broke off into a jitterbug and Pete swung Carrie out to the end of his arm and pulled her back and they were into a dance of rhythm and fun. Carrie loved to dance and Pete was such a great leader, there was no dance she couldn't do with him. Back and forth, under his arm, around his back, they laughed as the pace grew faster and faster. When the music ended, she was out of breath and begged for relief. "You are such a great dancer, Pete, and so easy to follow."

"Thanks, Ginger, you're not so bad yourself."

They stayed just a short while longer to finish their drinks and then walked back to the Hilton. Carrie's anticipation of their lovemaking, matched that of a kid waiting for the next reel of a serial at a Saturday afternoon matinee. She did not want to add to Pete's guilt, but she loved him and wanted him so.

As they entered their room, she switched on the light inside the door and Pete immediately shut it off, took her in his arms and kissed her.

"What's all this riff raff you have on?", he teased and began to help her remove her dress. Like a game of tic tac toe, they each in turn undressed the other and Pete took her hand and led her to his bed. No sofa, no returning to the hospital at midnight, they held each other, caressing and whispering their hearts' secrets until sleep took them both to their dreams.

When the morning light peaked through the hotel window, it took Carrie a few minutes to orient herself as to where she was. She looked next to her to see Pete still fast asleep. She leaned over and kissed him quickly and then took refuge in the bathroom so she could straighten out her hair and brush her teeth.

"What do you want to do today?", Pete cried out from his bed.

Carrie came out and sat next to him, holding his hand.

"I'd like to go shopping in one of the big Japanese department stores. I'd like to see if I can buy a ready made dress. I'm getting tired of the same old custom made styles and I think I am small enough to fit into the larger Japanese sizes."

"Sounds good to me. I'd better get up and get ready."

There was no better place to get lost in a crowd than the Tokyo Ginza. A maze of traffic and color, the streets and sidewalks were jammed with thousands of Japanese and other multinationals. Cameras, stereos, cigarette lighters, kimonos, china and silk, all beautifully displayed in windows caused mini traffic jams on the sidewalks. They finally came to Takashimaya, one of the largest department stores and went immediately to the dress department. Carrie looked through the selections until her eyes fell upon a black and white sundress with thin spaghetti straps over the shoulders. The skirt was quite short. She was dying to buy her first mini skirt.

"Here, would you please hold my bag while I try this on." Once in the dressing room, she slipped the pique dress over her head and loved it. I think I'll show Pete, she said to herself. Walking back out into the department, her eyes were searching for him when she heard a soft wolf whistle.

"How do you like it?"

"Makes you swing and sway like Sammy Kaye. Get It."

Carrie felt beautiful and knew when she added her long pearls to the dress they would swing back and forth as she walked. She paid for the dress and Pete tucked the box under his arm.

After lunch, they discovered that "South Pacific" had recently reopened in Tokyo. She asked Pete if he would enjoy seeing it and he said that he would as the music was some of his favorite. Later, sitting in the darkened theater, Carrie heard the show's words like she had never truly listened to them before. When Rossano Brazzi sang, "This Nearly was Mine," she was grateful that the darkness of the theater hid her tears.

After the movie was over, they were both tired. It had been a long day after an exciting night. They agreed to stop at the Sanno for a quick early dinner and to go back to the room and just relax.

"I think we should find out about church in the morning. Tom Paige told me about a Franciscan chapel that is by the American Embassy."

"Did you tell him we were coming up here?" Pete asked with shock in his voice.

"Heavens no! Not us specifically. He asked me what I was doing for the weekend and I told him I was going to Tokyo with a friend. That's when he suggested the chapel."

After a light supper, they stopped at the desk at the Sanno and had the clerk write out the directions in Japanese, to the chapel and back to the hotel to give to the taxi driver.

By the time, they had showered and put on the cotton yukatas provided by the hotel, it was nearly nine o'clock. Pete called room service and ordered two drinks for them. They were both exhausted. The day had been full and the excitement of being away together had drained them of energy. Propped up against the pillows on Pete's bed, they relaxed with their drinks and cigarettes. Pete loosened Carrie's yukata and gently rubbed her back and shoulders.

"Feel good?" he asked.

"Hmmmm, wonderful. You should be the nurse and I should be the patient."

"There are so many things I love about you. I've never told you that one of them is your name, Caroline."

"I like it now, too. At first I thought my mother got a little carried away. My twin sisters are Candace and Catherine and then, me, Caroline. When I was a kid, I was teased with Scary Carrie and Fairy Carrie but then I suddenly achieved elegant status when both Jacqueline Kennedy and Princess Grace named their baby girls, Caroline."

"What do your sisters do?"

"Candy lives in San Francisco and is an airline stewardess. Cathy is married to a Navy dentist and they live in San Diego. I'm due to be transferred in June and I've asked for San Diego as my next duty station. I really love California and it'll be great living near Cathy and David, David Peterson, her husband. Actually, Candy and I look more alike then she and Cathy. For some reason, I've always gotten along better with Cathy. Candy and I always seem to be competing."

"Where do you think you'll go after Vietnam?"

"Oh, there's no mystery to that. The Marine Corps has a pretty standard career ladder. I strongly suspect that I'll go to an advanced school at Quantico and then to duty somewhere in the Washington, DC area."

They looked at each other. No words were needed. Their faces said it all. Pete lifted the yukata from Carrie's shoulders, along with his own and they climbed under the covers. The warm shower, and the drink added to their fatigue so that at the end of a long hug, they were asleep in each other's arms.

As they walked into the chapel, Carrie thought they could have been back in the States. It was jammed with Americans. She looked around and was quite taken by the hand painted mural on the wall behind the altar. The line of people started with Christ handing a loaf of bread to St. Francis, who handed it to an Asian, who handed to an African and so on all around the chapel.

As she turned to follow the mural, she saw the lights over the confessional lit up. She desperately wanted to receive Communion but she felt confused after her weekend with Pete. Her mind started playing ping-pong. I'd rather go here than back on the base with someone I know, but part of the sacrament is the firm purpose not to sin again. She knew she was not strong enough to stop seeing Pete. She prayed for a few minutes and decided to go to confession because she suddenly remembered the words of Father Paige with Mr. Phelps, "Did you do the best you could?" She leaned over and told Pete that she was going to confession and he looked around toward the back. When he saw the lights on, he rose and joined her in line with those waiting.

Entering the confessional, she could feel her heart pounding and when the priest slid open the small sliding wooden window on her side, she told him as best she could what her sins had been since her last confession. The priest was a very old monk and when she had finished, the only thing he said, was, "tell God you are sorry, try to do better, and please say a prayer for me." Carrie was so relieved, she left the confessional with tears streaming down her face.

As she cupped her head in her hands and said her penance prayers, she desperately asked God to help her, she was so much in love. She felt Pete return to the pew and kneel beside her. She opened her eyes to see him staring at the altar, saying his prayers, his lips moving ever so slightly. She knew at that moment that she had never loved anyone as much as she loved this beautiful man.

After church, they had breakfast at a small European cafe and decided to check out and return to Yokosuka. The weekend had been wonderful but they were both tired and wanted to go back where they could relax and unwind.

Just as expected, on Monday, Dr. McLean returned from leave and made rounds acquainting himself with all the neurosurgical patients who had been admitted in his absence. Like many neurosurgeons, he was a nice guy but very highly strung and often misunderstood. He carefully listened to Pete's story and then he examined him.

"Well, Captain, this doesn't look like anything we'll have any trouble with if we are cautious and take our time but I have to tell you, if it's all right with you, I'd like to wait 'til the end of the week to put you on the schedule. There's a backlog of patients for me and most of them have more serious illnesses than you, besides, I want to get some more x-rays, and perhaps do a dye study or two so I'll know exactly what I am going after."

"Yes, Sir, that's fine, Sir," replied Pete. "I'm not going anywhere and I certainly understand the need to take care of the guys with the bad wounds first."

Carrie was delighted when Pete came over Monday night and relayed the news.

"Wonderful. You'll be here at least three more weeks after the surgery which brings us to the end of October."

Pete hugged her and their joy at their new lease on life and love filled the room along with the music from the stereo.

"I just hope I don't have to go on night duty during that time. Next week is my week to work evenings and that'll work out just right because if you have your surgery, you'll be tied down anyway."

By now, Betsy and George Gleason and Carrie and Pete had spent a lot of time together. The men hit it off right away and Betsy was so supportive of Carrie as she poured her heart and her concern about what would happen when Pete finally had to leave. The Gleasons were there so they understood the dilemma of lovers being thrown together during war and it was a real gift for Carrie and Pete to be able to socialize with another couple in their home rather than the constant party atmosphere of the Officers' Club.

Finally, the day arrived for Pete's surgery. Dr. McLean had reassured him that all the preoperative studies were fine but that the fragment was considerably deeper than his records had led him to believe. Carrie was working three to eleven and spent the morning in her room trying to hold down the anxiety she felt with concern about Pete. She imagined every type of horrible medical complication from total paralysis to a slip that would rupture the carotid artery causing him to bleed to death.

Finally, she decided to go to noon Mass. Kneeling before the tabernacle, she begged God to watch over Pete and to take care of them as a couple. After Mass, Father Paige said he was heading to the club for lunch and would she like to join him.

"Oh, Father, I'm such a wreck. I don't know if I can even eat. Pete is in surgery right now and I'm scared."

"Come on, have a cup of tea anyway and keep me company. You've really got it bad haven't you?"

"You don't know how bad, Father. I never thought this would happen to me, goody two shoes Carrie."

"He certainly is a fine fellow. I've enjoyed him every time we've been together. Just don't loose your head, my dear."

"I think I've already have, Father. I have never loved any man the way I love Pete. Believe me, he's not like a lot of the other married guys just getting what they can while they're here."

"When it comes to affairs of the heart, I try to stay away from advice but I'm always here if you need a shoulder to cry on, remember that. He may be different, Carrie, but I'm afraid the outcome will be the same."

"I know, Father, you're right but thanks for understanding."

Walking up the long corridor of the hospital to head for the club, they passed a nurse pushing a gurney coming out of the recovery room.

"It's Annie, wait Father, I'm going to ask her if Pete's in the recovery room yet."

She ran ahead and as soon as she rejoined him, Father Paige knew everything was okay.

"Annie says he just came in. The case took longer than expected but that he is fine but very groggy."

Father Paige put his arm around Carrie. "See nurse, sometimes you have to leave it to the other fellow to do some of the worrying for you."

55

Father Paige was not unaware of his own feelings for Carrie. She was his favorite nurse and when he was honest with himself, he admitted his attraction toward her was not just professional.

When Dr. McLean made rounds on ICU that evening, Carrie told him about her and Pete and asked how he had done.

"What a nice guy," said Dr. McLean. "You know, after I got in there, I realized they took a chance letting him run around. That piece of shrapnel had multiple jagged edges. He could have been hit in the neck and who knows what artery or nerve could have been severed."

Carrie felt a chill run through her.

"Anyway, I had to put a lot of retraction on his neck to get good visualization so he is going to be both bruised and sore not to mention swollen. I hope he doesn't develop an infection."

"How long do you think he will be here?"

Dr. McLean looked at Carrie and winked.

"Oh, I think I can send him back the end of the week........no, don't panic on me, he'll be here at least three weeks and by the time the Marine Corps straightens out their paper work, who knows?"

Carrie breathed a sigh of relief, in fact, two sighs, one for the fact that Pete was okay and one for the joy of having him around another month.

"Thanks Roger, thanks a lot. You've taken a big load off my mind."

"Nothing's too good for our Navy nurses and their weeping hearts," he said, poking her in the ribs. She wished everyone knew Roger like she did. He was so warm when it counted but he could be so gruff if things did not go his way. I guess that's what comes from poking around inside people's brains, she thought to herself.

Pete had a rough time the first two days. As Dr. McLean predicted, he had a lot of swelling and a considerable amount of pain. With a huge pressure dressing around his neck, he looked like a turtle gasping for air. Carrie did not want to be too conspicuous visiting him on the ward, so she wrote him long letters but only visited him a little while each afternoon before she went on duty.

On Pete's sixth post-op day, the dressing was reduced to just a light gauze and Dr. McLean said he could have liberty as long as he didn't do any jitterbugging.

"Everything is fine in there but the tissue has really been traumatized so I'd just as soon baby it for awhile."

Having Pete back was wonderful and the first evening that he came over, they just stood still and held each other.

"Thank you for the beautiful letters. You have such a way with words."

Carrie held Pete so tight and kissed him with renewed passion. The week without his company had given her time to reflect. She knew they were in a no win situation. Neither of them could marry outside the church and she didn't think she could live with the fact that she had deprived children of their father. She loved him deeply and had come to the decision, just as Annie had, that she would cherish his love and company as long as she could and then go through the pain of separation later. By now, it was near the end of October, her favorite month.

Stepping back, Pete made a little bow, and said, "The gentleman has something to present to the lady," handing her a cream colored formal looking envelope.

Puzzled, Carrie took it looking askance at Pete. She carefully opened it and read:

>
> THE COMMANDANT OF THE MARINE CORPS
>
> AND
>
> THE COMMANDER, MARINE BARRACKS, YOKOSUKA
>
> CORDIALLY INVITE YOU TO ATTEND
>
> THE MARINE CORPS BALL
>
> THURSDAY, NOVEMBER TENTH
>
> COMMISSIONED OFFICERS MESS
>
> AT SEVEN O'CLOCK
>
> DRESS, FORMAL

Carrie was dumbfounded but at the same time overjoyed.

"Does this mean you will still be here November tenth?"

"I'm taking a chance, Dr. McLean said I'd be here three weeks post-op and it's only seven days, that gives me two more weeks. To be honest, I think we'll just make it under the wire. I think I can manipulate the paper work to keep me here until the Marine Corps Birthday but that's about the limit, besides, Princess, I really need to get back to being a Company Commander. I have a lot of devotion and loyalty to my Lieutenants and troops and if I am away much longer, I'll loose their trust and loyalty."

A pain seared through Carrie's gut. It was the first time they had talked about his leaving using a real date.

"Come here," Pete said, as he reached for her. "Carrie, my life will never be the same because of what you and I have shared. I know I love you and I will live with that pain as I adjust my life now to living without you. Besides, it isn't fair. You need to get on and meet someone with whom you can have a full and loving life."

Carrie couldn't bear to hear his words. She knew they were true and really were the only option but she had grown so close to this man in the past five weeks that she did not know how she was going to survive without him. Admittedly, she had let a lot of her relationships with her girlfriends slip and it was nearly two months since her last trip to the orphanage. She couldn't remember the last time she had a real visit with Paula or anyone else for that fact, except for the time they spent with George and Betsy. She had no idea of how often Pete wrote to Rita, whether he called her or not and what he said. It was simply too painful for her to know those details.

Carrie could tell that Pete was tired so they made their first evening back together a short one. Now that she knew she had at least three more weeks with him, some of her panic subsided and she didn't feel the need to be with him every moment.

Back in the hospital, Pete fell into bed exhausted. He was growing stronger by the day but still had a long way to go to get back the strength he had before the injury and surgery. He knew he should write Rita tonight but between his exhaustion and his growing love for Carrie, he was finding it increasingly more difficult to correspond with his wife. He was filled with guilt, guilt for his infidelity to Rita and guilt for the hurt that he knew he would ultimately inflict on Carrie. He couldn't believe how close he felt to her and he knew from being married that they would have had a terrific marriage. He quickly banished the thought from his mind. It just couldn't be and there was no need torturing himself with those thoughts. They had even discussed the possibility of stopping seeing each other and decided that neither one of them was strong enough. They rationalized by saying that life was intense enough in Japan with the war bringing new casualties every day that they might as well enjoy each other as long as they could. He started a letter to Rita and when he awakened the next morning, the pen and empty paper had fallen to the floor beside his bed unfinished.

4

Yokosuka, Japan
October, 1966

Pete and Carrie asked Paula to join them for dinner at the club. As usual, the cocktail lounge was a madhouse when they arrived and it gave Carrie a great feeling. She was so grateful for the idea to join the Navy. She felt alive and involved and shuddered when she thought of the boring job she had left behind. "To think, I could still be stuck back there day after day."

They were sipping their first round of drinks when Paula said, "Hey, guys, I had a letter from Yale today. He wants me to meet him in November in Hong Kong. The ship will be in for five days."

"That's great, Paula. Hong Kong. How romantic."

Paula was positively glowing.

"Why don't you see if Ed can get you a ride? Speaking of the devil."

"How about a dance Paula?"

"Now, there's a catch," said Carrie. "The only trouble is that every single woman on base is after him."

"What's his story?" asked Pete.

"His name is Ed Walker and he's on the Admiral's staff. Rumor has it that he was engaged right out of the Naval Academy and before he could get married, his fiancee was killed in a boating accident in Florida. He has dated a lot of the nurses but he always avoids involvement by saying it's not fair to the girl because he has to travel so much with the Admiral and his staff. I don't know. I went out with him twice and had a great time but he never asked me out again."

"Didn't know what he was missing," Pete winked at her and squeezed her hand. "Let's join them."

"Dance?, you can hardly walk!"

"That's what I mean. Let's just stand on the dance floor, hold each other and rock back and forth to the music."

The dance floor was jammed as they inched their way to the center where they could hide in the crowd. As Pete held Carrie to his chest, the band softly started, "The Shadow of Your Smile." He held her so tight, she thought she was going to crack. It felt wonderful.

"How do you like this dancing?" he asked. Carrie just lifted her eyes and smiled to him. She was so much in love.

When they returned to the table, Paula came over and said that Ed had asked her to join his party at another table and would they mind if she left them.

"Great, go ahead, " said Pete. "Don't forget to work on him for a free plane ride."

When they returned to Carrie's room, around eleven thirty, the closeness between them was explosive. As soon as he closed the door behind him, Pete took Carrie's hand and led her toward the bed. Somewhere, in a moment on the dance floor, his mind shifted and he allowed himself to think of changing his future and making this girl his wife. By now, he knew he was not just caught in a web of a fling but that he was very much in love. For the first time, he thought honestly about Rita, things about their marriage that he had dared not admit before. He admitted he hardly knew her when they married and he was disappointed in her lack of affection and sense of humor. He had never dwelt on these problems because he loved her but there were, indeed, rough spots in their marriage. Spending the last five weeks with Carrie made him face these truths he had repressed for a long time. Tonight, he was going to make love to Carrie and share with her his thoughts and dreams of the future.

As they lay on the bed slowly removing each other's clothes, Carrie sensed a change in Pete. Along with his usual tenderness, she felt an aggression to his lovemaking. At the point where they usually came up for air and had a cigarette to gain some control over themselves, he continued to caress and love her, his passion passing beyond anyplace they had been together before. It frightened her. He seemed like a different man than the one that had just entered the room with her. At the height of everything she felt for him, she clung to him, caressing him and returning his kisses with all the love she had. Suddenly, she pulled away and sat up.

"Pete?", what are you doing? Are you sure you want to do this?"

She had dreamt of and longed for this moment but the change in him, the feeling of power and aggression was so strong that it had introduced an element of fear into their lovemaking and she could not let it continue.

"Here, sit up and have a cigarette," she said striking a match.

"Carrie, all along we assumed that our love was temporary and when I left, it would be over but tonight on that dance floor, I realized that I will never be able to forget you and what we have. For the first time since I met you, I've thought about leaving Rita."

Carrie was dumbstruck.

She cast her eyes down in the darkness of the bedroom.

"It just seems so unfair that we would meet and become so close and love each other so. I know how you feel, but to actually get a divorce?"

Her head was spinning. She thought of her family, her upbringing. They would never accept a divorced man. Her most visual thought was of two little children, Pete's children, who would not have a father and not understand. She held on to Pete and started to cry.

"We can't do it, Pete, we just can't do it."

Exhaling a long sigh, Pete said, "I'm not so sure anymore. I'm just not sure about all the rules."

Carrie looked at him.

"All the rules seem to be changing and I don't know if I've changed enough to marry you if you get a divorce. I love you. You know that and it will take a long time for me to forget you, if ever. Knowing that you feel the same and are willing to tell me, means a lot. I trust you and I think we are both doing what we have to do to live with ourselves. These talks help a lot. They clear the air but I don't want to spend out last two or three weeks together crying every night. Can we lighten it up a little?"

"How about another weekend away? Do you think we can go up to the Mount Fuji area next weekend? I'll be feeling better by then and it will be beautiful this time of year with the leaves changing against the rich blue Japan sky."

"Sure, there are some great old hotels there or if you like we could stay at a ryokan, a Japanese inn. That might be fun."

"Okay let's plan on it."

Carrie felt the tension go out of Pete. They had made it, barely, through another evening together. She knew the only thing working in their favor now was that both of them had not weakened at the same time.

When Pete was back in bed, waiting to fall asleep, he was frightened. He knew that for a moment that evening, he had made a decision to leave Rita and marry Carrie and it was only Carrie's quick pickup on his change of behavior that brought those thoughts to a temporary stop. Tonight, I know, he thought, that because I have met and known Carrie, I will carry a pain in my heart for the rest of my life.

Mount Fuji, Japan
October, 1966

They decided to wait until Saturday morning to leave for Mount Fuji because the drive on the mountain roads in the dark was treacherous. They left at six o'clock and about mid morning stopped at a small restaurant in Gotemba. Carrie immediately recognized the name of the town because of her trips to the orphanage. The ride down was beautiful and the fall in the Japan mountains looked like the fall in New England.
Sipping his coffee and eating a sweet roll, Pete asked, "Well, what will it be, a Japanese Inn or a fancy hotel?"
"Let's try an inn. What would really be nice is if we can find an inn near a big hotel and then we can use the facilities of both."
Pete called over the young man who had served them coffee and in a combination of English and Japanese was able to get the name of a good ryokan near the Fuji Lake Hotel on Lake Yamanaka, one of the five lakes in the Fuji area. They found it easily because of its lovely gardens which set it back from the street. After Pete registered, they were led to their room by a lovely Japanese woman, who invited them to remove

their shoes before stepping onto the large tatami covered floor of their room.

"Please, sit and wait and I bring you hot tea," she said as she backed out of the room bowing.

"Where do we sleep?" asked Pete looking around at the stark plain room. Carrie started to laugh.

"The Japanese don't want bedroom space all day like we Americans. They roll up their beds and put them away in the closet. Tonight after dinner, they'll put the futons down on the floor where we will sleep. The room looks plain to us, but its simplicity is beautiful and relaxing to them."

The windows and sliding doors were covered with translucent rice paper and on one side of the room was a recessed alcove with a Japanese scroll on the wall and a vase with an arrangement of flowers on the floor.

"The whole purpose of the Japanese inn is to provide a place of comfort and serenity, thus the lack of color and noise. We might find it drab and boring but to them, the setting allows them to relax and meditate. Wait 'til we take our baths."

"I took a shower this morning, what bath?"

"After we return from exploring the countryside today, we'll remove our clothes and put on yukatas provided by the inn. Then we'll go to the ofuro or hot bath and soak and relax. If we want the woman will then come to our room and give us a massage. Also, there is no dining room in the inn. The woman comes to our room, sets up a hibachi and cooks and serves our dinner right there."

"I can't wait for all this," said Pete. "I've heard all the hotsi bath jokes, but thought that type of thing only went on in the red light districts."

"Oh no, the Japanese inn and its routine is the pride of Japan. Let's get started on our day. It's gorgeous out."

Mount Fuji was so overpowering. No matter what course they took on the mountain road, it seemed to loom over them like a watchful mother. In certain areas where they parked the car and got out to walk, they took pictures that were breathtaking. Looking across the lake at the mountain, Carrie could look through her lens and see her photo framed in long dried grass as if an artist had put in there just for the photos. She took several pictures of Pete and when they meet a young Japanese couple, the asked them to take a few of them together.

About one o'clock they drove into the parking lot of the Fuji Lake Hotel. Nearly every car had a military sticker on the windshield.

"What should we do? Suppose we run into someone who knows you?"

"No sweat, hon. As long, as we are within one day driving distance of Yokosuka, it'll look like we just drove down for the day."

The large dinning room was jammed with Americans but fortunately no familiar faces. Carrie decided on a big American lunch telling Pete that regardless of their upcoming romantic Japanese dinner, she wasn't sure what the entree would be and it would be too late and dark in the mountains to get anything else to eat. She then remembered a story the Admiral's aid had related to her concerning Japanese food. Whether it was true or not, she wasn't sure but, nonetheless, it was one of those stories that had been passed down in Yokosuka over the years, always being attributed to the current Admiral's wife.

Because of their high position, Admirals and their wives are continuously invited to dine with high Japanese officials both in their homes and in public restáurants. The meal is usually always Japanese cuisine. It seems that this one admirals wife, no matter how hard she tried, just could not eat nor stand to take even small bites of Japanese food. The whole concept of raw fish, seaweed, octopus, squid and the like was abhorrent to her that she found herself with a real problem on her hands.

On day, she promised to buy her young son a goldfish and when she saw the merchant place the goldfish in a small plastic bag with some water to assure its survival for the ride home, she was suddenly struck with a brainstorm. As soon as she got home, she opened her closet and took out her five favorite dresses, all of which she had made by Meiko, the dressmaker, in Yokosuka. She was so excited she took the five dresses and drove straight to see Meiko. As she entered the dressmaker's, all the seamstresses bowed with their usual graciousness.

"Konnichiwa Oksan", they replied in unison.

"Konnichiwa", replied the Admiral's wife, returning their bow and afternoon greeting. She quickly located Meiko in the group and pointing to her five dresses asked her if she had any of the left over fabric.

"I give to you, Oksan," replied Meiko.

"Of course, you did, how stupid of me. Well, let me tell you what I want. I'll go home and see if I can find the scraps and if I can't then we'll just have to match fabrics the best we can. I want you to make me a medium size draw sting purse to match each dress and to line it completely with plastic."

Meiko looked puzzled.

"Plastic, Oksan?"

"Yes, Meiko, let me explain." She then proceeded to tell Meiko her social predicament and had just that day discovered a solution to her problem.

"Meiko-san, now I can got the Japanese banquets and little by little slip all my food into my purse. After dinner, I can go to restroom and empty purse."

Meiko and the girls went into titters of giggles.

"Oksan, you so funny. Sure, I make purse. you bring me fabric, okay?"

Carrie finished her story laughing herself and told Pete not only did the Admiral's wife survive the Japanese dinners but she probably improved international relations by not insulting the hosts.

The afternoon drive back to the ryokan was lovely. Carrie looked about her at the scenery and didn't know if she was in New England or Japan, in heaven or in hell. She tried to concentrate on enjoying the day but she was plagued with the thoughts of Pete's leaving in less than two weeks. She found herself ready to abandon all her long and rigidly held morals and standards. She suddenly jolted herself with the realization that there was also another practical consideration, and that was what would she ever do if she got pregnant. If she did, she would have to get out of the Navy. She could never go back home and live in that stifling New England environment after being out of there for two years. I guess I would go to San Diego and be near Cathy and David. An abortion would be out of the question.

She was startled by Pete asking her about the baths again.

"Are you up to a coed hot bath?" he winked at her.

"I don't know, I guess there's always a first", but then she remembered how shy she was when Pete had seen her naked walking across the room in Tokyo.

By the time they pulled into the Japanese inn, it was nearly five.

"I need a stretch after the drive. Let's walk through the beautiful gardens." suggested Pete.

Hand in hand they strolled the pebblestone pathway engulfed in quiet and peace except for the faint sound of a brook running through the short twisted bonsai trees. Finally, reaching the door, they removed their shoes and entered.

"Konnichiwa" said the innkeeper. "You are ready for bath?"

"We sure are", grinned Pete.

"Please, go to room and take off clothes and put on yukata. Lady go to front and gentleman to back to wash and then to big bath to relax."

Hmmm, thought Carrie, a compromise. We do our washing separately but we soak together. I guess I can handle that.

They went to the room, both acting so sophisticated and cavalier. As they disrobed and put on their yukatas, they looked at each other and started laughing.

"I guess I'm not the only one who's nervous," said Pete.

"You're wonderful. I've been dreading this all day after I went and acted like it was nothing. Actually, now I feel fine about it. Let's go get the grim of Mount Fuji off us."

The Japanese hot bath was so different from the American bath and shower. As Carrie entered the bathroom, the young female attendant invited her to remove her yukata and handed her a towel and small washcloth, asking her to please sit on a small stool in the middle of the tile room. She then proceeded to assist Carrie in washing herself. When they were finished she poured clean rinse water over her and told her she could now wrap in the towel and go to the hot bath to relax.

Pete was already in the large pool-like bath when Carrie entered the room, along with six other guests. Without as much as a word, Pete came over to her and stood in front of her so that his body hid hers from the other guests as she dropped her towel and stepped into the steaming hot water. Once she was submerged, she felt comfortable and the tension start to leave her body. The heat of the bath was hypnotic and she felt herself growing sleepy. Sitting next to Pete in the bath, recalling his protection of her and his concern for Rita, she allowed herself to admit for the first time that he was probably a more sincere and honest person than she was. Although she agreed with him in their discussions of his marital fidelity, in her heart she knew that it was the fear of pregnancy more than the protection of her virtue that concerned her most. Slowly, the admission of her dishonesty made her all the more protective of him and she knew now that she would try even harder, in spite, of her growing love and longing to possess him, to help him maintain his fidelity.

She was awakened from her reverie by the quiet voice of the innkeeper asking if they would like to go to their room for a massage.

"Sounds great," said Pete.

When they returned to the room, the futons had been placed on the tatami covered floor and the maid invited them to lie down. First with Pete and then with Carrie, she proceeded to massage their reddened relaxed muscles. The effect was magnificent. Carrie searched her mind for the proper words to describe what she felt. Sensuous, relaxed, pampered, naughty; all of them together. With Pete beside her, she drifted off to sleep.

Sometime later, she awakened in the dark room to the touch of Pete's hand on her bare back and so thirsty from the hot bath, she thought she had crossed a desert rather than climbed a mountain.

"I need something to drink," she said, but Pete pretended he did not hear her and rolled over her, clutching her close to him. He had been awake for fifteen minutes and had lain watching the rhythmic rise and fall of her chest. He could no longer stay away from his love. He adored her and on a Japanese futon in a foreign land, he knew now that he would fully express that love with all he had to give.

Carrie held him tenderly in her arms whispering her love in his ear. She sensed what was happening within him and returned his kisses and caresses with a gentleness, a blending of their bodies amid the serenity of their surroundings. Later, melancholy and dreamy, she looked at him and said, "Now can I have a coke?"

They both burst out laughing.

After asking the staff at the inn, they located and attended Mass at a tiny chapel run by missionaries. Once again, the experience of being away with Pete and going to church with him only added fuel to the passionate fire burning within Carrie.

"God, why did you send me this man and not let me have him?", she prayed. She was a mess of emotions and as she counted up the days she had left with Pete, she felt a sort of panic start to build within her. She didn't know what to pray for. She wanted all of it and she wanted none of it. She just knew that she had grown so attached to him that she could not bear to think of him gone from her life, sin or no sin.

5

On Monday, Carrie cut out a picture of a dress from Vogue magazine and took it out to Mieko, her seamstress. She knew exactly what she wanted so she sketched it out for the seamstress along with the clipping. She wanted a pale blue light satin sheath gown with duel gossamer thin spaghetti straps just like the one that Grace Kelly had worn when she accepted her Oscar for her performance in, "The Country Girl". She had been in high school then and adored Grace Kelly. She loved that dress for it had an air of sensual elegance. Meiko assured her there would be no problem in copying it and told her to return in two days for a fitting. The ball was ten days away. There was plenty of time.

For some unexplainable reason, Carrie lucked out and was on the day shift and, according to the advance schedule, would continue to be so until Pete left. The casualties were increasing and for the first time she started to equate their injuries with the possibility of the same things happening to Pete when he returned from Vietnam. My world is slowly coming apart, she thought, and I am such a mixture of emotions that I can't, in any way, begin to sort them out until Pete leaves. Once again, she felt badly about the times that she had judged other nurses who became involved with married men. How can I have been so cold and heartless, she thought.

One week before the ball, she picked up her dress. The pale blue color caused her eyes to shimmer and softened the blondness of her hair. When she tried it on she decided that she would not wear any neckline jewelry so as not to detract from the elegant bare shoulder design. Her only jewelry would be a single strand pearl bracelet with single pearl earrings.

"How do you want to spend our last weekend?" asked Pete, who was waiting by her room when she returned from the seamstress.

The question almost made her throw up. There was no denying it.

Pete was leaving.

She thought for awhile and said, "I think I'd like to stay here. For one thing, we won't want a lot of hours traveling and I'd like to go to the club with George and Betsy and spend the weekend like we've spent most of our time rather than do something different."

"I agree," said Pete.

"Let's build on what we have and what we know rather than introduce another whole set of memories."

Taking her in his arms, he held her close and said, "Young lady, we have to talk. You are pulling away from me. You don't smile anymore. Is this how we are going to be with each other our last week?"

Carrie started to cry.

"I'm sorry, I'm just so upset. I feel like we belong together and now that you are leaving, I'm having all sorts of terrible feelings like what a jerk I was to get involved and how rotten you were to Rita to cheat on her. My mind is turning all the beauty of our love into wretched hatred and I don't want that to happen."

Pete just held her closer.

"I know. I've been doing the same thing. I'm not much of a shrink, but, I think it's a way our mind helps us so that the separation will not be so painful. Let's just sit down and try to talk it all out.

For an hour, they sat on the sofa, the scene of so much of their life the past two months. They reviewed who felt what when, where they went and gradually over the hour, the heaviness was lifted from their hearts and they were both smiling again.

"Can I see your dress?" asked Pete.

"No, I want you to be surprised on Thursday night when you call for me."

"Well, at least tell me the color so I won't get you flowers that scream out that I'm colorblind."

Carrie told him the dress was pale blue and Pete murmured, "like those pale blue gorgeous eyes", and was all over her like the Yokosuka mosquitos. The levity was back in their love.

Finally, Thursday, November tenth arrived, the Marine Corps Birthday. Fortunately, the unit was not too busy and Carrie got off on time. Stopping by her room to change out of her uniform, she drove out to the beauty shop. As Fumiko-san brushed back her hair before the shampoo, Carrie rather liked the look so she decided that she would have it swept back in a French twist. Not only would it look more formal but it would highlight her pearl earrings. At five, she took a quick shower and then took extra pains applying her makeup. This would be the last time that Pete would see her dressed up and she wanted it to be a picture etched in his memory forever. When she finally put her gown on, she stepped in front of the full length mirror and smiled at her own reflection. The feel of the satin against her chest was sensuous.

When she heard the knock on her door, she quickly opened it and there was Pete in his dress blues. "Oh Pete, how handsome."

Pete was so struck by the beauty of the girl before him that he just stood there staring at her.

"You are the most beautiful woman I have ever seen."

Carrie blushed. It was one thing for her to think she looked nice but to actually have another tell her startled her and she didn't know how to respond.

"Here, I hope you like these."

He handed her a flower box. He had selected a wrist corsage of baby white rosebuds and lilies of the valley. Carrie had never seen anything so delicate and once again it reminded her of Pete's sensitivity and tenderness. Looking her over once more, he said, "Your neck is bare. For two weeks, I've been looking for the perfect gift for you. I know what I want but I can't find it. I may have to buy it later and send it back to you."

"You don't have to give me a present and besides, I purposely left my neck bare tonight. I like the look."

"Hmmmmmm......so do I," said Pete as he nestled his lips against her neck.

"No, no, we can't start that now, this is no time for you to get horny after the hours it's taken me to get ready."

"Why don't we just forget about the ball and stay here?"

"Pete, you lecher! Come on, let's go over to the club."

The dining room of the Officers' Club had been transformed into a fairyland. Thousands of tiny twinkling lights had been strung across the ceiling and the Marine colors of scarlet and gold were used as a theme in all the decor. Each table had a gold table cloth with a small vase of scarlet baby carnations. The band wore scarlet dinner jackets and the Japanese waitresses, gold kimonos. At the entrance of the room, there was a receiving line where the Commander, Marine Barracks and his wife, along with other dignitaries greeted the guests. Carrie had met Colonel Schneider several times when he came to the hospital to visit patients but when she was formally introduced to him by his assistant, his eyes widened and he said, "This can't possibly be the same girl that works in the hospital."

"Yes, Sir, it surely is," beamed Pete. "Good evening, Sir. Captain Pachulis, up from Vietnam, Sir."

"Welcome, Captain. I see you lost no time cashing in on the best Yokosuka has to offer."

"Yes, Sir, I'm a lucky man, Sir."

"Pleased to meet you, Captain. Enjoy the evening."

"Thank you, Sir."

The dinner was elegant and somehow, the Officers' Club chefs had managed to come up with something different for the menu. The entree was stuffed cornish game hens, with wild rice, spiced apple, and baby green peas. The dessert was ice cream that somehow they had managed to color scarlet and gold, decorated with tiny Marine Corps flags. After dinner, they had the traditional ceremonial cutting of the cake by the oldest and youngest Marine present. The poor young second Lieutenant looked as if he wanted to fall on his sword he was so nervous standing up there with the Colonel.

Finally, with all the preliminaries out of the way, the band began playing and Pete took Carrie's hand and led her to the dance floor. The music was slow and romantic and the first medley swooned with songs of other wars.

"I'll Be Seeing You", "Far Away Places", "What'll I Do?".

Pete held her close to him and sung the lyrics softly in her ear. Carrie could never remember a time in her adult life when everything came together so perfectly for her as this evening. The people, the dinner, the decor, the music, but most of all, the man she was with guiding and gliding her across the floor.

Her thoughts were suddenly clouded by the realization that in just forty eight hours, Pete would be gone, but, she banished the idea from her mind. She would not let that dread ruin the beauty of this evening. Finally, at one o'clock, the band played "Good Night Ladies", for the last dance.

As Pete led her out of the dining room into the lobby, Carrie reflected on her first Marine Corps Ball. She did not know how many she would attend in her life but she knew for sure that this would be the best of them all.

"This is our last night together," said Pete, back in Carries room.

"What about tomorrow night?, you're not leaving 'til Saturday morning."

"You know the rules. Patients going out on the med-evac flights have to spend the last night in the hospital. I've thought about it and I've come up with this plan. You probably didn't notice but I brought a pair of khakis and a sport shirt over tonight so I could stay. I didn't think it would look too swift for me to cross the base tomorrow morning in dress blues. That's like wearing a sign that reads, 'Guess where I slept last night?'. We can spend all day tomorrow together and decide where we want to have dinner. I spoke to Betsy today and asked her if I could bring you over there tomorrow evening. When I leave, I want you to be with friends, and I'd like you to stay with them tomorrow night so that you are with someone on Saturday morning."

"You're thoughtful, Pete. Regardless of your plan, your leaving is going to be terrible but I agree, it will help if I am with my friends. No one could be better than George and Betsy."

"Enough of this departure talk, let's get undressed and down to serious business," said Pete. He unhooked the back of her gown and carefully slid the thin straps off her shoulders. She, in turn, opened the long row of Marine Corps buttons on his uniform. The elegant apparel which served the evening so well now lay in a combined heap on the floor as the two lovers held each other tightly in the dark. Removing the last of their clothes, they fell on the bed grasping each other in what each knew was their last night together. Their time together was over, a dreamworld, in which each of them had learned and loved like they never dreamed possible.

With the sharp edges of their consciences filed smooth by alcohol and passion, they clung to each other caressing and loving until sleep took them to their final day together.

"What would the Commandant think of this, Sir," asked Carrie as she stood above the pile of clothing on the floor. She had wakened before Pete and had run down the hall for a quick shower and to remove last night's makeup and cigarette smoke from her body.

"Aye, aye, Sir," replied Pete, "I think he'd love it." referring to her nude body and ignoring her intention of the clothing on the floor.

"Come here."

"No, no, I'm going to get dressed and so are you. I want to get out of this room before we get into the sadness of this day. I'd like to walk out in town and buy you a Yokosuka souvenir."

"What kind of a souvenir?"

"I don't know, but I'd like you to have something that you will always have from me, something that will survive in the jungles of Vietnam and yet be ambiguous enough for you to have at home without looking like it came from a girlfriend."

"Sounds fine. You know what I'd like to do with you just one more time?"

"I'd like to go to noontime Mass with you today. I'd like to say goodbye to Father Paige."

"That's a great idea, I'd like that, too. With your leaving, I need to reattach myself to my conscience and take time to sort out a lot of my feelings."

As things turned out, their last day together in Japan was quite ordinary just as they wanted it. In the morning they went shopping and decided on the plain and mundane gift of a cigarette lighter with *Yokosuka, 1966* engraved on it. It met the criterion Carrie had established. Pete did not buy her a gift. He told her once that he knew exactly what he wanted and hoped to find it later and mail it back to her. At noon, they went to Mass and ended up going to the Officers' Club to lunch with Father Paige. Carrie was so taken by his kindness to them and his total lack of judgement of their togetherness as a couple. At the end of lunch, as they were parting, Father Paige extended his hand and told Pete how much he enjoyed knowing him and wished him well in Vietnam. Pete returned the compliment and then added, "Father, watch over this lovely girl for me." Carrie's eyes brimmed with tears, suddenly aware that she had just witnessed Pete's first goodbye.

They didn't know what to do in the afternoon. Carrie did not want to spend it in her room for she knew that the tension would probably cause them either to cry or fight. She did not want either of those choices to be her last memories of Pete.

They decided on a long walk around the outer perimeter of the base which passed by the bay in several areas. When they tired they sat on the seawall and it turned out to be a perfect activity for the day. By four, they were both tired, so they decided that Pete would return to the hospital to pack and Carrie would take a nap.

"How about a drink, dinner and a dance tonight? Not too late, just a touch of each for our memories," asked Pete.

"I'd like that." Carrie wasn't sure she wanted to go through all of that at the club, but she instinctively knew that they were better off with activity then just hanging around waiting for that fateful final hour of departure to arrive.

The evening was lovely. They had a leisurely dinner, danced to their favorite melodies and around ten-thirty, they left the club and headed for the Gleason's home on base. George and Betsy were still up but were ready for bed. They said their goodbyes to Pete and left the living room. There were no more words to be said. They had said them all thousands of times and reviewed their options over and over. The time had come for their separation and though neither of them spoke it, they both knew it was probably final, that there would be no reunion. What had happened had happened because of the war and Yokosuka and it could not be recreated in another time or place.

"Look at me," Pete said. He lifted her chin and kissed her.

"Just like my first kiss," he said. "I want to remember you with that shy, selfconscious look on your face. You must promise me you won't come to the bus tomorrow. I want you to stay right here with Betsy and let me just leave with the other troops."

"I promise," said Carrie.

About one o'clock, Pete rose from the sofa, took her in his arms and said, "I love you dearly," and kissed her tenderly, holding her close to his chest.

"I love you, Pete, and I probably always will." She started to cry.

"That's okay, you can cry. It's for a worthy cause," he smiled at her. They walked to the door. Pete once again gently lifted Carrie's chin, kissed her lightly on the lips, turned and walked down the Gleasons' sidewalk back to the hospital.

6

When Carrie awakened Saturday morning, the clock said nine and she jumped out of bed.

"Oh my God!, I've got to hurry, the bus will be gone."

"Didn't you tell me you promised Pete you wouldn't do that?" asked Betsy.

Carrie stopped. "But I have to see him one more time."

"Carrie, you've just finished telling me how beautiful your last minutes with Pete were. Don't go and ruin it with a scene at the bus. Please Carrie. Let it be."

"Oh, Betsy, what would I do without you? You're right and I did promise and agree with Pete. Let's have some coffee."

The two friends talked for over an hour. "You'll do fine, my friend. You always do. Oh, it'll hurt for awhile, but you have so much spunk, you'll be out on the market again in no time."

"Not this time, Betsy. This time it was the real thing. I know now, that he will be the standard by which I judge future men in my life and that is going to be hard."

"Not only hard but unfair to other men. Pete was uniquely Pete and other men will have their own fine qualities. Do what you want, but at least give others a chance if they come along and are interested."

"Dating is the last thing on my mind right now, believe me. I could not go out with someone else now, I just couldn't."

"I know. It'll take time. Just be patient with yourself and gradually, the wound will heal."

"How I hope you are right."

About eleven o'clock, Carrie gathered up her clothes, thanked Betsy with a hug and drove across the base to her quarters. As she entered her room, she was overcome with emptiness and sadness and began to cry. Looking around her, everything in her room was now a reminder of Pete and the hours they had spent there. The rest of the day and weekend loomed before her like a vast wilderness of time that she had no idea how to fill. For eight weeks, she had spent nearly every available minute with Pete. Suddenly, she hated Japan and she wanted to go home. She was tired of trying. Trying to be a good nurse, trying to be a good friend and trying to be a good Catholic. She knew she would feel terrible when Pete left, but this was ten times worse than she ever could have imagined. She was so depressed and overcome with inertia that nothing, no activity appealed to her. The though of going to the club tonight and partying with the officers from the ships repulsed her.

She wiped her eyes and looked in the mirror. I look terrible. The strain and sadness of her mood was reflected in her eyes and face. She knew she had to get out of her room but had no desire to go anywhere or see anyone. She looked down at her chipped nail polish and decided to go to the Yokosuka beauty shop for a shampoo, set and manicure. She was void of energy and that would give her a place to go as well as kill some time.

The beauty shop turned out to be a good idea because the Japanese beauticians were so kind and accommodating and she needed the pampering they so generously gave her.

As she opened the door to there room upon her return, her phone was ringing.

"Hello."

"Hello, Carrie, this is Father Paige, Tom. How are you doing?"

"Oh! Father, how nice of you to call. Actually, I'm not doing very well. Pete left this morning and I'm a mess." She started to cry.

"I'm so sorry, Carrie."

"The reason I'm calling is that three of the women from the Wives Club and their husbands and I are leaving early tomorrow morning to drive to the orphanage in Gotemba. It's a little early in the year but we want to talk with the sisters and find out what their needs are for Christmas for the children. There's an empty seat in my car and I wondered if you would like to come with us. You haven't been there in a long time."

"Oh Father, I'd love to. That sounds just like what the doctor ordered. Maybe I can get my mind on something else beside my own broken heart. What time are you leaving?"

"I have the eight-thirty Mass and we plan to leave right from the church. Why don't you come to church and just leave with us?"

"Fine, I'll do that. I'll see you then."

"Carrie, are you going to be okay the rest of the day?"

She started to cry again and could not speak. The only sound Father Paige heard in his ear was that of sobs and sniffles.

"It hurts a lot, doesn't it Carrie?"

She pulled herself together to answer the kind priest.

"Father, it hurts something terrible. I feel like I don't have the right to be sad or to talk about it because I should have known better and I know a lot of my friends are thinking, 'I told you so'. I never meant for it to go as far as it did. We even tried one time to stop seeing each but the attraction was so strong that we just couldn't stay apart. Now all the feelings of joy and laughter and fun are gone and I'm just full of sadness, depression and remorse. I'm all mixed up. I don't know whether to be angry at Pete, to forget him or to try harder to marry him. I'm obsessed with thoughts of him today. I have a headache and my stomach is in knots."

"Stay right where you are, I'm coming over there. You need to talk about this thing and you are not going to be able to do it tomorrow with the other couple in the car. Put on your coffee pot."

Tom Paige hung up his phone and thought about the mission ahead of him. He had seen it happen over and over and the result was always the same. The men left the area and the nurses were left brokenhearted. Maybe the men were broken hearted too but he hadn't had an opportunity to observe that end of the romance. There was an air of innocence to her but it was well hidden in the midst of her competence and sophistication. Knowing her Irish background, and the part of the country she came from, allowed him to make some generalizations about the state of her faith and morals.

So many of the Catholic nurses he had met from that area were guilt ridden and fearful of God. Somewhere along the way, they had missed the message of God's everbounding, everlasting love. He had no agenda for his visit to Carrie but to listen and answer any questions she had. His only goal was to be a soothing presence for that Almighty Soothing Presence, the One Whom he had pledged his life to work for.

It took him just a minute to walk over to her quarters from his in the next building. Entering her room, he said, "I thought you were supposed to look terrible. You look beautiful to me," aware, once again of his attraction toward her.

"I just came from the beauty shop. You should have seen me before I went. What would you like in your coffee?"

"Cream and sugar, please. I'll never get used to Navy black mud."

Carrie fixed their coffee and sat in the easy chair opposite the sofa from Father Paige.

"Father, I never thought it would be this bad. I don't even like my room anymore. It's like Pete took all the joy out of it with him when he left."

Once again she started to cry, but this time she launched into a running narrative of their whole relationship from the night he arrived as a patient to the last night together when they said goodbye. Along the way, she interspersed the conversation with her feelings both good and bad about various aspects of the romance.

"Carrie, I'm not saying what you did was right, but it wasn't all wrong either. By taking the risk and falling in love with Pete, you exposed a part of yourself that you didn't even know existed. You now know the great capacity to which you can love. I suspect you feel guilty about the physical aspects of being with Pete, regardless of how much or how little. Sex does not exist in a vacuum but is an integral part of love. May I have some more coffee?"

Carrie walked into her bedroom and poured him another cup, his words swirling around in her head.

"All around us the rules seem to be changing and it is particularly difficult for you girls who were educated by the nuns, all of whom seemed to receive their education in Ireland. God loves us as a whole person and that includes the sexual part of ourselves."

The tenderness and compassion of Father Paige touched Carrie so deeply that it just made her cry all the more. She wiped her eyes, caught her breath and looked up at the priest.

"Father, I don't know where you get the words, but they sure are the right ones this afternoon. Tell me something, did you like Pete, did you think he was a nice guy?"

Pausing, he looked up at her smiling and said, "I thought he was as nice a guy as I've met in a long time. You know, he had his concerns too. We had a few chats. Yep, you met a winner. Unfortunately, someone else met him first. Now what are you going to do tonight?"

"Gosh, all of a sudden, I really do feel a lot better. Thank you so much, Father. I have some food in here and I think I am just going to stay in and write some letters. I am way behind because I spent all my spare time with Pete. I'm really looking forward to the trip tomorrow. It'll be tiring so I'm going to go to bed early."

"That a girl. You'll do fine. It's just the initial panic that is so overwhelming for you. I'm glad I called."

Carrie did feel better. Being able to tell her entire story from start to finish had helped enormously. She was in awe of men like Father Paige; handsome, strong, attractive men who chose to commit their entire lives to working for Christ, and helping save the souls He created.

She decided to write the first letter to her parents. She had really slacked off on her correspondence with them while she was with Pete because without mentioning him, her letters seemed so empty and vacuous. Yet, there was no way they would ever accept or even begin to try and understand her having a relationship with a married man. Their rules were inflexible based on years of blind obedience to church rules. Today, she would fill her letter with news of the Marine Corps ball saying she went with a friend and also tell her folks about tomorrow's upcoming trip to the orphanage. Her thoughts kept drifting back to Father Paige's words. He was right. Things just were not so black and white to her anymore. Gradually, she was starting to question principles and morals she had always accepted blindly. But, there was so much vagueness in her thinking, that she put it aside and closed her letter, sending her love to all the family.

By now, it was seven o'clock. She decided she had written enough and heated up a can of chili. She would start the weekend crossword puzzle in the Stars and Stirpes and then go to bed early. She had finished the across words and was halfway through the downs when the words started to blur on the page. She checked her watch. It was eight fifteen. She hadn't gone to bed this early in a year but she was sure she would sleep. She was physically and emotionally exhausted.

The alarm awakened her at seven thirty and she felt refreshed and eager for the trip to Gotemba. Thinking about it immediately brought her to thoughts of the wonderful weekend in the Fuji area she'd had with Pete. I wonder where he is today, she thought. She didn't know if he was still in Okinawa or if he had been sent immediately to Vietnam.

After Mass, the group met in the parking lot. She had seen two of the couples in the club frequently but did not know who they were. She was happy to be doing something with people from outside the hospital staff. Perhaps it would brighten her perspective. God knows she was mired deep enough in her present one.

All three couples were from the supply depot, the men all Supply Corps officers, the supermarket and department store folks for the ships and bases. The couple in Father Paige's car was Ruth and Bill Lane. Bill was a Lieutenant and Ruth, a school teacher who taught first grade in the grammar school on base. The ride down was so intense with conversation, that Carrie could not believe it when Father Paige said, "Well, here we are."

Bill and Ruth married the week they graduated from high school. They had been married eight years and acted like honeymooners. The conversation covered everything from the war, to assessing the benefits of various duty stations, to the new birth control pill. Ruth was what Carrie always referred to as a high energy person. She just radiated strength and activity and seemed to be a fountain of suggestions and new ides. Bill was rather quiet, obviously in love with his outgoing wife. The thing that impressed Carrie the most was there was not one word of gossip in the two hour drive. She had never met anyone quite like them. They had so many interests and could talk about subjects like photography and stamp collecting in such a way as to draw her interest with them. No wonder they are so happy she thought. They are so stimulating to be around.

After meeting the Sisters and enjoying a welcome snack and cup of tea, they met up with the folks from the other car and went into an enormous playroom. Carrie was taken back by the number of children there. Where do they all come from? she thought. Immediately, two little girls about three years old, came over and took her hands, pulling her outside to the swing set.

"Push, push", they said.

These kids are adorable, she thought. Soon, half the playroom was gathered around her at the swings and she could feel the hunger for love and attention. The language barrier simply did not exist when it came to children. They could read adults so accurately.

The Sisters served a scrumptious lunch of noodles and fish and after the children were put down for their naps, the group met with them to plan a Christmas program. Sister Regina, the superior, said that what she would like is for every child to receive a toy and an article of clothing, like mittens, a winter hat or socks. They discussed age appropriate gifts and reassured Sister that they didn't think they would have any trouble filling her request, in fact, they felt that they could provide more. Because there would be so much merchandise, they thought they would probably make a few more trips before Christmas.

Carrie was spellbound by Sister Regina. A young nun, her porcelain skin and Irish brogue made watching her and listening to her fascinating. She was soft spoken but direct and Carrie thought what a perfect person to be in charge of an orphanage, remembering the contrast with some of the ogres from Charles Dickens' stories.

"We really need another swing set," said Sister. Do you think there is anyway you could help us with that?"

Bill Lane spoke up. "Sister, many times ships are looking for a project like that. The guys are willing to contribute and they like it when it is an item they can visit and see. I'll ask around. My guess is we will have no trouble at all. There are a lot of ships in and out of port right now. Chances are not only will they buy it, they'll come down and set it up with an engraved donor plaque on it, and give a party to celebrate!"

Father Paige suggested they start back early as he wanted to have the unfamiliar part of the trip over before dark. The ride home was even better than the trip down. As soon as they got into the car, the Lanes were abuzz in the back seat.

"What's going on back there?" asked the priest.

"Tom, where do all those children come from?" asked Ruth.

"They come from various situations. Some are born out of wedlock to Christian girls. Abortion is widely used in Japan but the Christian girls usually have their babies and put them up for adoption via the orphanage. Some are half Japanese, half Caucasian or half Black. These racially mixed children are scorned by Japanese society so they are given away. Then, there are the children, who sad to say, are always present in every society, the abused and abandoned children who are victims of someone else's problem."

"Gosh," said Ruth, "I never would have imagined the scene in that orphanage if I hadn't seen it for myself. Do they allow any of them to be adopted?"

"On occasion, they do, but not very often. Although the guardians do not want them around, the are reluctant to sign the papers that set them free forever."

Ruth thought a minute.

"We don't usually discuss this out of our home, but Bill and I planned to start our family the year we both graduated from college. After two years when I didn't become pregnant, we went through a infertility workup to no avail. Don't get me wrong, we are very happy together but we do want to adopt. Just as we were getting ready to go through the adoption procedure last year, Bill received his orders here and they took us off their list."

"I can speak to Sister the next time I go down," said Tom. Do you feel you could be happy with a Japanese child?"

"We've never discussed it because we didn't realize it was a possibility. I guess we need to think that over and talk about it ourselves."

What a day, thought Carrie. It was a perfect tonic for her, nothing could have taken her farther from thoughts of Pete and the hospital. Here was a new group of friends totally different, with different interests and problems than her nurse friends. She remembered Annie's advice about making friends with people from outside the hospital staff. By the time they returned to the base, they were all exhausted and agreed to forgo dinner together for the quiet of relaxing and getting ready to return to work the next day. When Tom Paige pulled the car up in back of Carrie's quarters, she turned to him and said, "Father, um, Tom, gosh I don't know what to call you. It's very hard for me to call a priest by his first name."

"Call me whatever is comfortable for you. I was Tom a long time before I was Father."

"Anyway, Father, I don't know how to thank you for today. I know it is unrealistic to think I can forget Pete in a day or even a week or a month, but today has given me a different perspective of life here and gotten my mind off my own problems."

"One thing I do know for sure, Carrie; that is if you do something for someone else, it will always make you feel better about yourself. Perhaps the best thing for you to do for awhile would be to get involved in some group activities rather than to try and immediately replace Pete with another man. With Christmas on the horizon, there will be lots of functions. We'll be going back to the orphanage in two weeks and then again just before Christmas. I hope you'll join us for those trips. You're always welcome, anytime."

"I'd love to. Don't forget to remind me when the time comes."

She said goodnight to Father Paige and this time when she entered her dark room, the jolt of its emptiness was not quite so unnerving. Father is right, she thought. The only way to survive this heartache is to stay involved with other people.

On Friday, Carrie received a letter from Pete. Since it was just a short walk to her quarters from the hospital, she waited until she was in her room to open it.

> November 13, 1966
> Dear Carrie,
> I am writing this from Okinawa but by the time you receive it, I will be in Vietnam with my old Company. I'm going to be here on Okinawa just long enough for some paper work. I expect to leave for Nam either tonight or tomorrow morning.
> Today, I finally found the gift I have been searching for and will put it in the mail before I go. I hope you will be pleased with it.
> You have been in my heart every minute of the day and night and now that the time has past, I can't believe that it happened and is over. You are a special woman and I miss you dearly. There are so many things I want to write but to do so I have to think and

thinking about you makes me very sad.

I know these days must be very hard for you and I beg you to go out and get involved with your friends that I so selfishly deprived you of while I was there.

I miss you more than you can ever know and I will write to you as soon as I arrive in Vietnam so you'll be sure of my correct address.

Love,

Pete

Carrie held the letter to her heart and noticed that her hands were shaking. She was so happy to get the letter but, in it's words, she could feel the beginning of a goodbye, between the lines. Maybe he was in a hurry. She found herself making excuses for it brevity and lack of, lack of she wasn't sure, but she felt the letter was superficial and didn't express what Pete was really feeling. In particular, she missed the fact that he didn't refer to anything they had shared together. Could he have forgotten all of that so soon or was it just his way of coping with their impossible situation? What did you expect? she asked herself. A long love letter filled with promises of the future? The letter in her hand did not sound like it came from the Pete she loved.

She changed out of her uniform into a yukata and wrote a letter to Pete. At first she felt constrained by Pete's reserve and her writing was stilted. After thinking about it, she tore the letter up and started a new one pouring out her heart and feelings about their time together and her love for him. She knew he loved her and the brevity of his letter was due to other factors she reassured herself.

At six, Annie came by and asked her to go to the beach club for dinner.

"We haven't talked in ages, Carrie, come on, get dressed, let's get out of here."

When Carrie sat at their table and looked around she was slowly reminded of the feelings she had before Pete came to Japan. She usually ate her dinner with her friends two or three nights a week and met and made so many friends from the base here, her first year in Japan. Now, being back in that setting reminded her just how lucky she was to have all those friends. She wasn't going to cease living just because of her heartache.

"Annie, I have a confession to make to you, an apology."

"Don't be silly, Carrie, what could you possibly have done that calls for an apology after what you did for me."

"It's not what I did, it's what I thought, my attitude. After you told me about your affair with Paul, and out little trip to Tokyo, I felt a little superior, morally, I mean, and gave myself a pat on the back for not being stupid enough to get involved with something like that. Now, I'm sorry for those thoughts. I know now, it is nothing one plans. The powerful chemistry of love just about wiped away every good intention I had never to get into that kind of a situation."

"Oh, that's okay, Carrie. I felt the same way before I fell in love with Paul. I only hope that I have learned the lesson not to let it happen again. I learned a lot about myself through that pain. One of the biggest lessons I learned is that I like the thrill of excitement in my life and an affair certainly provides that with the sneaking around and melodrama of the whole thing. Naturally, an open date with a single guy can't provide that so now I know I have to be more patient in dating and realize that the excitement will come with getting to know someone well and building a romance with him."

"I never thought of it that way, Annie. Being with Pete was certainly exciting and made romance with the base bachelors pale in comparison. I'm so glad I have you to talk with about all of this. I know now that unless someone has been through it, there is no way they could understand how we got involved and what a strong factor it was in our lives."

Annie placed her hand on Carrie's.

"Thank God for friends, especially for you."

7

Futema Marine Corps Air Station
Okinawa, 1966

As Captain Pete Pachulis entered the air terminal at Futema Maine Corps Air Station in Okinawa, he dropped two letters into the mail, one to his wife, Rita, and one to Carrie. It had taken just a little over twenty four hours to process his papers at Camp Haig and now he was going into the war zone for the second time.

When he checked the departure board he saw that he would be flying to DaNang on a C-130, a camouflage painted, pregnant looking monster of an aircraft. As he was pondering the schedule, the desk sergeant erased the departure time and made the announcement that the plane was now ready for boarding. The terminal was abuzz with activity as Marines poked their buddies to wake them up while another small group of men headed out onto the tarmac.

Pete tried to find a comfortable position on the plane. The C-130, which was primarily for cargo had no passenger seats. Instead, along both sides were weaved strapped seats, beach chairs without the beach. One sort of sunk one's body into them. The C-130 assaulted every sense. The position was physically uncomfortable and the atmosphere reeked of the odor of fuel. There were small windows too high to look out of, and any communication with the man across from you was impossible because of the cargo. Today, they were carrying two huge generators bolted to the center aisle of the plane. The engines seemed to roar in his ear as if to say if you think this is bad wait 'til you get to where you're going.

Actually, Pete was glad to be going back to Vietnam and thrilled that he was returning to his own Company. He had been assured of that in Okinawa.

The twenty four hours in Okinawa had passed quickly for which he was glad as it gave him little time to think. He was delighted with his gift for Carrie, as it was exactly what he had hoped to find.

As the plane reached cruising altitude, his thoughts turned to Japan and the past seven weeks. He never in a lifetime could had predicted that his orders to Vietnam would have included a love affair and a Marine Corps Ball. But, now, removed from the situation, he started to feel remorse for his behavior and guilty for having involved a innocent lovely girl like Carrie. He wondered to himself why he couldn't have been stronger and resisted the first impulse to date her. He knew now that life would be difficult and sad for her alone in Yokosuka. He was heading back to the job he wanted to do but life would continue for her among the memories that they had created together. He tried to project his thoughts forward to when they might meet again but it was impossible for it always forced him to the conclusion that he either had to tell Rita and end their marriage or stop seeing Carrie all together. With the war raging about him, he knew he could make neither decision at this time.

He must have fallen asleep in spite of the noisy plane for when the sergeant in charge of the cargo poked him and said they were preparing to land, he couldn't believe they were there.

When they departed the aircraft, it was nine in the evening and he was nearly overcome by the stench of DaNang. Looking off toward Monkey mountain, he could see the constant glow of tracer flares and already behind them, another plane was landing on the airstrip. Off in the distant, the sounds of mortars punctuated the already noisy air, and the humidity was drenching. For a minute, Pete struggled to draw a breath. As he looked about, he was struck by the unbelievable contrast of the life he had lead the past seven weeks. The buildup of troops and equipment in that time was obvious to him. The surrounding scene was that of a bone fide war zone regardless of what the politicians called it.

DaNang was always a busy place but tonight there seemed to be a frenetic urgency of activity. Surveying the airfield, he said to himself, 'this war is growing, and he tried to think of the word from geometry, ah, exponentially. It is no longer a little battle in which I can hope to earn a few medals.'

As he stood trying to collect his thoughts, a young corporal approached him, "Captain Pachulis?"

"Yes, Corporal."

"Good evening, Sir. I'm here to take you to Battalion Headquarters to see Colonel Jamison."

The trip was short but provided Pete with a first view of the night time war. All around the sound of mortars continued and the sky looked like the Fourth of July.

"We're glad to have you back, Sir."

Pete looked at the young Marine.

"Do I know you Corporal?" he asked.

"I had just reported to your company when you were injured so we never met, but the troops sure talked a lot about you and are really glad that you are coming back, Sir."

"Well, thank you, Corporal, I'll try not to let them down. What is you name?"

"Corporal Nathan Rubin, Sir."

"I just finished a three week patrol and now I'm back at the Command Post for two weeks. I was sure glad to get out of that patrol alive. We were ambushed twice. We lost two men, Sir."

"I'm sorry to hear that, Rubin. When one Marine dies, a little bit of all of us dies."

"Yes Sir, Captain. I never thought of it that way but that's just how I felt."

The jeep pulled up to the quonset hut with a makeshift sign, "Command Post Ist Battalion, Fifth Marines."

"Here you are, Sir."

"Thank you, Corporal, thank you for the ride."

"Yes Sir, anytime Sir. Welcome back."

Pete entered the Command Post to find only a desk sergeant on duty. Greeting the sergeant he handed him his orders.

"Do you know how to handle these, Sergeant?" he asked.

"Yes, Sir. I've been on desk duty for two weeks and I've checked in about a hundred men. They are coming and going everyday, Sir."

"Well take good care of these, Sergeant. As you know, there's no bigger catastrophe in the Corps than a misplaced set of orders. One missing piece of paper and you can find yourself on the other side of the world."

The sergeant laughed.

"You're right, Sir. It may be a bit of an exaggeration but your point is well taken."

"Sergeant, where can I find Colonel Jamison?"

"Sir, the Colonel and the other Company Commanders are over at the MAG 16 Officers' Club."

"Oh, over there playing with the Marine Air Group, huh?"

"I guess so Sir, I think it's a farewell party for Captain Woodworth, his year is up in two days."

Pete did not want to go to the Officers' Club. He was tired and needed a shower after the taxing ride on the C-130.

"I think I'll pass up the Club, Sergeant. When the Colonel returns, would you please tell him I've checked back in and will see him in the morning."

"Yes Sir, why don't you go to hooch number four. It's right across the way. There are three of four empty racks in there."

"Thank you, Sergeant."

Luckily, the Marines had hoisted a fifty gallon drum on the roof of the hooch so there was enough hot water in it for a shower when Pete went outside. As he scrubbed away the dirt of the plane, it was so muggy that he felt it would only be minutes before it would be replaced by the grime of Vietnam. He dried off as much as he could and fell, exhausted onto his rack in the darkened hooch but sleep did not come right away. The transitions of the past months kept running through his mind and slowly the guilt that he had suppressed in Japan started rising to the surface now that he was removed from Carrie and surrounded by the danger of war. The long ride and oppressive environment were working on his emotions and as he said his prayers he asked the Lord to forgive him for not being stronger, not staying faithful to Rita and most of all being unfair to Carrie by involving her in his life.

Throughout his married life, he had occasionally fantasized about infidelity. He imagined an encounter with a femme fatale, a siren, an irresistible broad. Never in his most far fetched dreams did he consider that his fall from grace would be with a person that he could love. He knew, now, that he had to use the remaining months of his tour in Vietnam to bring Rita back to the place in his heart where she was when he left her in the States. As for Carrie, it was too painful to think of just cutting the romance off, although in his heart he knew that was what had to be done.

He made the Sign of the Cross, a silent prayer with no words, for he did not know what he wanted. He would place it in the hands of the Lord.

Tom Paige reviewed his day as he got ready for bed after the long trip to Gotemba. The faces of the children lingered in his mind as he thought of how wonderful it would be if he could help the Lanes adopt a child. He was thankful that it had been a good day for Carrie. He had not always been a priest and the memory of the few heartaches he had endured during college freshened his feelings for the heartsick nurse. He found himself becoming angry with Pete as well as all the other men that came in here throwing their marriage vows to the wind, involving single girls, and then leaving them in a puddle of tears.

But, when he was honest, he had to admit that he was very fond of Pete and felt that probably Pete had gotten caught up in a situation that he was not looking for and once entwined could not extract himself. He quizzed his mind on the single men and women stationed here permanently in Yokosuka. So few of them dated each other and in all the time he was here, only one base couple had married. Perhaps the atmosphere of war did change people's ethics. He did not want to place himself in the position of judge and jury but wanted to remain a gentle, comforting presence to stand ready to pick up the pieces anyway he could when the breezes of battle blew caution to the wind, leaving in its path, sadness and despair.

On Wednesday, when Carrie went to her mail box, there was a note to call at the window for a package.

The postal clerk handed her a rather small package. Carrie snuck into the restroom off the main corridor. She wanted to be alone when she opened Pete's gift. Inside the mailer, was a small jewelry box. Slowly she lifted the lid and gasped. Before her was the daintiest, most feminine cross and chain she'd ever seen. It was white gold with a small diamond in the center. Folded in sixteenths was a note. Carefully, she opened it and read:

> Dearest Carrie,
> This may be the only diamond that I am ever free to give you. Wear it and know that is surrounded by my love.
>
> Love,
> Pete

Fighting back tears, she undid the clasp and put the necklace on, carefully hiding it beneath her uniform. It was a perfect gift summing up their eight weeks of love.

She remembered that she was on duty and quickly rushed back upstairs to the Intensive Care Unit. As usual, it was crowded with young Marines with brutal injuries. The war was escalating, no doubt about it. When she cared for her patients now, she felt a different bonding with them. Anyone of them could be Pete, she thought, anyone of them.

It seemed as if each day in ICU got worse. When she went to work the day after she received her gift from Pete, the senior corpsman took her aside.

"Miss Craig, come here please."

"Thanks Lyons, what's the problem?"

"I just wanted to warn you about the patient that we have in the back unit. He's the worst one we've ever had up here."

"What's the matter with him?" asked Carrie.

"Just about everything. He has lost both his legs, one arm and a facial injury that is disturbingly distorted and, well, quite repulsive."

"Thanks Lyons, I'll go have look at him."

For the first time in her career as a nurse, Carrie lost control of herself. She walked over to the injured Marine's bed and touching his hand, took in his multiple injuries. She then went into the bathroom and lost her breakfast. Dear God, she said to herself, please take this dear boy home. Don't make him live like this and please give me the strength to take care of him and be a good example to my corpsman. She breathed a sigh of relief knowing his parents were too far away to ever see him like this.

About ten o'clock, Lyons came to her and said, "Miss Craig, I think he has stopped breathing."

Carrie quickly rushed to the patient's beside with Doctor Carlisle, one of the orthopedic surgeons behind her. One quick look told Carrie the young Marine was dead.

"Doctor Carlisle, should we get the ambu bag?"

Doctor Carlisle put his hand on Carrie's arm. "Let him go, Carrie, let him go."

Carrie stood at the bedside of the dead Marine and tears poured down her cheeks. Nineteen years old, she thought, his life ending on a bed in a foreign land, far from those who love him. She placed her hand on his forehead and made a small cross. God Bless you Marine and thank you.

After she regained her composure, she looked up to see Father Paige standing behind her.

"He's already dead, Father."

"That's okay, Carrie. I'd like to give him last rites and conditional absolution. We never know just when the soul leaves the body. Besides, when I write to his family, it'll mean a lot to them to know he had the last sacraments."

"I didn't know you did that."

"I may not always be able to, but as long as we have so few deaths here, I try to send the parents a letter."

The staff prepared the body for transfer to the morgue and afterward, Carrie called the staff together.

"I don't know about anyone else, but I need to talk about this." The unit was not busy, so the staff pulled chairs into an empty room and for about a half hour, everyone sat and poured out their feelings about what had happened. I'm no psychiatrist thought Carrie but if I don't unload some of this, I'm going to boil over.

"The worst part for me," said one of the corpsmen, "was his face. I can take anything but the face."

"Me too," piped in another, "plus I looked at his birthdate he was two days older than me. Geez, this is getting bad, Miss Craig. I see this and everytime one of them drafts comes in for corpsmen, I get so antsy, I'm a mess."

"Does anyone else feel that way?" asked Carrie. She looked around and every head was bowed.

"Hey you guys. You don't have to be ashamed of feeling scared. Come on, let's fess up, no one wants to come back from Vietnam looking like that."

The group, one by one, shared their feelings and their shame at being repulsed by the patient's look and odor. Carrie then told them about her trip to the bathroom after seeing him and that seemed to help them all.

Before he left the unit, Father Paige asked Carrie if she could go with him to the orphanage on the weekend but she had to refuse as she had weekend duty. He brought her up to date on the progress of "Operation Santa Claus." He had contacted a chaplain friend on one of the destroyers in port and the crew had jumped at the chance to be involved in Christmas at the orphanage. They had taken up a collection and had purchased two swing sets.

"They are going down this weekend to assemble them."

"Oh, I sure wish I could go. I bet it'll be a lot of fun."

"We'll be going down again so you'll get another chance. Oh, guess what Carrie? The chaplain down in Sasebo has to have some elective surgery in January so I've been ordered to relieve him temporarily for two or three weeks."

"Great Father, are you looking forward to it?"

"I am. It'll be a nice change and I've heard it's really easy to get airplane hops to Korea from there. My only concern is that I've had plans for some time to meet my folks and brother and his wife in Hawaii the end of January for a vacation. I guess it'll work as long as the chaplain has no complications with his surgery."

"Sounds like we won't see much of you around here the beginning of the New Year." said Carrie.

"I thought about that too, but Father Kilkenny from the Catholic hospital in town said he would help Father McSweeney out with Sunday masses and that made me feel better."

Father Kilkenny was a missionary who had been in Japan twenty years, ten years at the local hospital. He always maintained a relationship with the base chaplains. It worked to everyone's advantage. He got to go to the club and enjoy the relationship of English speaking friends, and then, in turn, helped the priests out when he could.

"By the way, how's the old spirit, Carrie?"

"A lot better, Father. Time does help."

That afternoon, Carrie received another letter from Pete. He had now been back a little over three weeks and that very night was to begin going out on patrols with his Platoon. In the letter, he told her about Operation Attleboro, a blood bath that he had just missed, in fact, it was the week of the Marine Corps Ball. He said he was feeling well, except for the oppressiveness of the heat and dust and was anxious to get back into the swing of his job as Company Commander. Their goal on this patrol would be to search and destroy the enemy in villages as they went along, eventually hoping to conquer Hill 22 off the perimeter of DaNang. He mentioned a few buddies he had seen including one Major who had also been a patient on the ward in Yokosuka. He closed by asking Carrie to say a prayer for him and told her he missed her a lot, signing it, "Love, Pete."

Carrie could not control the shaking of her hand. Witnessing the young Marine's death this morning followed by the knowledge that Pete would now be making night patrols overwhelmed her. As she went off duty, she saw the large air evac bus pull up to the emergency room entrance. Another busload of casualties, she thought. It just didn't make sense with what she was reading in the paper and the weekly news magazines. But, at least, she thought, we are keeping Communism out of another country. Charlie. It was amazing how her vocabulary had adapted to those of the Marines. Charlie, VC, Gooks, C-rations, Number 10, hootch. Every war needed and developed its own lexicon for communication.

"Hey Carrie, wait up."

She turned to see Paula coming out of the hospital side door. "Where you going?"

"Just to my room, why?"

"Nothing special, just asking. Letter from Pete?" she asked looking at the envelope in Carrie's hand.

"Yeah, it's scary, Paula. He's going to start going on night patrols. You know, I just had a very selfish frightening feeling. If Pete was ever killed, I guess the only way I would ever find out was when his name appeared in the Stars and Stripes. I'm certainly not listed as any next of kin."

"Golly, are you morbid or what?", responded Paula. "What brought all this on?"

"I guess it was a combination of the death we had today and his letter. Paula, I miss him so much. I look around this base everyday and his memory is all over the place. I know I have to get involved in more activities. I just can't pass the time moping around between now and the summer when I rotate back to the states."

"Come to Yokohama with us tomorrow night. We're going to the Alte Liebe, a great German restaurant. There's a whole group going, a gang of guys and girls from the Q, Father Paige, even Greta is coming."

The trip to Yokohama turned out to be a riot. They all had so much fun drinking beer and signing German Beer Hall songs. The irony of the whole thing struck Carrie as hilarious. Here they were, a bunch of Americans, in a Japanese German restaurant waving their steins and singing, "Du Du Liegst Mir Im Herzen". Slowly the lights dimmed and the room quieted. A beautiful Japanese girl stepped to the microphone and sang the most beautiful rendition of "Lilli Marlene", that Carrie had ever heard. It was fun to be back doing things with the old crowd again. The day by day pain was easier to bear but the thought of a life without Pete was still too painful for her to dwell on.

The next day, Miss Mullaney put up a notice asking the nurses whether they wanted Christmas or New Year's off. Carrie volunteered to work Christmas because she knew she would be invited to George and Betsy's in the evening. She felt that by being with the Marines on Christmas day at work, somehow, she would feel closer to Pete. Christmas and New Year's were on Sunday this year, so they would be given Monday as holiday time and by the time New Years came, she would be ready for a three day weekend.

8

DaNang, Vietnam
December, 1966

Pete strained his ears next to his radioman trying to hear the incoming message from the platoon out on the hill. This was the final night of their three week patrol and he was exhausted. The rain was relentless, causing a constant feeling of steam heat and filth from the knee deep mud everywhere. VC Charlie never seemed to run out of rockets and Pete had to admit to himself that he was surprised that the Command Post, from where he directed operations hadn't taken a hit. They found the old shack on their way to their position three weeks ago and had set up headquarters there.

As patrols went, this one wasn't too bad. Nine of the Marines had sustained injuries, but none were too bad and no one was lost. Pete was also glad to reaffirm within himself his ability to lead and carry out a successful operation.

Suddenly, the panic coming over the radio signaled trouble.

"Man down, man down, serious, send chopper."

"We read you, sending help, only one casualty?"

"No, multiple, but one serious. We've taken direct hits from snipers."

Pete was deflated. Just like the last ski run when people break their legs, all hell was breaking loose on their last night.

"CP, this is wetfoot. Correction. We have five men down, one gone. Hurry. Send chopper. Over."

"Roger, chopper on way. Relay position for artillery coverage."

Pete called for the artillery to help out by plummeting the enemy position with mortars but at best, in this ground squirrel war, it was a hit and miss operation. What a bitch, he thought, the last night. The dammed VC loved night duty.

At the thought of night duty, a flash of Carrie crossed his mind for he remembered she hated it so. Carrie, sweet Carrie. That seemed a million years ago from tonight he thought.

In the morning they returned to headquarters South of DaNang and he briefed the Colonel on the operation.

"It's a real crapshoot, Sir. They come at you from all directions so you're at a loss to tell the artillery coverage where the hell to aim the mortars."

"You hit the nail on the head, Pete. Couldn't have expressed it any better myself. Lose anybody?"

"Yes Sir, one, plus six or seven injuries. If I may be excused, Sir, I'd like to go over to the hospital now and see how they are. I also want to find out who I lost."

"You're excused, and Pete, you did a great job out there. With you there, I knew there was one Company I didn't have to be concerned about."

"Thank you Sir. Any reports of damage on the other side yet?"

"Body count forty five and multiple injured."

"Well, it doesn't make me feel one bit better about the one I lost but at least we got rid of a good chunk of the sons of bitches."

Leaving the headquarters, he bumped into two sergeants with clipboards in their hands, heading for the Colonel's office for the daily death and injury report.

"Good morning Sergeants. Do you have the name of the casualty from Hotel company last night?"

"I'll check, Sir," replied one of the Sergeants, saluting smartly.

"Here it is Sir, Hernandez, Corporal Raphael Hernandez, Sir."

"Thanks Sergeant."

Pete recognized the name of the young dead man. When he returned from Japan, he spent time trying to get to know at least each man's name and faces.

Nineteen years old he thought, nineteen damn years old.

After he left the hospital an hour later, he wondered who was better off, Hernandez or two of the injured from the Platoon. One of the men had lost a leg and the other was in surgery having his belly contents rearranged to keep him from bleeding to death. The others had various fractures and shrapnel wounds. None would stay at DaNang. Four were being sent out to the hospital ship this afternoon and the two seriously injured ones would be air evaced to the States to the military hospital closest to their homes.

The chaos at the Naval hospital in DaNang was overwhelming. Every patient was acutely ill and the staff rushed around exhausted trying to save lives. The casualties never stopped coming. The triage area was just a quonset hut of two rows of sawhorses. Strung from above on wire, were IV solutions all set for infusion. As soon as a litter arrived, it was placed on a saw horse, and the patient quickly evaluated or triaged by the physicians, placing them in priority order for treatment. They were then plugged into IV fluids and moved on to the next step. Thoughts of a movie showing the assembly line at General Motors that he had seen once, flashed thought Pete's mind.

In the Intensive Care Unit, the nurses had somehow found time to decorate with a few silver bells and red and green crepe paper. God Bless 'em thought Pete. You really have to have faith to see Christmas through all this carnage. His heart skipped a beat when he saw a young blond navy nurse on the unit. He still had difficulty believing that he had really been with Carrie for seven weeks. He left a war and was now back in the thick of it and through an injury, he had been given seven weeks that were the farthest thing from war.

Gradually, through the time he had been back in Vietnam, he had allowed himself to think about his love affair with Carrie. He still did not feel right about it and he knew that he would always love her on some level. She wasn't out of his heart or his soul. He thought that sometime during the next three weeks while he was at the Command Post, he would try to speak with one of the Catholic chaplains. Father Paige had been great but Pete knew he could not stop seeing Carrie so he never really got into to it very deeply with Tom.

Vietnam, also had its version of a social life. Like Yokosuka, American women were at a premium but they were there. There were the military nurses, the Red Cross workers, and some civilian nurses who were there with the Aid to the International Development program.

In the DaNang area, the Officers' Club at MAG 16, the Marine Air Group, was the arena for parties and pairings but Pete had learned his lesson. Regardless of how innocent, refreshing and fun an evening with the nurses over there would be, he had promised himself that he would not put himself in a position where that could happen again. He was wiser now, with a new knowledge of his own vulnerability and he intended to use his new found wisdom.

Back at headquarters, he started to draft a letter to the parents of the dead trooper when the Colonel entered his office. Pete stood and greeted Colonel Jamison.

"What was the damage, Pete?"

Pete told the Colonel of his grim visit to the hospital and his frustration at the young age of the men they were losing.

When he heard Pete's report, the Colonel turned stone faced.

"It's a damn shame Pete, a damn shame. Sometimes I feel they send us over here to fight this goddamn mess and then half way through they act like they were just kidding. Goddamn fucked up politicians."

Pete shared the Colonel's frustration although he had yet to form his own political assessment of the war. He just hadn't been well enough informed to make a judgement at this point.

"You got any great need to be around here for Christmas?" the Colonel asked Pete.

"No, Sir, none at all."

"I've got to go up to Quang Tri to be briefed on the situation at the DMZ. Colonel Dick Bowen, a buddy of mine is the top man up there. How about coming along?"

"Yes, Sir, that would suit me just fine. I don't care if I'm in the Demilitarized Zone or here. The only Christmas I'll have is what's inside of me and I can take that anywhere."

"Well, you've got some brains between those two ears of yours and I'd like you see as much of the screwed up mess as possible. I hate to admit it but I can see it coming. I sat and froze my ass off in Korea fifteen years ago while the politicians cloaked themselves in political horseshit. It's going to be the same goddamn thing here. They only thing missing is the snow and ice. Search and destroy. Now, I ask you, isn't that as close as playing hide and go seek as you've ever seen and to top it all off while you're doing it, you're likely to get your goddamn arm blown off by a hanging booby trap from a tree. Shit, Pete, I'm tired of this already. I thought I was coming over here to use my experience and lead a Battalion into battle."

Pete did not know quite how to respond to the Colonel's tirade. He was probably right because he had access to information that Pete did not have.

"Sir, I noticed a tremendous change in just the seven weeks I was gone. This thing is suppose to be winding down but you'd got to be blind not see the daily buildup."

Winding down!" the Colonel screamed. "Shit, they just announced that they are sending in 100,000 more ground troops. Blind? You'd have to be goddamn Helen Fucking Keller to think this mess is going anywhere but full bore. I'm anxious to meet with Dick at Quang Tri and see if it is the same up there. I'll plan on your coming with me."

"Yes Sir, thank you, Sir."

"You're a good man, Pete, a real Marine. I don't want to loose track of you."

As Pete showered, trying to clear his mind as well as body, his emotions were sliced in two. The visions of the horror over at the hospital passed before his eyes while at the same time the thought of having the Colonel as a mentor was a plus for him and his career. He liked the crusty old Colonel and he knew that he could learn a lot from him. He was enormously grateful to be getting out of DaNang for Christmas. He did not feel like attending any drunken brawl Christmas parties, in fact, he would be just as happy to fall asleep on December twenty fourth and wake up on the twenty sixth. Going up to the DMZ with the Colonel would provide a chance to throw himself into his work and forget the whole holiday. His only reservation was leaving the company without a leader. "Oh hell", he thought, "the troops don't need me around when they're trying to party".

Yokosuka, Japan
December, 1966

Carrie felt terrible. Pete had been gone seven weeks and the permanence of his absence was now settling in her mind. After he left, she busied herself trying to fill the time but by now she had run through all her diversions and she was left with the bold truth that he was gone and she would have to get on with her own plans. He continued to write her faithfully and his letters were loving but they were just that, letters. In four months, he would return to the States and his family. Looking at her favorite photo of him and fingering the cross around her neck, her eyes filled with tears. She felt so empty, so alone. She felt so in tune with Pete that now she felt ripped apart, like a part of her was gone, a part that she really liked and she didn't much care for the part that was left.

Christmas. Who needs it? she asked herself. For the first time she had not sent Christmas cards, a tradition she had loved. She was miserable and just didn't care about any celebrations. The hospital was full of visiting volunteers and celebrities to entertain the troops.

Her faith provided little comfort. She tried to pray but was always distracted with thoughts of Pete and then felt angry with God for sending him and then taking him away.

It was only nine o'clock but she felt tired so she decided to go to bed. Her one blessing was that she could escape in sleep. At least that had not been taken from her. As she crawled into bed, eyeing the clock, she thought, nine o'clock on Christmas Eve. Who would ever believe it?

Christmas wasn't bad at all, much better than she thought it would be. The hospital wasn't busy. The doctors had given liberty to everyone possible and many of the base families had opened their homes to the ambulatory patients for Christmas dinner. ICU only had two patients and her two best corpsmen were on duty so Carrie was able to break away for noontime Mass in the hospital chapel. There was a scant group at Mass also, so many having attended Midnight Mass. She tried to put her self pity aside and concentrate on the wondrousness of the birth of the Christ child and its meaning in her life. Father Paige's sermon was about new life and new beginnings and how change is difficult. She felt like he was taking to her and vowed that she would try to get a better hold on herself asking for God's grace in this New Year, maybe the grace for a new attitude.

Dinner at George and Betsy's was fun. They just had six people in, all close friends, and just before dessert, Betsy announced to the group that Santa Claus had brought them a very special gift. She was pregnant. The group was delighted for them. When the day was over, Carrie realized that in spite of herself, she had found joy in this Christmas, a Christmas she had dreaded.

Quang Tri, Vietnam
December, 1966

Christmas at Quang Tri was pretty much what Pete had expected. In the morning, he attended Mass celebrated at a makeshift altar, set up outside. The Chaplain asked for a volunteer altar server and when there was hesitation, Pete stood up and for the first time in twenty years, was with the priest as an altar boy. He was grateful that the Mass was now in English because he would have been hard pressed to remember the responses in Latin, responses the Irish nuns had drilled into the young altar boys before they would give then their seal of approval to serve the priest at Mass.

Kneeling with the priest in a short meditation before Mass, Pete was filled with the Spirit of Christ and this celebration of his birth. He was sorry for his sins and asked God's forgiveness. The message in the Chaplain's sermon was one of faith and hope, of holding onto those virtues in times of struggle and turmoil.

"God never changes." he told them. "Never forget that, especially here. When all seems lost and hopeless, God never changes."

Just what I needed to hear, thought Pete, as the priest returned to the alter. At the Offertory of the Mass, he thanked the Lord for the wisdom of sending him on the trip up here. Just being at this particular Mass had made his Christmas, a Christmas he had tried to deny and avoid.

The Saturday morning of New Year's weekend Carrie went back to the orphanage with Father Paige. She was anxious to see the swing sets and to visit with the children once again.

On the way down, Tom asked Carrie how she was adjusting to Pete's absence.

"I don't know, Father. I'm a mixed bag of feelings. Some nights I cry myself to sleep and other times I'm so angry about the whole thing. It just doesn't make any sense."

"Sure it does, Carrie. It means you are perfectly normal. You had an intense love affair with Pete and then a sudden split. It will take your emotions a long time to catch up with the calendar."

"You have the best way of putting things, Tom. Where do you find the words."

"I don't. The guy upstairs finds them for me."

Their conversation next turned to the future when Tom asked Carrie where she wanted to go for her next duty station.

"San Diego," she replied. "I'm a New England girl, but I sure love California and the Far East. I have a sister in San Diego and another in San Francisco. I'm due to go back in June so my orders should be coming in about March. I had to give two choices so I also put Camp Pendleton, but I really don't want to go there. It's too far from everyplace, too South of Los Angeles and too North of San Diego."

"How about you Tom. Where do you want to go?"

Tom laughed.

"Oh, I know what I want, not only for the next set of orders, but for the next twenty years. One of my favorite past times is to sit down and plot out all my future duty stations. Talk about a fairytale, huh?"

"I should say. The way some of these orders come through, you wonder if they even look at the dreamsheets we all send in."

"The Officer Preference Card. The Navy sure has a way of giving papers a fancy name. I've often wondered what would have been wrong with calling it the 'duty station request card'. No wonder everyone calls it the 'dreamsheet'."

"Anyway, if you're interested in listening, I'll tell you my dream career."

"Try me," said Carrie, "and I'll tell you how close to reality I think you'll come."

"Well, for starters, when I leave here, if I'm not sent to Vietnam, which is a very likely possibility, I'd like to go and be the Chaplain at Annapolis. It's great duty and I'd be back close enough to my family to visit. They're in Pennsylvania. After that, I'd like to see Europe and probably the best chance for that is a ship out of Norfolk, Virginia, besides, I'll be due for sea duty anyway. Following that, I'll have been away from formal education for nearly twelve years so I'd like to go to graduate school in either psychology or some similar branch of human relations."

He lowered the car window as the sun was quickly heating up the cool car.

"Wow, the Naval Academy, the Mediterranean and Graduate school. Sounds realistic and a great seven or eight years. Tell me more."

"When I finish graduate school, I'll be ready for promotion to Commander and I'd like to be in a job where I can use my new education to effect some changes. I guess a tour in Washington would fit nicely there. I know I can't have a full career and escape Marine duty. I'm hoping it'll be Camp Pendleton instead of Camp Lejeune because I want to slowly work my way back here. The way I see it, I may have to do one more tour of duty before I do that and I wouldn't mind the Northwest. Everyone seems to love it, and there's no reason that I shouldn't. Of course, all of this is predicated on us not getting ourselves into another war. This next part may surprise you but eventually, after I trotted or sailed or crawled all over the globe, I'd like to return here as Senior Chaplain. The Orient has gotten in my blood. If I keep my nose clean, I'll be a Captain by then and just the right age. My final choice will be a duty station in the San Diego area from which I shall retire. There are plenty of jobs there, so that should be no problem."

"Wow! I'm tired just listening. How on earth did you ever figure all that out?"

"Carrie, sometimes we chaplains are worse gossips than nurses. When we get together at conferences, everyone brings all the tidbits of every duty station, the good and the bad. It's sort of become a game with me."

"I think it sounds like a great career. What you should do is write it down and file it for safe keeping. Eighteen or twenty years from now, take it out and see how close you came."

They continued along in their drive to Gotemba. Mount Fuji was radiant in its winter attire, a glistening snow cap leaking down its sides like a child's vanilla ice cream melting on a sugar cone.

Quang Tri, Vietnam

As the H-34 chopper lifted off from the airfield at Quang Tri, Pete and the Colonel adjusted their light helmets and microphones. The chopper was so open and noisy that this was the only way they could communicate with the pilot up in front. Pete was lost in his thoughts. He would only have one night back at DaNang before he would lead his platoon back out on another three week patrol.

The visit to Quang Tri had been good for him. He ran into a few buddies and got a first hand look at the problems of the war from their prospective in the North. This was not one war. It was one hundred wars being fought in on hundred different ways. The rules of beach landings and battle lines simply didn't apply here. He felt discouraged and a bit afraid. He knew he was not prepared for this type of jungle warfare.

"Not a bad few days, huh, Pete?" asked Colonel Jamison, nudging Pete in the ribs.

"Just what the doctor ordered, Sir. I'm most grateful to you for taking me along."

They took advantage of their position following the curves of Highway One for awhile, as the chopper headed South for DaNang. Like a venomous snake, Highway One slithered its way the length of Vietnam. The chopper was only at about one thousand feet but it was high enough to provide a broad vista below them. Up ahead of them, he spotted some smoke and motion below in the rice paddies.

"Can you drop this baby lower?" he shouted into his mike.

The pilot dropped to eight hundred feet.

As they approached, they could make out the camouflage uniforms of Marines and the black pajamas of the VC.

"Looks like an ambush. I bet they came out of the hills by way of Laos. Look at them, Charlie and his sleazy band of gooks. Lieutenant, do we have any ammo on board?"

"No Sir, just the machine gunner in the door."

"Well, how about radioing back to Quang Tri with their location. Lets let the boys give them a little 'rockets red glare, bombs bursting in air', to add to their party."

"Yes Sir."

Pete heard the pilot call in their position while he was trying to assimilate the enormity of this war. Out of the hills, up from the tunnels, booby traps hanging from trees. What a mess, he thought.

"Pete, it's like trying to take a crap squatted down with your pants on, this goddam war. If we could just go it with all we've got and forget the political horse pucky, we'd be out of here by Washington's Birthday. Old George must want to puke when he looks down and sees this candy ass operation."

Pete chuckled to himself with amazement at the Colonel's command of the English language. You sure don't have to ask him twice what he means, he smiled to himself.

Just as he turned to ask the Colonel a question, the chopper started to vibrate. When he started to speak, the vibration was so strong, he could not control the motion of his jaw.

"What the hell's happening?" shouted the Colonel but before the pilot could respond, the chopper went into a counterclock spin. Suddenly, the Colonel who had been sitting next to Pete was lifting up above him.

"It's the rear rotor."

The Colonel fell on Pete.

"The back rotor must have been hit by a sniper," shouted the pilot.

"I've lost altitude control."

"Son of a Bitch." screamed the Colonel. "Son of a fucking gook bitch. See if you could put this mother down on something soft."

Pete knew. He just knew. The chopper was out of control. He looked up and saw the earth and down saw the sky. This was it. A quick look around him told him there was no way out. The helicopter spun toward the rice paddy.

In his last moment, it was neither Rita not Carrie that filled his heart and mind. His dying thoughts were of his God. He made the Sign of the Cross.

"I tried dear Lord. Please forgive me."
He closed his eyes and waited for the crash.

9

Yokosuka, Japan
January, 1967

    The week after Christmas, Carrie received a letter from Pete and then another one ten days later. Both were written and mailed from Quang Tri, where he was on his trip with the Colonel. The mail was a real problem. People communicating between areas in the Pacific wrote "Inter island" on the envelope so the letter would not go all the way back to the Fleet Post Office in San Francisco. All duty stations and ships in the Pacific, had a FPO San Francisco address. Pete's first letter had come directly from Vietnam but the second one had gone all the way to the States and back and with the two long holiday weekends had taken forever to find it's way to her.

    She was glad that Pete had been able to get out of DaNang for Christmas and she was moved by his story of serving at Christmas Mass. The second letter, written just two days after the first related his reunion with some old friends and his initial feelings of the futility of the war, feelings she herself was starting to realize as the patient census at the hospital continued to rise. The letter was loving but Carrie felt a certain distance or cautiousness in it. What did I expect? she asked herself. He's a married man and I am no longer around to distract him from his family. How I miss him.

    In his closing sentence, he said that he expected to return to DaNang the next day and to go out on another three weeks of night time search and destroy patrol as soon as he got back.

"This looks like a recurring routine", she thought to herself. "It looks like I'll have a spring of three week clumps of fear and terror", remembering her feelings during his last patrol.

She chuckled to herself and her mood lifted as she looked at the address again remembering the story that Annie had told the group about her Southern grandmother.

"My grandmother never recovered from World War II. She was terrified of the Japanese. When I told her I was awaiting orders, she made me promise I would not go to Japan. I desperately wanted to come here so for two years, because the address says, 'FPO San Francisco,' she thinks I've been in San Francisco. Why break an old woman's heart?"

She and Annie spent a lot of time shopping for their major purchase like china, stereo equipment and other bulky items, that most people delayed until they were nearly ready to return to the States because of the storage problem. Annie's longed for orders to Jacksonville arrived so shopping created another interest for them to share besides the trauma at loving married men. After looking at china patterns in the exchange for nearly two years Carrie decided on a simple pattern, a white plate with a tiny green flower trimmed in gold. She thought it elegant in its simplicity. The same day, she saw an elegant strand of cultured pearls and thought she might treat herself to these before she left.

The intensive care unit was busier than ever. They had recently admitted two seriously burned Marines who had been riding in an armored tank and were trapped in its' fire when struck by a rocket. Each patient required the care of two full time corpsmen and was seen by a physician in consultation from just about every service. Though saddened by their horrible injuries, Carrie seized the chance to use the experience to teach her staff. A burn patient was a lesson in physiology at its most basic level, in every system of the body.

The corpsmen were both tired and jittery. The mental drain of caring for dying men their own age and the constant fear of receiving orders to Vietnam themselves, often resulted in quick tempers and fighting among the staff.

While Carrie tended to her patients on the unit, Annie was in her quarters curled up on her sofa looking through her "Welcome Aboard" pack that had arrived from Jacksonville. It was early evening and she was studying a map of the city trying to pick out what looked like a nice area to live. She had saved a lot of money in Japan and was thinking about buying a three bedroom house. By taking in two roommates, she'd have help with the mortgage payment. She would soon be ready for promotion to Lieutenant Commander and she knew if she did not get some property, she'd pay and enormous income tax.

Suddenly, she was jolted from her reverie by a pounding and yelling at her door.

"Annie, Annie, Annie!" She recognized Paula's panicked voice.

"Come in girl," she said. "Whatever is the matter with you?"

"Oh Annie, did you see it, did you read it?" she cried waving the Stars and Stripes.

"See what, what are you taking about?" Paula looked like she had seen a ghost.

"Annie, Pete has been killed. His name is here on the casualty list in tonight's paper. Look, it says he was killed on December twenty ninth. That's a month ago. Obviously, there's a lag between the Marines' deaths and the reporting in Stars and Stripes. Carrie did mention she hadn't heard from him in awhile, but she knew he was out on patrol. God, what an eerie feeling. Remember the time that she told us she wondered if anything ever happened to Pete how she would find out because she wasn't his next of kin? Well, I guess we know how she'll find out."

"Paula, she's on PM's. We can't let her come home at eleven thirty and pick up her paper and see this. What do you think we should do?"

Paula lit a cigarette and thought for awhile.

"Let's call Father Paige. He knows her pretty well and maybe he can help soften the blow."

"He's not here, remember? He's in Hawaii on vacation with his family."

"Oh God, no. Oh Annie, what do you think we should do?"

"You and I are going to have to tell her." Annie paused in thought for a minute.

"Let me think. I've got an idea. Let's call George and Betsy. They were fond of Pete and a real support to Carrie when he left. How about you and I going to the hospital and waiting for her to come off duty. We'll tell her and then we'll drive over to the Gleasons'. That way she can spend the night with them, instead of being along in her room."

"I think that's a good idea, as good as any I could come up with."

Annie dialed Betsy's number and George answered the phone.

"How's my favorite southern belle?" he asked.

"Not too good, George. I'm afraid I have real bad news." Annie related the news of Pete's death and added in what she knew about how long ago Carrie had received her last letter. She told George that Carrie was at work and their plan to tell her when she got off duty at eleven.

"I know she thinks the world of you two," he said. "I guess you should be the ones to tell her but then go ahead and bring her straight over here. Betsy and I will be waiting with good stiff drinks for all of you. What terrible news, a truly superb guy."

"Thanks George. We knew we could count on you and Betsy. We feel so bad. Carrie was never happier than when she was with Pete."

"He was one hell of a guy, one hell of a guy. Betsy and I thought the world of him and we really ached for them caught in their dilemma. They really did love each other."

"I know." said Annie. "They really did."

"Okay George, we'll probably be there about eleven thirty."

"Fine, see you then."

Annie hung up the phone and just looked at Paula.

"Oh, Paula, what a mess our lives have become overhere. No one seems to end up with the right person. Betsy was telling me that it's no bed of roses for the married people either. Some of the wives just can't adjust to the life here and it puts a real strain on their marriages. When they first arrive, they're all excited. They get a maid and a sew girl and then, they all sign up for the flower arranging classes. But, I guess you can arrange just so many flowers. A lot of them want to work but there's only a handful of jobs available. There are a few civilian jobs in the hospital and school, for those who are nurses or teachers."

Suddenly, Annie remembered that Paula did not know about Paul Gutierrez. She decided to trust Paula and tell her about her summer affair.

"You know, I never told you, Paula. Carrie is the only one who knew, outside of Father Paige that is, but I had an affair with Paul Gutierrez last summer. When he left, I was a mess."

"I'm sorry, Annie. If I had known maybe I could have helped."

Paula did not want Annie to know, but she did know about her affair shortly after Paul left for Bremerton. She heard about it from one of the doctors, one she couldn't stand. There was no need to hurt Annie any further now by telling her that.

"Are you over him, Annie?"

"Yes, I guess, well, no, not really, well, heck, I don't really know. It was great, Paula, great while it lasted but I don't think I'll ever do it again. It just wasn't worth what I went through afterward."

"I hate to tell you this but it is a quarter to eleven," said Paula, glancing at her watch. "We'd better get over to the hospital. We can't take a chance that this would be the one night that Carrie gets off early."

"I'd rather take a beating than do what we have to do."

Driving the short way to the hospital, they decided on the logistics. They would park the car next to Carrie's and then they would go into the hospital and wait in the corridor outside ICU. When Carrie came out they would make small talk about picking up their mail or checking the new time schedule for the reason they were there. When they got outside they would tell her.

The plan went off like a well written script. The three of them chatted down the hallway, Paula bitching all the way about finding out she was going on nights again in just four weeks.

"Geez, I just got off. One thing I'm looking forward to is being senior enough to do the schedule.

I know I could make it fairer than this mess. I just got off nights."

As the approached the two cars, Annie knew that the time had come. The chill of the January night air lay heavy on the sad frost covering her heart and she was afraid she would be unable to speak. When she reached her car, she turned around and leaned on the trunk.

"Carrie, something terrible has happened, that's why Paula and I are here."

"What, huh, what, you mean bad news from home? What's terrible, what do you mean?"

"No, not from home, Carrie. Everyone at home is fine. Carrie, its Pete."

Carrie gasped.

"Pete? How do you know about Pete? Is he hurt?"

"Carrie. Pete is dead. He was killed on December twenty ninth. It was in the Stars and Stripes tonight."

From somewhere deep in Carrie came the most painful moan that Annie had ever heard.

"No, no, no. Oh God!, no, not dead. No."

Annie pulled her into her arms and just held her. All three girls were crying.

Paula spoke up.

"Carrie, we are so sorry. We only found out about eight o'clock and we didn't know the best way to tell you. We called George and Betsy and they want you to come over. They're up waiting for us."

"Pete dead, no, Oh God, he can't be. Are you sure?"

"Well, we're as sure as we can be on any name that's published in the 'Killed in Action' column. It said Captain Pete Pachulis, New York."

"Oh God, and I thought the reason I hadn't heard from him was because he was out on patrol. December twenty ninth? I think he was still in Quang Tri then or maybe that was the day he left to go back. I wonder if there is anyway I can find out what happened. Oh what am I saying? What does it matter?"

The ride to the Gleasons' took only a few minutes. They rang the Gleasons' door bell and George answered immediately.

Suddenly, upon seeing George and Betsy, Carrie lost all control. She fell into George's arms screaming and crying from a painful place deep within her. George led her to the sofa and just cradled her against him and let her cry herself out. He didn't say a word. Annie and Paula went with Betsy to the kitchen and helped fix brandy for everyone, each girl silently suffering her own version of Carrie's grief. Each had suffered a broken heart but both Paula and Annie knew that they had not endured the loss that Carrie was feeling right now. They felt helpless. They all loved Pete so their sadness was not just for Carrie alone. Each of them felt his loss in her own way.

By the time they brought the drinks to the living room, Carrie was sitting up next to George.

"Here drink this. It's not much but it'll help calm you down," said Betsy. Carrie took the brandy and nodded her head. The five of them sat silently, sipping their brandy, all teary eyed. Poor Carrie, thought Annie. Fifteen minutes ago, she came bouncing out of work, a smile on her face and now, in such a short time, her whole world has changed.

Carrie started to talk. "Pete is dead. I know that. I believe you. I don't know how he died or if I ever will. I loved him like no one else I ever knew or right now feel I ever will know. I'm all messed up inside but I am so lucky to have,...to have," she started to cry again overcome with sadness, ".....to have four friends like you. I just sat here and thought about what this evening must have been like for you as you found out the news and tried so hard to find an easy way to tell me. I love you all."

With that, all five friends cried their hearts out, hugging each other. Finally George asked Carrie to stay overnight and Annie and Paula got up to leave. It was nearly one o'clock.

Carrie went into the guest room and put on one of Betsy's nightgowns. She did not kneel on the floor to say her prayers but instead got right under the covers. She blessed herself and could only think of five words to say, "Oh God, please help me."

10

Tokyo, Japan
February, 1967

As the taxi raced through the streets of Tokyo, Carrie's thoughts raced through her mind. As the got closer to the hospital, the memories of the trip with Annie became more vivid and she felt her fists clench on her lap.

In her mind, she could see the hospital in back of the American Embassy and when she pictured it, at the same time, she pictured the Franciscan chapel around the corner where she and Pete had attended Mass their wonderful weekend in Tokyo.

When she thought of Pete, an overwhelming feeling of shame overcame her, not because of their love but because of her mission today. Suddenly, she knew what she would do.

She tapped the driver on the shoulder and tried to make him understand that she didn't want to go to the hospital but between the traffic and the language, she could not communicate with him. Finally, the arrived at the door of the Kanto Women's Hospital. Carrie took her overnight case, paid the driver and got out. Looking around, she tried to get her bearings. She could see the American flag flying over the Embassy so she headed in that direction. She knew if she stood in front of it, she could then locate the chapel. Later, she would never look at an American flag the same way again, knowing that day, that it was a beacon that changed her life.

"May I help you?", asked the Monk at the front desk of the chapel.

"Yes, Father, I would like to talk with a priest."

"Certainly, have a seat in the second room on the left down that hall and Father will be right down."

Carrie started to perspire waiting in the small cubicle for the priest. She had no idea what to say or what she would do. She was always one for drawing up plans, having everything all figured out ahead of time. The door opened and she looked up to see an obese, middle age, red faced man enter.

"Hello, I'm Father Cyprian," he said extending his hand.

"Hello, Father, I'm Caroline Craig, how do you do." She thought he looked like an alcoholic.

"Can I get you a cup of coffee?" Carrie was dying for a cup but did not want the priest to leave to get it. She wanted to get right on with her story.

"No, thank you Father, not now, maybe later."

"Now what can I do for you?"

She started to cry.

"Oh, now dear, it can't be all that bad. Why don't you just start at the beginning and tell me the whole story."

"Father, it's not the beginning, it's the end that's so bad. I came up here today to have an abortion and I just can't go through with it but now that I've decided that, I don't know what to do, I'm back where I was before I decided to have it."

"And where is that?" asked the priest.

Carrie preceded to tell Father Cyprian about her family, the Navy, Pete, Vietnam and all her dashed dreams that having this child would cause.

"Have you talked with Miss Mullaney?"

Carrie was shocked.

"How do you know Miss Mullaney?"

"I've known Miss Mullaney for years. She trained at Bellevue, you know, and I first met her way back in New York when I was at the chapel there. Now she's part of our guild and I see her every month or so when she comes up for the meetings."

"No, I haven't talked with her, I haven't talked with anyone. She's so intimidating and besides, I don't think she likes me to begin with, she's the last person I'd go to."

"I think you have her pegged all wrong. Kate's a swell gal. Her management may be a little tough but she rates high with me on compassion and kindness. Why don't you give her a chance? Tell her you talked with me. I'm sure she'll figure out the very best thing for you to do. Chances are, she's been through this before. It's new to you but I'm sure it's not new to Kate."

"Father, what a small world. I guess I did write her off without giving her a chance."

Suddenly lost for words, Carrie asked, "Could I have that coffee now?"

The priest left to get the coffee and Carrie's thoughts went to Miss Mullaney. She could take the train back and talk with her this afternoon. But, there was something Miss Mullaney could not change. She would still have to get out of the Navy. That was the part that hurt the most. What would she do with the rest of her life?

"Here you go, feel better?"

"Oh, yes Father, I do. We haven't solved everything but I still have my baby and I don't feel like such a bad person."

"Your a beautiful person, Carrie, inside and out. I'm so glad you came in to see me and I'll help you in anyway I can. Do you have enough money?"

"Yes, Father, money is not a problem. What I wish is that I had someone like you to talk with my family. I probably will end up giving the baby up for adoption and not even telling them."

"That's a decision you don't have to make today. Today, all you have to do is go back to Yokosuka and speak with Miss Mullaney and then maybe, you can try taking it one day at a time after that."

"You're right, Father. I'm such an organizer. I want to have everything all planned out months ahead."

The train ride back seemed to take forever. By now, it was two o'clock and the gray clouds gave an added chill to the air. Back on base, Carrie dropped her case in her room and immediately dialed Miss Mullaney's quarters. She knew if she put it off, she would talk herself out of it.

"Miss Mullaney, this is Caroline Craig. I'm sorry to bother you but I was wondering if I could come over to your quarters and talk to you this afternoon."

Without even a second's hesitation, Miss Mullaney replied that, yes, she could and she could come right now if she liked. Carrie, thanked her, said she would be right over and hung up the phone.

Carrie walked along, her hands in her coat pocket. The cherry blossom trees lining the main street that would dazzle everyone in April now looked like skeletal sticks poking at each other in the wind. Out on Sagami Bay, the wind puffed up white caps in sharp contrast to the glistening sparkle of last Summer's bay. Walking near the bay made her feel close to Pete. She'd only had a short time to get used to the news of his death. Misty eyed, she stopped and looked over the water. You dear man, you dear, sweet man, she whispered to herself. He was so young, she thought and tried to find some meaning in his death. Her thoughts went to one of her favorite poems, *To An Athlete Dying Young,* by A.E. Houseman, in particular, she thought of the words of the fifth stanza:

> Now you will not swell the rout
> Of lads that wore their honors out,
> Runners whom renown outran
> And the name died before the man

No, Pete would not outlive their love. Tears streamed down her face, tears of both sadness and fear. Pete was gone and the task before her now filled her with fear and terror.

She entered the building and walked to the end of the corridor. She knocked on the living room door of the two room suite. Miss Mullaney answered immediately.

"Hi Carrie, come in, I'm just heating some water for tea. My, its blustery out."

"Miss Mullaney, I'm sorry to bother you like this."

"No bother, come in, come in. I wish more of you girls would stop in. By the way, I haven't had a chance to tell you how sorry I was about the death of your friend, Pete. I didn't know him well but I admired him. I don't know if you knew it or not but while you were in the ladies room at the Marine Corps Ball, he asked me to dance and we had a lovely visit."

"No, I didn't know that Miss Mullaney. Pete wasn't the type to tell nice things on himself, but thank you for thinking of him."

Miss Mullaney fixed the tea and decided to let Carrie set the pace for the conversation.

Carrie looked around the suite. There was a warm feeling in the decor and lots of photos of friends engaged in fun and good times. She immediately got a different picture of Miss Mullaney.

"You've fixed your place up beautifully. Looks like a real living room."

Catherine Mullaney served the tea. Carrie took the spoon and placing it in the cup stirred the tea back and forth like the pendulum of a ticking clock, her tongue searching for the right words.

Casting her eyes downward, she said, "Miss Mullaney, I'm so ashamed, so upset, so scared." She was only able to get one sentence out before her tears blurred her vision.

In all her wisdom, Catherine Mullaney said nothing.

Carrie looked at the waiting woman. "Miss Mullaney, Pete's death is not my only problem."

"What is it Carrie? What could have you this upset? Is it one of the doctors giving you a hard time?"

Carrie shook her head back and forth.

"May I please use your bathroom? The cold wind and the hot tea seemed to have produced a diuretic."

While Carrie was in the bathroom, Catherine Mullaney refilled their tea cups. She was genuinely found of Carrie.

Carrie returned to the sitting room and let out a deep sigh. Looking up at her chief nurse, from somewhere at the back of her throat, she rushed out the words, "I'm pregnant."

As soon as she said the word, Carrie felt an immense release and her tears flowed freely. She had tried to deny it, to pray it away. She had shared her suspicions with no one until today. Finally another person knew and she felt her burden lighten.

"Oh Carrie, no. Are you sure? Are you sure you're not just upset or scared? Of all the problems I considered since you entered my room, I never considered that."

"No Miss Mullaney, I'm sure."

"Who else knows about this, Carrie?"

"Just you and me." She decided not to tell her about her visit with Father Cyprian. She did not want her to know that she had been to Tokyo. "I haven't told any of my friends. One thing I always remember our grandfather told us was 'if you wanted to keep a secret, you didn't tell anyone, not even your best friend'."

"Your grandfather gave you good advice."

"Carrie, how can you be sure? Have you seen one of the doctors?"

"No, but yesterday, I brought my first voided urine into the lab with a false name on the specimen and one of the doctors name on it. Last night, after the evening corpsman put the lab slips in the hallway boxes, I came over and retrieved the slip. The pregnancy test was positive."

"Well, I can't give you my whole hearted approval of your tactics but I admire your ingeniousness at thinking it up," Catherine Mullaney smiled.

"Miss Mullaney, I know the rules just as well as you do. I know I have to get out of the Navy. That's why I came up here, to talk about that and how I can best do it without a whole lot of people knowing. I want this kept as private as possible. That's why I've come to you."

"Oh, that's no trouble," said the chief nurse. "That'll be no trouble at all."

Carrie looked shocked. "I don't understand."

"Carrie, dear. You underestimate me. I wasn't always a chief nurse twenty years older than everyone else. You forget that once upon a time I was an Ensign and JayGee too. I certainly don't mean to diminish your problem but you are not the first Navy nurse to become pregnant on active duty or overseas for that matter."

Carrie smiled.

"Of course. I never thought about that. I guess you're right."

Miss Mullaney became serious for a moment.

"Carrie, I will not invade your privacy and I will help you as much as I can but before we talk about what you are going to do, I have to ask you, is there any chance of a wedding?"

"No, Miss Mullaney, no chance."

"There are no other men you know, men who would....."

"No, Miss Mullaney, I couldn't do that. I'm alone in this."

Miss Mullaney paused and looking at Carrie, said, "Caroline, I will help you all I can but I want you to know how genuinely sorry I am that this has happened to you."

"Thank you, thank you for telling me that. I know I have let you down and I feel very ashamed."

"Carrie, your only sin was in loving too much. You haven't let me down. Now, lets talk about how we can best handle this."

Miss Mullaney put her hands up to her face and thought for a few moments.

"I will have to tell the Commanding Officer but that is the only person that'll have to know. Captain Spaulding is a kind man and I know he will be both discreet and helpful. Tomorrow morning, I want you to spread the news that you had word from home that your father has had a heart attack. Try to carry on like it is quite serious and you are waiting for further word. I will go to personnel and speak to the Personnel Officer, who will cut you Emergency Leave Orders for four days from now. On that day, we will say we received a message saying that your father has taken a turn for the worse and we will let you go on emergency leave."

Carrie listened intently, not wanting to forget a word.

"Now the next thing to do is to set up a way for you to get your personal effects back. We can't do it the regular way. There isn't enough time for housing to do that. Thank God for friends. The skipper on the USS Delaware is an old hospital shipmate of mine from Korea days. I'll ask him if he will take your shipment back for you. They'll be heading for San Diego in about three weeks."

"Miss Mullaney, I'm overwhelmed. I never knew all of this could be arranged."

"Carrie, I've been in the Navy a long time. There isn't much I haven't seen. You forget there is no limit to imagination and ingenuity of the American sailor when the going gets tough."

Carrie smiled, nodding her head in agreement.

"Now, have we covered everything?"

"I think so, and thank you so much."

Miss Mullaney continued. "I am going to give you Monday off. Don't worry about the schedule. I'll see to it that the unit is covered. Make sure that you tell a few people either tonight or tomorrow about the heart attack though. Get your household effects in some semblance of order. What will probably happen is that the Delaware will send a work party up to your place in the middle of the night and move your household effects out and on to the ship. So go shopping and get the last minute things you want so they can load them, or better still, if you go shopping and purchase large items, have them delivered directly to Captain Mauldin on the Delaware."

"You are so kind. I don't deserve this good treatment. I've caused you so much trouble."

"No trouble, no trouble. If we nurses can't be helpful to each other, how on earth can we be helpful to our patients? Now go along back to your quarters and try to sort some of this out in your head. As soon as I have word from personnel on when you are leaving, I'll let you know. If you need to talk, call back here anytime."

"I don't know how to thank you."

"You can thank me by being courageous and by helping someone else out sometime down the road who is in the same boat."

"Oh, I will, I certainly will."

Walking across the base back to her quarters, Carrie couldn't believe how smoothly the visit with Miss Mullaney had gone. She felt so guilty for the nasty thoughts she had harbored toward her chief nurse. What a wise and companionate woman, she thought. Suddenly, her mind went to Paula, Annie, Betsy and George. Should I tell them she asked herself? She quickly decided she would tell no one. The Gleasons would be in Japan for another year. Annie was leaving in a week or two for Jacksonville and Paula was due to leave in June and had asked for Great Lakes Naval Hospital near Chicago. Chances are she would not see any of these people in the next year so they would never learn of her pregnancy. As long as the baby was going to be adopted, there was no reason for any of them to ever know she was pregnant.

"Good evening, Miss Craig."

Startled, she looked up to see two of her corpsmen heading out for a night on the town.

"Hi, you guys going window shopping?"

They both laughed. All three knew they were probably headed for the alley and a night of bar hopping ending up in the arms of a Japanese bar girl.

Carrie hugged her arms across her chest. The wind had picked up as early evening set in, and a winter chill tore through the weave of her woolen coat. As she passed the Officers' Club, she could hear the band playing, "The Girl from Ipenema." Her mind traced the memory of the hundreds of fun filled nights she had spent in that building and it saddened when the thought struck her that those nights were now a thing of the past. If that building could talk, she thought. She felt like the club was almost a person rather than a building.

Entering her room, she looked around and tried to collect her thoughts about the role she would have to play the next two or three days. She felt exhausted so she changed out of her uniform and into a comfortable yukata. Lying on her bed, she started to relax as she lined up the activities of the next few days when suddenly she stiffened as she thought, 'Oh God, what do I do when I get to San Diego? How do I handle that end of it?'

The deceptive plan that Miss Mullaney devised to get Carrie out of Japan went off like a well rehearsed drama. As the two major players, they even started to believe each other as they talked the last three days. Both Paula and Annie were on the evening shift so she didn't even see them before she left. The word spread quickly among her friends about "her sick father", and when the second message came to come home, few were surprised.

"Hey, Miss Craig," said LTJG Greg Cortes as she passed personnel. "I got you a seat on Pan Am out of Haneda Airport. It's a military contract flight. Sure beats riding in a car or bus three and a half hours to Tachikawa Air Force Base."

"Thanks, Greg, that's great. Thanks a lot."

The night before she left, four sailors from the Delaware arrived at her room at midnight with a truck and loaded all her goods. Off went her clothes, her china, her brass table, her woodblock prints, her stereo, all memories of shopping trips in Japan. As each item went through the door, the pain of the separation from Pete and Japan intensified. If she could just hold herself together until tomorrow.

At six o'clock the next morning, the Commanding Officer's driver arrived in the command sedan and drove her the hour's ride to Haneda airport, orders in hand to proceed to San Diego for separation. She was in an "On leave" status until then.

When they arrived at the airport, the driver helped her with her luggage and bidding her goodbye, said, "See you in a few weeks Miss Craig. I sure do hope your dad recovers. You being there is sure to help."

"Thank you. Thank you kindly both for your thoughtfulness and for the ride."

"Yes, Ma'am."

Carrie walked through the automatic door to the Pan Am counter. Checking in for her seat assignment, the airline clerk asked, "Going back to the good old U S of A, Lieutenant?"

"Yes, I am. I'm anxious to see the things that I've been reading about like hippies and flower children."

"Well, there's no shortage of them in San Francisco, that's for sure," replied the friendly agent. He handed her her boarding pass and wished her a comfortable flight.

She had an hour to kill so she went to the news stand and bought several American magazines, some gum and chapstick for the long flight. Finally, she heard the announcement that her flight was ready for boarding. Handing the agent at the gate her boarding pass, she proceeded toward the plane. The sun was just breaking through the clouds this chilly February morning. She walked slowly up the portable staircase to board the plane. When she reached the top step, she stopped turned back and took a last look at Japan. Strains of the love song, "Sayonara", echoed in her head and her eyes filled with tears. She turned and entered the aircraft.

"Goodbye, Japan. Sayonara."

11

Commander Mullaney sat at her desk reviewing the nurses schedule for next month. First on the agenda, she thought, will be to assign a new nurse to take charge of ICU but I can't do it yet because the staff thinks that Carrie is coming back. She forgot or just plain had not thought of what to tell Carrie regarding a cover story for her failure to return. Last night she had mapped out a feasible story and today she planned to send it to Carrie so their stories would not conflict.

She got up and looked out the large window in her second floor office. The sight made her shiver. It was pouring rain with the wind blowing so hard, it slammed sheets of water like buckets of paint up against the buildings.

She would write Carrie today at her sister's in San Diego and tell her that in three weeks, she would tell the staff that because she was so close to returning to the States anyway, she had received the orders she wanted to the Naval hospital in San Diego a few months early. That way, Carrie could begin to write to some of her friends and not worry about the San Diego postmark, when she was supposed to be in New England visiting her father.

She hoped she had handled Caroline correctly. Her thoughts went back nearly twenty years. She was stationed at St. Alban's Naval hospital in New York, when one of her friends became pregnant. The chief nurse was so furious that she withheld the girl's request for discharge until her seventh month when she was popping out of her uniform. The young nurse was so embarrassed as she worked each day trying to cover as much of her pregnancy as she could with a sweater. She had vowed that if she was ever in that position to prevent something like that from happening, she would vindicate that wretched memory.

She quickly wrote a short note to Carrie and walked downstairs to the mailroom. She wanted her to get her story line to her as quickly as possible so Carrie could match it on her end in San Diego.

Aboard Pan Am Flight #18
February, 1967

Carrie awakened with a cramp in her neck. She looked at her watch and saw that she had been in the air four hours, just under halfway there. I'm in the middle of the Pacific she thought and it occurred to her that the expansive ocean was about to demarcate two phases of her life.

The flight attendant brought her a cup of tea.

"Did you have a good rest?"

"Yes, thank you I did. This tea looks like it's just what I need to clear my head."

"Are you returning for duty in the States?"

"No, I'm on Emergency leave. My dad has had a heart attack and isn't doing well at all."

"Oh, I'm sorry. I hope he recovers. I'm sure having you there will help a great deal."

Carrie was amazed at how easily she lied to the flight attendant and suddenly realized that the story of the heart attack was now worthless. That was a story created to get her out of Japan. Now, she had to take some time and decide on what she was going to tell her family. Her problem was not limited to her family. She knew she would have to get a job immediately to start earning money and that would mean co-workers. If she was only clear about what she was going to do with herself, it would be easier to handle the innocent questions of others.

Her mind drifted back to her last two days in Japan. She knew Paula, Annie, Betsy and George well enough to know that they must be puzzled and upset with her for not calling before leaving. She wrote them all notes before she left that they would receive today, begging off a visit by claiming she had so much to do. She added that being upset about her dad had placed her into a state of inertia.

She expected the plane to land at Travis Air Force Base, north of San Francisco, but because it was a contract flight, it landed at San Francisco International Airport. With the time change, it was midnight the day before when they finally arrived nine and a half hours after leaving Japan. Carrie decided to splurge and take a taxi into the city to the Mark Hopkins Hotel. She wanted to take a day to recover from jet lag and to decide on an unshakable story before she called Cathy and proceeded to San Diego.

Looking out her eighteenth floor window atop Nob Hill at the city lights and spans of the bridges, she felt a great sadness. This was the city of her first duty station filled with wonderful memories of friendship and love. When she left here nearly two years ago, sailing under the Golden Gate Bridge, it was with excitement and joy at heading for the Orient. She recalled how shocked she was at Paula's behavior and how she had changed since then. How did I ever allow this to happen? she asked herself. At this moment, Japan, Vietnam, all of it seemed unreal, like a time period she had only dreamt. She opened the San Francisco Examiner scanning the pages for the casualty list. After going through the paper twice, she was astounded not to find one. At last, she felt sleepy. She took a hot shower and went to bed.

The next morning, she bought the San Francisco Chronicle and again searched for the casualty list. When the waiter brought the breakfast she ordered from room service, she asked him about it.

"No Ma'am, I don't know what you are talking about. There's never been any list like that in the paper."

Carrie moved over to an easy chair in the room and looked out at the spectacular San Francisco scene. She took the complimentary writing paper and a pen to doodle her thoughts and to plot out her story. From past experience, she knew the simpler she made a story the less trouble she was apt to get into defending it. Few would ask about the baby's father, at least not directly to her, but for those who did, she had to be ready. After sitting there a half hour she was satisfied with her plan. From this day forward, she was Mrs. Caroline Craig, whose husband was killed in Vietnam. She met him in Japan. A few months later they met in Hong Kong on leave where they were married. He was then killed and she found out she was pregnant. That was the story for outsiders.

For her sisters, she was simply going to tell them that the baby's father was killed in Vietnam. She also decided that morning that no one, not her family or her best friend was going to know his name. There were too many people to be hurt by that and it was going to be one intimacy that she was going to claim for herself and her child.

After she created her cover stories, she felt a burst of energy, as if a burden had been lifted, and she thought she could now face Cathy. She dialed the phone and felt her heart racing as she heard the phone ringing in Coronado.

"Hello."

"Hi Cathy, guess who?"

"Carrie, Where are you?"

"I'm in San Francisco. We med-evaced a badly wounded patient and I had to accompany him on the flight. How would you like some company?"

"Great! I can't believe it. Have you talked to Candy?"

"No, I just got in last night."

Carrie gulped. Candy. She couldn't believe in all her anxiety and her focus on San Diego, she forgot she had a sister right here with the airlines in San Francisco.

"Oh, I forgot," said Cathy. "She's on a cross country to New York. She was going to try and get up to see mother and dad."

Carrie gulped again. Mom and Dad.

"Cathy, I'm all packed. I'll call a taxi and go right out to the airport. PSA has a flight just about every hour. I'll just go military standby. I'll call you if I can before I board. If not, I'll call from San Diego."

Pausing a moment, she added ".......and Cathy, until I get there, please don't tell anyone I'm here, especially mom and dad. I'd like some private time with you before the onslaught of calls and visits.

"Sure. You picked a great time for a gab. Dave is in New Orleans at a dental convention. He's not due back for three days."

Thank you God, Carrie prayed.

Carrie got the last standby seat on the flight to San Diego, beating out two barefoot, longhaired hippies.

"Military pig," she heard one of them say and she looked at him shocked.

"Baby killer," said his friend.

Carrie was completely confused. Who were these people who stood accusing of her of unthinkable acts?

The agent looked at her sympathetically and asked if she were a nurse.

"Yes, I am and I've just spent a year and a half taking care of Vietnam casualties."

"Don't even try to understand it Lieutenant, God know I've tried and I can't. To me they're a bunch of lazy slobs that need jobs."

"I was stationed here before Japan and there wasn't any of this before I left."

"Well, they're all over the place now and unfortunately, I think it's going to get a lot worse before it gets better. Have a nice flight."

Carrie enjoyed the flight, picking out landmarks of the California coast. Before long, they were over Camp Pendleton and Carrie felt her stomach lurch. Pete had said that Rita and the two children were staying a Pendleton. For a quick second, she thought of calling Rita and saying she was a friend of Pete's, but quickly stopped herself. Misty eyed, she had to accept the fact, there was no place for her in Rita Pachulis' life.

As soon as she left the aircraft, she saw Cathy's beaming smile. She hugged her sister until she thought they both would crack, tears streaming down her face.

"Oh, Carrie, how wonderful to have you here. You've been so good about writing but you know it's not the same. I couldn't sit there and wait for your call. I took a chance that you'd luck out and be on the first flight."

The sisters hurried to the car and down Pacific Highway to the ferry landing.

"This old ferry isn't long for this world. Did you know they're building a bridge?"

"No, I didn't. I guess it's better for traffic but the ferry is so quaint, so romantic."

"Most of Coronado is up in arms about it with people vowing in the press, that they'll never drive over the bridge even if they have to swim or take the long way round. Do you want to stop for lunch?"

"No, I'm not hungry, why don't we go right to your place so I can get out of this uniform?"

"Sure, you must be exhausted after a long flight like that."

"I'm okay. As long as I can lie back a day or two, my body will catch up with my head."

Cathy put the tea kettle on and Carrie changed into a yukata.

"What is that?" asked Cathy.

"A yukata. I felt the same way when I first saw them, thought they were the ugliest things in the world but they are so comfortable, I am forever hooked. I bought one for you."

"Thanks, now put your feet up and tell me what I've been missing by being married the last year and a half."

Carrie had to fight hard to avoid a smirk.

"I have a long story, Cathy, and I really would appreciate it if you took your phone off the hook. I'd like to be able to tell it to you without the fear of Mom calling in the middle."

"Oh, she never calls. With all three of us away, she said she decided way back to save money and limit the calls to holidays only and so she got back to letter writing. I'm sure you get the copies just like we do. I'll take the phone off, no problem, but you really got my curiosity up."

Mrs. Craig wrote one letter every week, then xeroxed it and sent one to each daughter. At the bottom of each she would write a small personal note.

"Cathy, first of all, erase everything I told you on the phone from your mind. I didn't come home because of a sick patient. I came in on Pan Am the night before last. I'm going to be discharged from the Navy because I'm pregnant."

Cathy gasped, then said. "I'm sorry Carrie, but it is a shock. What? Who?"

"Let me go on. I don't have any definite plans. I have to have some time of peace and quiet to sort out some things and make some decisions. I'm hoping to find that here. What I do know is that I am definitely pregnant and I will not be getting married. I'm ashamed and sad and very confused right now. I know you are curious but at this time, the only thing I am willing to tell anyone was that the baby's father was killed in Vietnam and that he was wonderful and special person. Everyone in Japan thinks I came home on emergency leave because Dad had a heart attack. The chief nurse was great and helped me get out of there.

Could I have some more tea?"

"Sure, hold on."

Cathy went to the kitchen, her head spinning.

"Everyone in Japan thinks I'm coming back, so in a few weeks, she is going to write me here and tell me the cover story she used so that we can be consistent. As far as mom and dad go, I only wrote to them every two weeks, so I am going to send the letters to Miss Mullaney and she is going to continue to mail them for me from Japan."

"God, they would just die. You remember how they nearly had a stroke when Sheila's baby was born in seven months. Poor Sheila, and she was married! We ended up with a darling cousin, but they'll never let anyone forget that Sheila had to get married."

"At this point, I don't know if I am going to keep the baby. If I do, they will have to know, but if I relinquish it for adoption, I want to get out of this with as few people as possible knowing about it. From this minute on, every person I meet here or that you happen to make mention of me to is to think that I am married, that my name is Mrs. Caroline Craig and that my husband was killed in Vietnam. If you are pressed for details, please just say that your sister is very upset and that you would prefer not to talk about it. I know things are changing but they'll never change enough for Mom and Dad to forgive a sinful daughter who is pregnant. They still hate the wonderful changes in the church. They drive thirty miles to go to a church where the Mass is still in Latin, and Mom still won't serve meat on Friday even though that is no longer a church rule."

Lighting a cigarette, she continued.

"Oh, I don't mean they aren't good parents but do you think it's an accident that they are on the East Coast and the three of us are out here? I can tell you exactly what they would do. They would pressure me to go away to one of those Catholic nuns homes or Florence Crittenden House, hide away, have the baby and give it up for adoption. Once, they had me away, they just wouldn't have to deal with it. That's how they've always handled unpleasant things."

Cathy smiled.

"I hate to say it, but you're right. I don't know what else to say but I feel good that you came to me and you can trust Dave and me. Stay as long as you like. You can either have the guest room or you can stay in the cottage in back. It's just a hole in the wall but it's private. Many of the homes here in Coronado have them and different people call them different names, mother-in-law, cottage, dollhouse. There's one large room with a small bath and kitchenette."

"Thanks, I'll take that. You and Dave need your privacy."

"Can I fix you another cup of tea?"
"No thanks, I've had enough."

"Carrie, if you don't mind me saying, you seem so cool and collected about all of this."

"Don't get the wrong impression. I loved him very much. I'm aching about having to leave the Navy and terrified about what's ahead. I want to get married but who's going to marry someone with an illegitimate baby. Name me one person you know who's done that. I have to get a job. I may seem cool to you but I've thought of nothing but this for the last three days waiting to talk with you. Do you have any suggestions?"

"No, it seems like you've covered everything although I have to admit I am going to feel like a cheat when I write to Mom."

"I have to make a decision about them real soon. I am going to tell them I got orders here early. If I am going to go home between duty stations, as they'll expect me to, I have to do it soon before I show."

"Oh, gosh, I forgot about that. There's so much to cover when you're..................I'm sorry."

"I know, when you're living a lie. I've been living one for quite awhile and it's scary to know how good at it I am."

"What about Candy? How often does she get down here?"

"Literally never. She flies a San Francisco-Chicago-New York route and has a boyfriend in Seattle so when she has time off, she heads North in the opposite direction."

Five days later, Carrie received the letter from Miss Mullaney explaining the cover story with a check for one hundred dollars to be used to help her over the rough spots. She was so taken with emotion and wished more than anything she had the chance to know Miss Mullaney again under different circumstances.

She answered the letter right away thanking Miss Mullaney and telling her that she could start telling everyone that her "Dad was doing great", and that she could pass on her San Diego address to those who asked.

Gradually, the mail started dribbling in. In one week, she received letters from Paula, Annie, the Gleasons and Father Paige, all chuck full of details of Yokosuka life, the latest gossip, whose orders were starting to come in, but most of all, how much they missed her. She carried them around the house, like a two year old dragging a blanket, her tie to her soul. She sat on the glider on Cathy's porch, the stack of letters in her lap. Tears streamed down her face as the memories of the past year and half flooded her mind. The patients, Tokyo, Fuji, Hong Kong, Pete, the Marine Corps Ball, the orphanage, the little mama-san who cleaned her room and ironed her uniforms, Miss Mullaney, all her friends. They passed before her eyes like a holiday parade. For awhile, she had fooled herself, thinking she made the transition smoothly and fairly painlessly, but the words of her friends quickly transported her mind to a place her heart had never left. The loving, caring, words from those who had shared a common experience and because of the intensity of the war, their lives and their loves would be bonded together in some way forever. Her heart was broken.

Glancing down at the tear stained stack of envelopes, she wept openly as she prayed silently, "Dear God, never have I felt so loved and yet, so very much alone."

BOOK TWO

JOHN

1

Coronado, California, 1973

    Carrie stood at the kitchen sink rinsing out the dishes from lunch. She was tired but content after a busy morning. The Fourth of July parade in Coronado was the best in San Diego County. They had taken their beach chairs over to the median strip on Orange Avenue and had enjoyed the parade in the shade of the eucalyptus trees in the park in front of the Catholic Church.

    "Mommy, Mommy, look at me," squealed the little girl's voice from the swing set in the back yard. Pushing herself higher and higher, her strawberry blond pigtails stood out straight behind her head, the yellow ribbons caught between the sun in the sky and the sun on her hair.

    "Yes, darling, I see, you're almost touching the sky."

    The scene in the yard touched Carrie so deeply and her eyes misted over watching her daughter. To think I almost gave her away. She shuttered at the thought. She's nearly six years old and how I love her.

    Maybe it was because today was a national holiday and celebration was in the air that Carrie was hit by a flood of her Navy memories, memories she had slowly buried in her need to adjust to her new life, but which would never completely leave her.

    She remembered her first visit with Sister Claire Louise from Catholic Charities and how kind Sister had been. She was happy to know that she would have a baby to place with one of the many couples she was helping.

After Carrie had time to think everything through during her pregnancy, she decided to give her child up for adoption. She gave Sister just two instructions; that the baby was go to a Catholic home and that both parents would be college educated. The rest she would leave up to Sister's good judgement.

She laughed at herself when she thought of the months she'd worked at the small Community Hospital on night duty. She, who despised every night she ever worked in the Navy ended up, by her own choice on nights. She was so ashamed, she wanted to limit her contact with people. By working nights, she would have fewer co-workers. She took an opening in labor and delivery which worked out well on many accounts, one being the loose scrub dress she was able to wear to hide her pregnancy until the seventh month. Among the night nurses, she was designated the nurse for the recovery area, so most of the time, she worked alone.

She stuck to her story. For the few people who asked, she simply told them that her husband was killed in Vietnam. The tale was a believable one in Coronado with its high military population, and it brought few further questions. Most people were not comfortable talking about grief and death so after learning she was a widow, they diverted the conversation to other topics.

Although she was eligible for free care at the Naval hospital for her delivery, she was terrified of running into old friends, so she chose to have her baby in the Community Hospital, paying for her stay with the health coverage she received as a full time employee.

She insisted on a private room and even though she made the decision to give the baby away, she had the nursery bring her child to her for her bottle feeding every four hours. On the third day, when the child came and the nurse left, Carrie looked adorasly into her baby's blue eyes, only to catch the baby returning her gaze. For some reason, the delivery room staff failed to give her the hormone shot to help dry up her breast milk. During the night, her milk came in and her breasts were swollen and tender from the engorgement. She held her child close and could not resist the maternal urge to put her baby to her breast. As she felt the baby's first suckling pull, she was filled with love for her child and in that moment, she knew beyond a doubt that she was a mother and that she had to raise her child. She was so overcome with the emotion of her decision, that when the nurse came to retrieve the child for the nursery, she was in tears.

"Whatever is wrong, Mrs. Craig?" asked the innocent nurse.

"Nothing, absolutely nothing, everything is wonderful. Could you please call Sister Claire Louise at Catholic Charities and ask her to come see me today?"

Sister became Carrie's greatest ally. She never for one moment made her feel that she had gone back on her word or had disappointed a waiting couple. On Carrie's second day at home, she came to visit and they sat down together and planned a new strategy for the new decision. With Sister's love and support, Carrie lost her shame and swelled in her pride as a mother. During the next week, she wrote to her close friends and her parents and told them the truth, that she had given birth to a daughter and was living in Coronado.

For some reason, she found it much easier to be a slim young mother with a baby than to be pregnant with a bump in front. The anxiety had passed so the recipients of the letters didn't have to dilly dally in their minds as to what she was going to do. All the decisions had been made. In the notes, she explained that she had hidden her pregnancy because she was going to relinquish her child but now that she was a mother, she wanted to share her joy.

Her parents response was predictable. They were angry that she had lied, were furious when she would not reveal the father's name and still tried to pressure her into giving the child up. Carrie tried to understand their feelings but by this time, she was more interested in protecting and loving her daughter than appeasing her controlling parents. Eventually, they'll come around she thought. They'll have to or they'll be the odd men out. Cathy and Candy adored the baby, and Cathy and her husband, Dave Peterson, were the baby's godparents.

Once she decided to keep the baby, she had to give her a name. Names were something she had refused to consider when she decided to put the baby up for adoption. She didn't want to think of her baby as a person with a name. But now, her daughter was hers to keep. She wanted her to have a pretty name, a name that fit in so she wouldn't be different. She reviewed a list of her favorite girls names and finally decided on Susan Catherine, Susan just because she liked the name and Catherine for Miss Mullaney, the first person to know about the baby, and the first person to support Carrie. She hoped little Susan would grow up to have the courage and compassion of Miss Mullaney. When she wrote and told Miss Mullaney that she was naming her child for her, she received a beautiful note and a promise that she would stop by and see "her" child when she passed through San Diego on her way to her next duty station in Florida.

All her friends responded immediately. They all said the same thing, that they felt terrible that she had gone through it alone and if only she had told them, they would have done anything to help her. She felt bad that she hadn't trusted them enough to tell them but she made what she thought was the best decision at the time. None of them had the poor taste to mention the baby's father. George and Betsy's baby arrived and Carrie received a darling birth announcement with "Made in Japan" on the cover. They too, had a daughter and named her, Stephanie.

They sent all the base gossip including news that Father Paige had left to be the Catholic Chaplain at the Naval Academy. Carrie tried to think back to their conversation about duty stations and thought she remembered that that was what he wanted. Betsy said that one of the last things he did before he left was to help the Lanes adopt a baby form the Gotemba orphanage, a boy that they called Michael Thomas, the Thomas for Father Paige.

When Carrie's maternity leave expired, she returned to her job on night duty. She just wheeled the baby carriage into Cathy's house at ten thirty at night and then she was home all day with Susan. It wasn't ideal but was the best situation available to support her and her child. Her first criteria was that Susan be tended by someone who loved her.

The Naval hospital was no longer able to deliver all the young women eligible for care there, so more started delivering at the Community hospital. Each night, she had at least two or three patients in recovery. She had now worked the night shift over a year and knew most of the obstetricians quite well. They'd drunk gallons of coffee together and had covered every conceivable topic of conversation in the wee hours when people's guards shrink and their vulnerabilities widen.

She was fond of several of the physicians but her favorite was Dr. Burton Ellington. Like Carrie, Dr. Ellington had served in the Navy. When he retired from the Navy, he began a private practice in Coronado. Carrie guessed he was about sixty years old but his handsome looks and fine physique belied his age. A tall man, he had dark brown hair with just a hint of grey and a smile that welcomed conversation and closeness.

She thought back to the time right after Susan was born. If it hadn't been for Dr. Ellington, she would have gone crazy. Learning to be a mother was a piece of cake compared to the changes in the world around her. It seemed like everything she cherished was now being torn down by a new force of power in the country. The first thing she noticed when she returned from Japan was the music. It was loud and she hated it. There was an anti-military feeling among the young so strong that at times she purposely withheld the fact that she had been in the Navy.

Everything was "cool", "groovy", or "psychedelic", and try as she did, she could not identify with any of it.

Martin Luther King and Bobby Kennedy were both assassinated and some people were quite open about the fact that they were glad. The attitude horrified her.

The recovery room was not busy the night the POW's started arriving in the Philippines from Hanoi so she turned on the television and she watched them deplane, tears streaming down her cheeks. Though she recognized just a few of the names, here were the men she had partied with in both Alameda and Yokosuka, returning now as Prisoners of War. She would never forget the attitude of the young orderly who came through the recovery room and asked her what she was watching. When she explained its meaning to him, he shrugged his shoulders and said, "Got what they deserved if you ask me." She felt lost as if caught in her own private time capsule.

She started to date when Susan was about a year old but each date was more of a disaster than the one before it. She looked forward to each time as a chance to get back into the social world she had left in Japan but it seemed to her that all the norms had changed while she was away. She recalled an evening in particular. She accepted an invitation to dinner from one of the young physicians. They went to Lubach's on the San Diego waterfront. All through dinner, his main topic of conversation was how he avoided the draft and how he thought the Navy doctors in town were incompetent. After dinner, they went to a disco to dance. As they entered, Carrie was struck in the face by whirling strobe lights and music so loud she could neither speak nor hear. After getting her a drink, her date pulled a marijuana joint from his sportcoat, lit it and offered her a drag. She couldn't believe it. She never thought of herself as a square but try as she would, she was unable to identify with this new world around her. Her precious values and memories made her feel isolated and lonely. She was a misfit in her own age group, something she had never been before. She longed for the ballads of Johnny Mathis, Barbra Streisand and Andy Williams and to be held in a man's arms dancing and swaying to "Chances Are" and "Moonriver." But, no one danced together anymore. There was just this awful gyrating and shaking four or five feet from each other, the whole dance floor taking on the look of caged monkeys engaged in some type of mating ritual. Her misery during the evening was compounded by memories of evenings in the Officers' Club with Pete and her old friends in Japan. She really did give other men a chance but deep inside she knew she had loved the finest and finding a match for him would not be easy.

It was during this time her friendship with Dr. Ellington grew. She teased him saying that his babies always seemed to be born at night and he kidded her back by telling her that was because they all got started at night. He was waiting for a delivery one night and came to visit her in recovery. He asked her why a pretty girl like her was working at night and not out having a good time. His question opened up a floodgate of frustration in Carrie and she told him her whole story, of feeling out of sync with the current social scene, but still sticking to the story that she was a widow, whose husband was killed in Vietnam. When she shared her disappointment in the dates and her felling of not fitting in anymore, Dr. Ellington said, "I know just what you mean", and went on to tell her how he was appalled by the lack of respect shown him by his younger physicians. Finally, she found someone who thought like she did.

"Carrie, I'm a lot older than you and I've seen some fads and eras come and go. This will go too, but it's a little stronger than most because its life and blood is rooted in the protest against the war in Vietnam. Don't you, for one minute, change any of your values and hook up with one of those creeps. You're a classy gal and if you are patient, some lucky guy will see that and move in on you."

She could have hugged Dr. Ellington.

Not long after that night, he asked her if she could come to his office some afternoon, that he had something that he wanted to discuss with her and he preferred to do it away from the hospital.

"Sure, I'd be glad to. Of course, I'm dying of curiosity."

"Nothing to be frightened of Carrie, just a little proposal I want to run by you."

That is how she started working for Dr. Ellington. When she went to his office, he showed her around all the rooms. It was a Wednesday afternoon, so there were no patients or staff there.

"Carrie," he said. "I'm quite interested in this nurse practitioner movement. I've watched you for nearly two years now and I think you are a wasted talent in that hospital recovery room. How would you like to come to work for me?"

Carrie was flabbergasted. The last thing in the world she expected from this meeting was an offer of a job. She told him that she would love to work with him but that she had a lot of things to consider. She had to admit that she thought being an office nurse would be boring although the anticipation of a daytime job was appealing.

"I wouldn't hire you to be my office nurse. I already have one nurse here. What I am talking about is either sending you to a nurse practitioner program or training you myself to see some of the routine patients. There's no reason in the world why you can't handle uncomplicated prenatal visits, pap smears and set up some teaching programs for the patients for me."

Carrie was thrilled with the prospect of the new role.

"Doctor, I have to be quite open with you about the job. I cannot take a pay cut and I have to have benefits. Also, my sister's husband has orders to Bethesda and we are going to move into her house but it also means that they will not be available for babysitting my little girl. As for school, I do not see that I could go away and do that now, perhaps later on, but I'd be willing to learn from you."

Dr. Ellington told her to take some time and think it over and also suggested that she speak with his wife, Kate, about child care. Kate knew everyone in the small community.

Through Mrs. Ellington, she found a kind and loving woman who would mind Susan. A grandmother herself, Mrs. Tobin took care of four little girls in her home and large yard.

Carrie and Dr. Ellington agreed on a salary and he put her on the group hospital plan at the office. She gave her notice at the hospital and three weeks later started her new job.

Over the next few months, she became a valuable asset to the practice and that summer, Cathy and Dave took Susan for ten weeks while she attended a formal course giving her certification as an OB/GYN nurse practitioner. She was amazed at how much she didn't know and when she returned she was able to take on additional duties which enhanced her professional status in the practice. Carrie loved her job, Susan loved Mrs. Tobin and gradually over time, she became like a daughter to the Ellingtons. Mrs. Ellington, became one of her greatest allies and confidants. In the lingo of the day, Carrie could not believe how "with it" she was and couldn't help but compare Burton and Kate to her own parents who seemed to refuse to grow and change with the times.

"Come on in now honey," she called through the window. "I think we'll both take a nap before we go over to Uncle Burt's and Aunt Katie's."

Susan loved Burton and Kate and they loved her. Not having any grandchildren of their own yet, they showered her with affection and spoiled her with gifts.

Every Fourth of July, the Ellington's had a traditional barbecue, followed by a stroll to Glorietta Bay to watch the fireworks. Carrie always had a great time at their home. The Ellingtons, they were masters at putting together a group of people who had both things in common and differences enough to stimulate a good conversation. Both Burt and Kate were excited about this year's barbecue because both of their sons would be there.

"Don't you dare miss this, Carrie. Both of my heroes will be here," said Kate on the phone to Carrie at the office.

Carrie had met both men briefly but couldn't say she really knew either of them. Burton, Jr., had followed in his father's footsteps and was a surgeon in the Bay area. John, the younger son, was an attorney and was a contracts lawyer for General Dynamics Electric Boat Division, in Groton, Connecticut.

Burt Jr. not only followed in his father's professional footsteps, he had the same handsome looks and appeal. John was a quiet man of medium height, with severe post-acne scars. He was already balding. Carrie could not help but wonder how these two ended up in the same family.

Living up to its past reputation, the barbecue was hopping with activity and conversation. All in all, there were fifteen people there and the topics ranged from what everybody thought of the new movie, "The Godfather", to some testy conversation on the recent Supreme Court decision on abortion. Some Cubans had broken into an apartment building in Washington and there was a lot of heat on President Nixon in what was being called the Watergate affair after the name of the apartment building.

Talking about abortion always made Carrie uncomfortable and was one issue that she and Dr. Ellington had come to terms with for the practice since the Supreme Court's decision. He wasn't quite sure how he felt about it and decided that at his age, he did not want to be bothered with controversy in his practice. When an abortion was requested, he simply said that he did not do them.

Carrie could not think of abortion without thinking and wondering what she would have done if that choice had been available to her when she first became pregnant with Susan. It made her shudder so badly that she was never to get beyond that in forming a decision on where she stood. She just assumed it was wrong.

"Your little girl is sure growing up," said the voice behind her and she turned and saw John Ellington pull up a beach chair. "How old is she now?"

"She's almost six, I can't believe it myself."

"Well, she's a real cutie, just like her Mom."

Carrie blushed and John added, "Especially when she blushes."

"How's it going working with the old man, Carrie?"

"Oh, it's just great. I must have the best job in the world. Your dad is a gem to work with. I don't know what I would have done without him and your mom these past few years."

"Yeah, I really did luck out in the parents department."

"How do you like living in Connecticut, aren't you a contracts lawyer, whatever that is?" asked Carrie laughing.

"I don't blame you for laughing, I think it's pretty funny myself. You know, when I decided on a profession, there were two things I was sure I did not want. After being on the river boat patrols in Vietnam and thinking every day was my last, I knew I wanted nothing more to do with the military. With Dad, of course, I considered medicine. I spent my whole life watching him get up at night, get called away from meals, and spend the weekend in the labor room. Maybe I'm selfish but I didn't want any part of that either. So, that's what lead me into law, sort of a process of elimination. I wasn't in school very long before I knew I didn't have the aggressive personality of a criminal courtroom lawyer so I decided to get into the corporate end of it. Where do I end up? Right back with an industry reviewing all their defense contracts with the military."

"How about a drink?" What can I get you?"

"I had one drink. I think I'll stick with iced tea for awhile."

"Sounds good. What about Susan?"

"Nothing. She's busy playing. Let's leave well enough alone. "

When John went into the house to get the ice tea, Carrie followed him with her eyes. What a nice guy, she thought and remembered the last time see had seen him. He stopped by the office for a minute and all she could think of was how plain looking he was compared to Burt, Jr. But, today, she felt a real warmness toward him. He was so genuine and totally without guile. The thing that made him attractive was the comfortable sense of self assurance that he radiated. Just like Pete, she thought.

"Here you go, let me finish my story. Mom and Dad don't know it yet, so keep it under your hat. I don't want Mom to get her hopes up and be disappointed but there's an excellent chance that I'll be transferred to the General Dynamics Convair Division out here. I'll find out when I go back this weekend."

"Are you glad about it?" asked Carrie.

"Sure, you bet I am. The four seasons are pretty back there but not for me. Once a Californian, always a Californian."

"I can sure identify with that. I'm from back there too. I love it here and can't conceive of living anyplace else."

The party progressed to a buffet dinner and after everyone ate, it was time for the fireworks. Carrie hunted up Susan and was ready to join the group when John asked if she would like to walk over with him.

"Come on, let this hometown boy tell you some of the secrets in these houses as we go by."

They walked the half mile to the bayfront, Susan between them, swinging their arms. Passing one house, John started laughing.

"We were such brats," he confessed. "The poor old lady that lived here was tough on us kids crossing on her grass so consequently we just tormented her. On night, she had her bedroom shade drawn and her window open about three inches. We reached in, grabbed the shade and ran it up the window just about scaring her to death."

"I think every neighborhood had its characters," said Carrie. "We didn't do exactly that but we did things that were certainly in the same ballpark."

The fireworks were spectacular as usual and by nine thirty, everyone was exhausted. After walking back, Carrie bid goodnight to the Ellingtons, thanked John for the guided tour, packed Susan in their car and drove the short distance to their house. She was so tired, she took a hot shower and went right to bed but she was unable to fall asleep. Scenes of the wonderful day kept replaying in her mind. For the first time in nearly six years, she found herself with a group of people that were like her. She enjoyed herself at a party with people and didn't wish she was back in Yokosuka. It was perfectly fine being just where she was. It was a nice feeling. She finally belonged.

A week later, on Wednesday afternoon, she was writing a letter to Cathy and Dave in Bethesda when the phone rang.

"Carrie, this is John Ellington. How are you today?"

"John!, I'm fine. How are you? Where are you?"

"I'm in Connecticut. I've got some good news and a question and I knew Dad closed the office on Wednesday afternoons."

Carrie couldn't wait.

"I bet you got your transfer."

"Right, your absolutely right and it's effective immediately. I'm coming home this weekend."

"John, I'm flattered that you called me with the news. You must be up to your ears arranging and packing and all. Believe me, I know all about that from my Navy days."

"My call isn't exactly all that selfless, Carrie. This Saturday night, General Dynamics is having a dinner dance at the Hotel Del Coronado and Henry Kissinger is the guest of honor. I'm calling to ask if you would go with me. I know it's a real late invitation, but I never thought I'd be back in San Diego so soon."

Carrie felt wonderful inside.

"I'd love to John. I'm a great admirer of Doctor Kissinger, especially his feat in finally getting our POW's home. What time is the dinner and is it formal?"

"No, dark suit for me and a fancy dress for you. No ball gown or anything. How's my favorite little girl?"

"She's great. She's out in the back yard with Debbie from next door and they are chattering away a mile a minute."

"Give her a big hug for me and I'll call you Saturday morning. I'm flying home Friday evening. I don't have much to pack. I rented a furnished apartment here so it's mostly clothes, books and kitchen stuff. The movers said they'll pick it up tomorrow."

"Okay, I'll wait for your call Saturday morning and thanks so much for the invitation. It sounds like an elegant evening."

She heard John hang up the phone and she held the receiver to her chest. She felt giddy and it felt wonderful. She had buried a lot of feelings about John all week and now they crowded her mind. What a nice guy, she thought. How many other guys would ask about Susan?

She heard a rap on the door and went to answer it.

"Hi, this letter was delivered to my house by mistake," said Betty Carson.

"Thanks, Betty, come on in. Got time for a drink or a cup of coffee?"

Betty and Fred Carson lived next door. Fred was a line officer stationed at North Island Naval Air Station at the tip of Coronado, and Betty was a nurse who was currently letting her profession rest while she raised their daughter, Debbie, who was the same age as Susan.

"Betty, I'm so excited, I can hardly contain myself." confessed Carrie.

"That is quite obvious. What's going on?"

Carrie told Betty about her call from John Ellington talking so fast that she tripped over her tongue getting out all the details.

"Hold on girl," said Betty. "You're acting like this is your first date. What's the big deal?"

"Betty, do you know how long it has been since I have actually looked forward to a date with any hope that it would actually be fun?"

"I know, I know, I'm just giving you a hard time. I think it's great. You are so overdue for some romance in your life, it's pathetic. You practically have mold growing on you."

"I'm just so excited about the whole thing, especially about hearing Henry Kissinger, and seeing who else is there."

"What are you going to wear?"

"I don't know. It's been so long since I've been to anything that fancy. The stores are open Thursday nights so I'm going to try and find something then."

On Thursday, Carrie found the perfect dress. Returning home, she tried it on and went to the full length mirror on back of the bathroom door. She loved it. The silk dress was light peach, nearly identical to the twenty's flapper dresses except that it was mini in length. The shoulders were bare except for thin straps that were a little darker in color, an apricot hue. She swayed her hips back and forth and loved how the fabric reacted to the move. She stepped into the silver sling back pumps and decided that the only piece of jewelry she would wear would be the white gold and diamond cross and chain that Pete had sent her from Okinawa.

The thought of Pete sent her back to the Marine Corps Ball, nearly seven years ago, the last formal dance she'd attended.

How different, she thought. How radical the changes in styles and the youth culture of our country. She toyed with her long hair that she'd worn straight parted in the middle, waist length, and decided it had to go. She was going to get rid of it. She'd been thinking of getting a shag for a long time and decided that tomorrow she would get it cut and have some blond streaks put in it.

When she fell into bed at ten thirty, it was with a feeling of contentment and excitement. She said her prayers thanking God for this special time. It had been so long since she'd cared about or looked forward to a date. John Ellington was only a friend but a friend who thought like she did. The excitement of an elegant evening at the Hotel Del kept her awake until midnight.

She finally felt drowsy and in saying her night prayers, added one prayer for the repose of Pete's soul, a prayer she'd added every night since his death.

2

Groton, Connecticut
July, 1973

John Ellington opened the oven door and looked in at the crusted remnants of charred steaks and spilled over casseroles. "The heck with it", he thought, "I'm not going to clean this thing". He decided to write a note of apology to the landlord and forgo his cleaning deposit.

After talking to Carrie, he sat for a moment and tried to prioritize his activities for the next two days. He had all day tomorrow and until three on Friday. He called and canceled his utilities and newspaper and made out a change of address card for the postman. What to do about friends was his big problem, not to mention, Pat.

John Ellington graduated from Stanford University with a degree in Political Science. Although unsure of his life's career at that time, he knew he wanted to head toward some field of law or foreign service and Poli Sci was as good a place as any from which to build a body of knowledge.

After graduation, he was commissioned an ensign in the Navy. He jumped in fast before the Army grabbed him. No way did he want to be a ground grunt with an invitation to Vietnam biting at his ankles.

After OCS at Newport, Rhode Island, he received orders to Amphibious Warfare school in Coronado, back in the old neighborhood. That should have been a warning but he still held out hope for assignment to an amphibious assault ship when with great shock came his orders to river patrol boats, swift boats in Vietnam. Outside of the Navy Corpsmen and fighter pilots, swift boat drivers probably held the best chance for a ticket to an early meeting with their Maker.

He spent nine months in 1967 in the slimy back waterways of Vietnam trying to intercept the VC as they brought in ammo from Cambodia via the many feeders of the Mekong River. Each time he took his boat and crew out, he felt it was his last. The crews of the boats weren't known for their brains or their charm. It was an accepted fact that the swift boat assignment provided a dumping ground for every misfit or troublemaker that other commands no longer wanted. His tour in Vietnam could only be described as nine months of stark terror. The last three months, he served as a advisor to the new area commander and the day he flew out of Ton San Nut Air Base, he considered himself the luckiest man on the face of the earth. As the big Air Force Plane lifted off, he looked out the window and thought, "What a screwed up mess and all those poor bastards still left there."

He returned to the states in April and after taking a few weeks off to think through what he wanted to do, he decided on law. He was a Magna Cum Laude from Stanford so he decided to shoot for an east coast Ivy League law school. He applied to five and was accepted at Yale and Columbia. He decided on Yale both for its reputation and its location. While at OCS, he had visited the campus and enjoyed the New England area.

When he was nearly finished in his senior year, there was considerable anxiety in the class. Many of his classmates were having difficulty finding jobs except, of course, those who were entering family practices or the top 5% who were offered positions with prestigious firms. By this time, John knew he wanted to practice

Dynamics offered him a position in Contracts and an attractive starting salary, he gladly accepted it.

His three years with General Dynamics had given him valuable experience in dealing with government bureaucrats as well as the military brass, not the least of whom was Admiral Hyman Rickover, the father of the Atomic Submarine.

The Electric Boat Division's name made it seem like a nautical version of electric trains, when in fact, the main project at Electric Boat was to build nuclear power submarines for the Navy. It was Admiral Rickover who convinced the Navy that they could put a nuclear reactor on a submarine that would deliver enough fuel to stay submerged for sixty days. The price they paid for his brilliant discovery was having to live with him and his dictatorial power within the submarine community. John could not believe how everyone quivered and shook when the Admiral was due for a visit and was sure he had made the right decision in leaving the Navy when he witnessed the total and absolute control one man had over so many lives. His thoughts were interrupted by the phone's ringing.

"Hey, Buddy, where are you? How come you're not out here screwing the Government out of another dollar?"

John laughed at the sound of his friend's remark.

"You will never believe it, Ted."

"Let me guess, chicken pox,.........or the Admiral's in town."

"Nope, no chicken pox and guess what, no more Admiral."

"Don't tell be the old tyrant is finally retiring."

"Fat chance. Hey, how many choruses of "California, Here I Come", can you sing before I count to ten?"

"No, you're kidding. You bastard, you really did it."

"Not only did I do it, but fast. I'm through as of today. I'm flying out Friday afternoon."

"Oh man. I'm sure glad for you but I'll miss you. Who am I going to tell my troubles to now that my own personal Dear Abby is leaving town."

"Come on out, jerk. I've been telling for a year to put in for a transfer. If you're lucky, you'll get out of here before another lovely icy Connecticut winter."

"Uh Oh, what about Miss Freckle Face. Have you told her the news yet?"

"No, I'm seeing her tonight. It's going to be a real bad scene. I'd rather take a beating than go through it."

For the past year, John had been seeing Pat Grant, an accountant at Electric Boat. He met her on a company ski club trip. Over the year, they shared a lot of time together, going into New York and Boston on weekends and fixing meals at each other's apartments. He really enjoyed Pat but he was not in love with her. When he knew that she was falling in love with him, he tried to break it off but the combination of her holding on tight to him and his loneliness kept him seeing her. It was a case of going with what you knew rather than risking a series of blind dates.

"Now I realize I should have broken it off," he answered Ted's question.

"You are going to have one basket case on your hands. Even though you told her how you felt and kept telling her you were trying for a transfer to California, that lady never gave up hope for one minute."

"I know and I knew that too. It's hard, Ted because I really like Pat and when I think about her, she's everything any guy could want but I just couldn't fall in love with her. For me, there's something missing."

Ted Daniels was John's best friend at Groton. He had served in the submarine service for seven years after graduating from the Naval Academy. After his second tour on a polaris submarine, he decided he didn't want to spend half of the next ten years under water. Electric Boat grabbed him when he applied for an engineering job. With his experience and top secret clearance, they were able to put him in charge of a top priority project that was in danger of loosing funding because it was so far behind schedule. He met John last winter when he gave him a jump start on his dead battery in the apartment parking lot.

John was surprised Ted had ever made it in the nuclear submarine service. He was such a practical joker and live wire. Most of the submariners that John knew were so bloody serious. John thought it was due to an overriding paranoia in the fleet about the security of the positions at the whim of Admiral Rickover. Sad, thought John. The Navy gives these guys a million dollar education in nuclear physics and then treats them like six year olds in first grade. One false move and you're in the corner, only their corner could be the ruination of a career.

"How about tomorrow night, can I have that and get a few folks together for a send off?" asked Ted.

"I'd love that, in fact, you'll really help me out because there's no way I can get around and see everyone."

"Great. Let me get off the phone, make a list and start calling. Good luck tonight."

"Thanks."

John drove to an older part of town where Pat had a small apartment in a renovated period home from the whaling days in New England. I'm going to miss this architectural charm thought John; this area has been good to me.

Pat opened the door and lifted her face for their usual welcome kiss.

"Let's go to Abbot's," she said. "I feel up to a battle with a big boiled lobster. It's too hot to cook inside."

Abbott's, an earthy place on the seacoast was known for its lobster and it's large picnic tables outside where diners sat and fought their meal.

"How about a gin and tonic here first. I want to talk something over with you."

"Sure".

Pat was flattered that John was asking her advise and going to discuss a problem with her. She was crazy about him. Meeting him on the ski trip was a dream come true. She hadn't cared about anyone for nearly two years. All the dates seemed to be the same, drinks, dinner and a battle of wits to get back in the house before the seduction started. She spent the whole weekend skiing with John. When they returned to Groton she asked him to dinner. He was like having an old shoe around the house. No one was more surprised than she when she fell in love with him. So far, she had been unable to get him to make a commitment to her but she knew if she worked on him long enough, she would win him over. Inside, she harbored a master plan. By working on him slowly but steadily, she hoped to be engaged to him this Christmas and married next June. After all, we're not kids, she thought and we ought to know what we want in a year.

John, on the other hand, knew exactly what he wanted and it wasn't Pat Grant. "I wish I'd had an extra belt before I left the house", he said to himself as he gulped his drink. He wished for all the world that he had stopped dating her when he knew he could not return her feelings. There was no easy way to do this.

"Pat, come over here and sit down."

Pat came in from the kitchen and placing her drink on the coffee table, sat next to John. She was ecstatic. Finally, she thought, he is going to admit that we have a future together.

"Well, John, come on, cat got your tongue?"

"No, not at all. It's just what I have to say is not easy and I'm afraid that it's going to hurt you.

"Pat, before, I tell you, you must try to understand that I never meant to hurt you. I never meant anything for us except the chance to spend some great hours together. You have been my salvation in this one-horse town. Our trips to the cities, the skiing, the sailing, all are terrific memories. I'll never forget them or you.

"I haven't talked about it in a long time but you've known all along that I requested a transfer to California, to the General Dynamics operation out there. Today my transfer came through."

Pat turned ashen.

"Are you still going to take it?"

"Yes."

"Will you be leaving before Christmas?"

"I'm leaving Friday afternoon."

"This Friday afternoon!"

"Yes, they want me right away."

The silence in the room was deafening. Pat could not, would not believe it. She had worked too hard to give it up now and let this slip from her life. Softly and seductively, she said, "That's all right, John, there's always the telephone and letters not to mention the fact that I could request a transfer too."

John took a sip of his nearly drained drink.

"Pat, none of this is easy to say. I don't want you to come to California for me. I have been honest with you and I hope I always treated you like a lady, and the good person you are. We have been over this before and quite frankly, I'm tired of the same conversation. You don't seen to be able to accept my honesty when I tell you that I am not in love with you."

Pat was furious.

"Well, thanks a lot, John. Good old Pat, good enough to go to New York with, good enough to hang around rotten Groton with, but forget it when it comes to the real thing."

"Pat, that isn't fair and you know it."

"Fair?, what do you know about being fair. You've tied me up for nearly a year but when it comes to marriage and commitment, I'm not good enough. You're off to California for some long legged blond Southern California bimbo. I should have known. You're no different than the rest. I've been such a jerk."

"Why do you put yourself down? There's nothing wrong with you. You're a wonderful woman."

"Right, wonderful for someone else. I can't believe you. How can you fly off in two days and leave me here like the canceled newspaper and the empty refrigerator?"

"Come on, you're not making this any easier. It's not like I'm never going to see you or talk with you again."

Pat jumped on the slight chance of hope.

"Let's see. The next holiday is Labor Day. Maybe I can tack two days' leave onto it and fly out for five days."

John sat silent.

"Pat, let me get out there and see what the situation is. I have to settle into a new job, find a place to live, buy a lot of new clothes. I'm going to be very busy for a few weeks."

"Right. No room to fit good old Pat in there. You're something John. You are really something."

John wanted to get up and leave. Pat's hostility made her so unattractive to him. He wondered if this was the real Pat and he was seeing it now because he had backed her into a corner.

Trying to change the mood, he said, "Come on, let's go over to Abbott's and get our lobster."

"You've got to be kidding. Do you think I can be bought off with a lobster. Give me a break. Talk about 'The Last Supper'."

John lost his patience.

"Pat, I am going to say it one more time. I have enjoyed you, and looked forward to all the times we spent together. I have been honest with you in my words and hopefully in my behavior. I'm sorry but I'm not in love with you and you have known that from the beginning. Now we either go to Abbott's or I'll say goodnight and goodbye now."

Pat panicked. She could not let him leave.

"I'm sorry, you're right, let's go."

The dinner was superb as usual but the tension in the air was thicker than the off shore fog. In the car on the drive over, John felt Pat slip into her sweet mood and knew he was being seduced. He was worn out from the battle with her and hoped that they could just have a nice New England summer dinner. He tried to talk about the upcoming move but she would only pick up on conversation when it involved something they had done together, a play they had seen, or a particularly good restaurant they had tried. Right there and then, John made a decision about the end of the evening.

Leaving the car in the yard of her apartment, they walked slowly toward her door. When they reached the step, he took her in his arms and held her tight.

"I'll miss you, Pat and I wish you the best. I'll be in touch real soon."

Pat was still in his arms but he felt a tightening of her muscles.

"Aren't you going to come in?"

"No."

"Right, John. Just cut and run away. You bastard, you weak using bastard, you unfair prick."

John had had it.

"Goodnight Pat." He turned, got in his car and drove home.

Pat watched in disbelief as the car pulled away and she started to shake. Her worse fears had come true. It was over between her and John. Her master plan passed through her head and her eyes filled with anger.

She stormed into the apartment slamming the door behind her. She walked immediately to the bathroom and looked in the mirror. She gasped when she saw how hard and angry she looked. Oh, I was awful. I've got to call him and apologize. I can't let him leave with this as his last memory or I'll never get him, she thought.

She waited ten minutes and when she was sure he had reached home, she dialed the phone.

When John answered, she told him how sorry she was and could he forgive her.

"You were just upset, Pat. It's fine, no hard feelings. Now get some sleep."

"What about tomorrow night, John?" she asked thinking that if she had one more night to work on him, she could change his mind.

"Ted is putting a party together for me tomorrow night and of course, you're welcome to come."

Pat's heart sank. He was going to spend his last night with a group of friends and not with her. Once again, she lost control.

"A party. Oh, that's just great, that's just great. Just what I need, an audience."

"An audience for what, Pat?" asked John.

"Forget it, just forget it." and she slammed the down the phone.

John did something he had never done before. He took the phone off the hook, took a shower and went to bed. He was a mixture of emotions. He felt bad about Pat but in a way he was glad that he had exposed a part of her that to date was unseen. He knew that she would not give up easily so at ten-thirty when the doorbell rang, he didn't answer it. He too, had a right to his life. He knew if he opened the door and let her in, he would not be able to get rid of her. The ringing persisted. Finally, in anger, he stood next to the door and asked who it was.

"It's me Pat. John, I have to talk to you. Please let me in."

"No, Pat, there's nothing more to add to what we already discussed. Please go home and I'll see you at work in the morning."

Pat persisted and begged and John stood firm. He knew now that he was dealing with someone who was desperate. Once again, he said goodnight and this time he turned off the outside light, leaving Pat standing in the dark. As he walked back toward the bedroom, he heard Pat shout, "You dirty bastard."

American Airlines, Flight #06
July, 1973

    Halfway across the country at 33,000 feet, John sat addressing envelopes. Because there had been so little time the past two days, he was unable to say goodbye to many of his friends. Last night, twenty people had gathered at Ted's for a farewell party but there were at least that many more who could not attend. When he went by the office today, he typed out a goodbye letter and made thirty copies of it explaining his sudden departure. He packed the letters with envelopes, his address book and stamps in his carry on bag, and passed the time on the flight adding a short personal note to each one. By the time his flight landed in San Diego, he had finished all his letters.

    His thoughts returned to Pat and he felt bad about the sad ending of their friendship. She had not come to Ted's party last night and called in sick today. When he arrived at the small Groton airport for his commuter flight over to Kennedy Airport in New York, he found her waiting by his gate. Fortunately, he spotted her before she saw him and he asked Ted to stay with him, not to leave him alone with Pat. By now, he did not trust her behavior and he was tired and tense. The last thing he wanted was a scene in the airport.

    "Pat, how great of you to come. I missed you last night," he said giving her a long hug.

    "I wanted us to have a fonder farewell than the one we had," she said sheepishly.

    "Don't give it another thought. The whole thing was a shock, even for me."

    John was eternally grateful that the plane was on time and waiting. The three of them walked to the gate. He shook Ted's hand thanking him for the ride and kissed Pat. She clung to him and whispered in his ear that she was sorry.

"Nothing to be sorry for, Pat. You can't help the way you feel anymore than I can. You take good care of yourself and I'll be in touch."

He boarded the aircraft without looking back.

Pat walked back into the terminal with Ted.

"I just feel terrible. John and I have had such a great time all year and I'm afraid I behaved rather badly at the news of his transfer."

"It's okay, Pat. John feels bad too. He thinks you're the greatest. None of us can drum up feelings that aren't there. I suspect after you have awhile to think about it, you'll be able to admit you hung on longer than you should have."

"I already know that. I refused to see the truth. I hate to admit I was desperate but I really loved John. I guess I thought I stood a better chance winning him over than starting new with someone else."

"You're no different from the rest of us. We all see what we want to see. Anyway, you hang in there, Pat. We're not going to drop you from the crowd. Before you know it, ski season will be back again." Winking he said, "It worked for you last time!"

Coronado, California
July, 1973

Carrie finished dressing fifteen minutes before John was to arrive. When she looked in the mirror, she decided that long pearls looked better with the mini chemise than the short chain and cross. She once again thought back to the Marine Corps Ball. Everything was so different. The blond french twist of that night was now a free and casual shag. Her pale blue formal gown exchanged for a mini skirted flapper dress. But, the biggest change in the evening was what was inside her. She was so in love with Pete the night of the ball and tonight, she was just going to a gala event with a friend. Looking once more in the mirror, she wondered if she would ever love anyone the way that she loved Pete.

When John rang the front door bell at six o'clock, Carrie developed an instant case of jitters.

"I'm a wreck," she said to herself, "who am I kidding?"

John entered the room, took a look at Carrie and gave out a soft wolf whistle.

"What a knockout you are."

"Thank you. It's been so long since I've gone to anything like this, I have to admit, I'm a nervous wreck."

"Oh, don't let all those fancy people intimidate you. I doubt there'll be anyone there who tops the way you look."

John's words were music to Carrie's ears, the old Carrie, the Carrie that loved to dress up and have fun.

The evening dinner dance was magical. John and Carrie were seated at a table with the other attorneys from General Dynamics. They were an interesting and stimulating group. She recognized one of the wives from her practice and the woman sang Carrie's praises to the entire table.

Her heart nearly raced out of her chest when Henry Kissinger commented on her dress as she met him in the receiving line. His talk about the behind the scenes at the Paris peace talks held the audience spellbound as he revealed the intricacies of international diplomacy.

But the best part of the evening was being with John. He took care of her as though she was a porcelain treasure. She was so comfortable with him, she felt like she had known him forever. He asked her so many things about herself, what she liked and what she didn't and sought her advice and opinion on where to live, and where to buy some new summer clothes. When the orchestra started to play, John led her to the dance floor and guided her around the room to the strains of "Misty". He was a wonderful dancer and led her with such skill and grace that she soon lost her self-consciousness at being an inch taller than he.

Since they were both strangers in the group, they preferred to dance all evening rather than sit at the table. When the beat changed to a rock song, Carrie started to sit down.

"Oh, no you don't, Miss. Come on, I'll show you how it's done."

Standing four feet apart, they held out their arms and gyrated their hips laughing and giggling like two high school kids. Carrie had no idea what she was doing but she was having a great time. She felt like something in her had been reborn. She was so glad John was back here. He was such a great guy and would make a wonderful friend.

Around midnight, John suggested that they go outside on the patio to get some fresh air. Giddy in their frivolity, they decided to walk on the beach. John took her hand in his and they strolled up and back talking and laughing, shoes in hand and sand creeping inside the feet of Carrie's panty hose.

When they finally arrived home at one thirty, Carrie was wide awake. She fixed some hot tea and they sat and talked another half hour. At last it was time for John to leave. They walked toward the front door and John took Carrie in his arms.

"I can't remember when I've had a lovelier evening. "Thanks so much for going with me."

"The same here. I haven't had a night like this since I was stationed in Japan during Vietnam. Thanks so much for asking me."

John pushed Carrie slightly away, looked at her and kissed her gently on the lips.

"You're one in a million, Carrie. Now let me get out of here and let you get some sleep. Your little one will probably be on deck early in the morning.

"Goodnight, thanks again."

Carrie undressed and fell into bed exhausted. She tried to identify what she was feeling but her head was filled with the evening's memories of light heartedness and fun and soon she drifted off to sleep.

John looked around his old room. His mother still kept all his junk there. Pictures of old prom dates adorned the walls and the jigsaw puzzle of the United States that helped him learn geography lay on the bookshelf. He thought about the great evening he had just spent with Carrie and couldn't help but contrast it to the horrible evening with Pat just three nights ago. Three nights and three thousand miles. Life changed and moved so swiftly these days.

3

Washington, DC
October, 1973

    Tom Paige sat before a pile of books at a table in the Georgetown University library. This fall semester would be somewhat easier because he was doing his clinical work in psychology at two different settings in town. But, there was no way to avoid a thesis and today he had promised himself to start the Review of Literature for his topic, "The Adjustment of the Vietnam Veteran to a Productive Life". He ran an initial search and cross referenced computer check and was discouraged at the few number of studies available on the subject.
    He looked up from his work out the windows at the beautiful fall sky. The leaves were a palate of gold and red and the sky sparkled with the reflective sun.
    His thoughts were interrupted by the librarian.
    "Excuse me, Father. You have a call from the hospital."
    Tom answered the phone. It was the emergency room at Georgetown hospital telling him that they had just received an seriously injured accident victim.
    "I'll be right there."
    A full time student, Tom was free of any chaplain duties in the Navy. He said his daily Mass at noon in the chapel at the university where he met Ray Marshall, a Jesuit on the faculty. A large man, Ray looked more like a full back for the Redskins than the gentle priest he was. Their friendship grew and blossomed both on the tennis court and in sharing many evenings together.

Tom loved the intellectual challenge of Ray's quick mind and he was happy to have the friendship of another priest while living amid hundreds of young students each day. When Tom found out that Ray had to cover the emergency room one weekend a month, he volunteered to relieve him for one of the weekend days.

Walking toward the hospital, his mind returned to his days in Japan seven years ago. Sometimes it seemed like seven hundred years and then other days, it seemed like yesterday. He missed hospital duty. Besides helping Ray out, taking this one day a month put him back in touch with people who needed him as a priest.

The two years in Japan held special memories for Tom. He still thought of his friends there often, and regretted that they didn't make an effort to keep in touch. When he first arrived at the Naval Academy, everyone exchanged Christmas cards the first year but then one by one, the original group all left Japan and the correspondence fell off as people got into their new lives back in the States.

His timing at the Naval Academy couldn't have been worse. After wishing so hard for those orders, his tour of duty there was a solid stress packed two years. He arrived in Annapolis at the height of the anti war protest marches, only to be followed by the assassination of Martin Luther King and Bobby Kennedy.

The midshipmen, like students everywhere, challenged all the rules, and the Naval uniform that he so proudly wore in Japan now became a source of mockery from others when he stepped outside the gates of the academy. What was worse than the pressure from the outside was the derision and undermining by the civilian staff on the faculty. Siding with the students, they turned every faculty meeting into a combat zone. His role as a chaplain was a difficult one and he found himself caught between wanting to help the students on one hand and resenting their attitudes toward the establishment on the other.

More distressful to Tom than the anti military movement was the division in the church that followed the release of Pope Paul VI's encyclical, "Humanae Vitae", upholding the long held rules against the practice of birth control.

Following the fresh breezes blown forth from Pope John XXIII in the Second Vatican council, both the laity and prominent moral theologians had hoped for a change.

There was practically an uprising at a Catholic University in the theology department with many of its prominent staff members openly voicing dissent.

All over the country, priests were leaving the priesthood. Five men in his ordination class of twenty-three left, three of them to marry. At the end of two years when his orders arrived for the aircraft carrier, USS John F. Kennedy, homeported at Norfolk, Virginia, he was ecstatic.

He threw the cigarette he was smoking in the gutter and stepped on it, promising himself that he would stop smoking on the day he turned in his thesis.

His tour on the Kennedy was just what the doctor ordered. Two weeks after he reported aboard, the ship left for a six month Mediterranean cruise. He was glad to be away from hippies, protesters, flower children, angry catholics, the whole mess. He loved the ship's duty and after two years aboard counseling sailors, he was more convinced than ever that good emotional health was necessary for one to attain a high level of spiritual health. That was what led him to choose clinical psychology for study in graduate school. His friend Ray's background in moral theology added another dimension to his education and many the night they debated for hours the earthly traps man had to leap over on his journey to spiritual perfection.

Entering the Emergency Room, Tom heard the low moaning sobs of a young woman. As soon as she saw him, she ran up to him.

"Oh, Father, he's not dead, is he?" she panicked at the sight of the priest.

"Who is he?" asked Tom.

"Bob, Bob Buckly, my boyfriend. We were just in a terrible automobile accident. I'm fine but he was unconscious. It wasn't our fault, the other car ran a stop sign and plowed right into the side of the front door at Bob."

"Let me check for you and I'll come right out and tell you."

Tom went through the doors marked, EMERGENCY STAFF ONLY. The nurse on duty came over and introduced herself saying that the patient was in the second room but that he was dead, from a broken neck. Tom entered the room and approached the table. He lifted the sheet and looked into the face of the young man. There was hardly a mark of evidence that he had been in an accident and Tom silently was thankful. He knew the sad job of helping the young girlfriend view the body would be left to him. He administered last rites and gave conditional absolution.

"Thank you, Father," said the nurse. "Are you new here?"

"No, I'm a full time student in the graduate school and I'm just covering for Father Marshall. If you don't mind, I'd like to tell the young man's girlfriend and bring her in."

"Sure, Father. I'll stay close by if you need some help."

Tom returned to the lobby and sat down next to the young girl.

"What is your name?"

"Barbara, Barbara Williams. How is Bob, Father?"

Tom put his hand on Barbara's arm.

"Barbara, Bob is dead. He died from a broken neck."

Barbara didn't yell or scream or carry on. She just sat quietly and suddenly every muscle in her body started to quiver as if chilled by a sudden icy gust of wind. Tom heard a quiet whimper.

"No, no, no."

He put his arms around her and just held her, saying nothing. In a little while, she asked if she could see her boyfriend and Father Paige took her to the room. He lifted back the sheet and stood with Barbara while she said goodbye to her man and her dreams. Tom thought back to Japan and realized that he seldom had to deal with this scene there. The Marines from Vietnam died alone. Their girlfriends and parents were all back here in the States.

Barbara gave the necessary information to the nurse and Tom offered to drive her home.

"I'd like to go to Bob's house," she said. "I'm very close to his parents and I want to be with them."

"I'll be glad to take you, just lead the way."

"Arlington, it's not very far if we go over the Key Bridge."

The afternoon at the Buckly's was a sad and draining one for Tom. By the time they got there, the family had been called by the hospital and had left to claim the body of their son. Tom took Barbara to one of the Hot Shopps and managed to feed her some soup and tea. He listened as the sad girl shared her dreams and felt them dash away in the memory of the body in the room at Georgetown. When, two hours later, they went to the Buckly's, their parish priest was there, so he told them he had given their son last rites and excused himself, calling the Emergency Room to make sure he didn't have any more calls pending before he set out back to the library.

Driving back toward Georgetown, his eyes were drawn by the rows of grave markers in the Arlington National Cemetery. He turned on his directional light and turned into one of the lower lanes and parked his car. He needed a few minutes of quiet reflection before he returned to the books. Leaving the car, he walked along the lane reading the stones. So many from Vietnam, he thought, and the sharply cut grass reminded him of the haircuts of the men in the graves, such a contrast to the longhaired students at the university.

He still ached at the changes. It had been a rough year for him and he was disappointed in his ability to adjust. Try as he might, he could not get used to the foul language, the drug culture, the ghastly music and the unkempt appearance of today's youth. He longed for the norms of his days at Princeton or later than that, the days in Japan. He thought of Pete, the handsome Marine that Caroline Craig had fallen in love with and the young Marine patients that died in the Naval hospital during his tour of duty there. His time in Japan was preserved in a special place in his heart. He was thankful that part of the clinical psych program included group therapy for the students. He still needed to work through his angry bitter feelings of the protesters. He wanted the old ways back but in his heart he knew that would never happen. Any changing that would happen would have to be from within himself.

When he returned to the library, his mind was too tired to study so he picked up his books and went back to his apartment on Wisconsin Avenue. On Monday, he would start a preceptorship at the Veteran's Hospital and he was looking forward to working with the young returning Vietnam Vets, a group he felt he knew something about.

He was awakened from a nap by Ray Marshall on the phone.

"What are you doing tonight, Tom?"

"I'm covering for you, dummy."

"I can't believe I forgot that. Hey, how about I pick up a pizza and come over? We can watch the World Series. I sure hope Oakland kills those arrogant New York Mets."

"Now, now, you're castigating this here kid's team. Sure, come on over, good idea."

"Did you have to go in at all?"

"Yeah, a traffic fatality, a young man. Really sad case."

"Gosh, I'm sorry Tom. Most Saturdays, I never even get a whimper from them."

"That's okay. It was good for me. I haven't been in a situation like that since my days in Japan. It's one of the special privileges of priesthood and reminds me how precious and tender life is."

The weekend passed quickly. On Sunday, Tom arranged his bibliography cards for his literature search and felt that he had tackled a big part of his thesis. He made a weekly timetable he promised to stick to that would allow him to complete his thesis by the week before Christmas. He had heard too many stories of Naval Officers who were sent to school and returned to duty before finishing their thesis. Somehow they never got around to it once the left the academic environment. Tom did not want that hanging over his head. He expected orders any day now and wanted to be free and clear of school, his degree in hand when he left. He had asked for the West coast but was afraid that he was going to be assigned to a desk job here in Washington. He did not look forward to that.

Tom walked into the lunchroom, a piece of paper waving in his hand and a grin across his face.

"What gives with you?" asked a classmate.

"Look what I've got." In his hand he held the first page of his thesis, the one that had two blank lines for the signatures of two faculty readers, signifying completion and acceptance. The two professors signatures were fresh in black ink.

"Man, do I envy you. How did you ever get it done in one semester?"

"By sheer discipline and torture," Tom laughed. "No, seriously, I made a timetable for a major task each week and I never let myself get behind."

"Have you found out where you're going yet?"

The group was as anxious about Tom's orders as he. Through their classes and their therapy group, they'd all grown close.

"Yes. I didn't get my wish for the West coast but I didn't get a desk job either. I'm going to the Marine Corps Base at Quantico, Virginia. The commanding officer was at a party with the chief of chaplains and it seemed that the topic of conversation shifted to the poor adjustment of the Vietnam Vets. The chief of chaplains mentioned that I was in graduate school working with such a group. Colonel McNamara, the commanding officer, reminded the chaplain that not all the Vietnam Vets got out, that we still had plenty in the service having some of the same problems. He asked how his chances were of getting me on his staff to work with the officers in their Senior Command and Staff program there. I'm excited about it. I might be the first guy ever to get a senior Marine to show some vulnerable feelings."

"That's great, Tom. It means you'll be in the area and we can all get together. Of course, it completely ruins the plans for the trips we all had to come out to California and see you."

Tom had to admit that after the initial disappointment, he was happy about the orders. When he started his clinical preceptorship at the VA, he could not believe the pain, anger and sadness he found in his small group. The same young innocent Marines he had worked with in Japan were now hostile and rebellious. Nearly all of them had turned to drugs and alcohol rather than deal with their pain. The country had let them down. The war might be over for the country but it wasn't over for these young men.

The first few weeks in the group, they attacked Tom unmercifully, accusing him of living in the special world of the officer. Through his training, Tom was smart enough not to become defensive but just let them get rid of some of the pent-up feelings they had. Gradually, they began to trust him and one by one they shed some of their anger in their tears.

"More coffee?" asked Cynthia, one of Tom's friends.

"Sure, thanks."

"We're sure going to miss you Tom-o," and she gave him a big hug. "I wish you could still be in the group."

"I do too. I'd be willing to come up each week for it but it's in the daytime and the Marine Corps isn't very generous about days off in the middle of the week."

"The Marine Corps isn't very generous about days off anytime." said Randy. Randy Webster was a Platoon leader in Vietnam. He had volunteered for the Marine Corps to avoid the Army. Tom was fond of Randy and he was helpful in providing the young officer's view of the adjustment back home.

Tom looked at his watch.

"Hey gang, it's a quarter to twelve. I'm going to head over to the chapel and say Mass and then head right out for home. Anyone want to join me?"

Two of the group got up and started toward Tom. He walked around the remaining three students and hugged them all.

"Thanks for everything and Merry Christmas."

During his final noon Mass in the Georgetown chapel, he reflected on his time here in graduate school. He was thankful he had grown both as a person and as a priest. He had not shirked the challenges of controversy but instead, he examined them closely, absorbing their effect on his life. Now, it lay before him to take his new knowledge home and help others make their way along the same journey.

He gave the last blessing, adding, "The Mass is ended, go in Peace."

The congregation answered, "Thanks be to God."

4

Coronado, California
April, 1974

As Carrie stepped into the entry of the church, she heard the strains of the "Ave Verum" fill the air. One of her favorites, it was the first piece of music she chose for her wedding. Betty Carson, her next door neighbor and matron of honor, helped her arrange her veil one more time.

Carrie looked lovely. Her white eyelet dress over white organza with its round portrait neckline accented her beautiful porcelain skin . Around the waist was a satin bow that fell in streamers to the floor in back. The long puffed sleeves and ruffled bottom added just the right touch of elegance. In her hair she wore a circle of white roses and babies' breath that caught a short veil. She carried a small basket of white daisies. Betty's dress was identical except that it had a pale blue underskirt.

The organist finished playing the prelude and then, the sound of the wedding march filled the church. Dr. Ellington offered his arm for the walk down the aisle and kissed her.

"Carrie, this is one of the happiest days of my life. I'm gaining a daughter and a granddaughter. With two sons, I never thought I would have the privilege of escorting a bride down the aisle."

Carrie kissed him and told him she still didn't believe it. They walked down the long aisle of St. Mark's Church, Carrie following Betty before her. Halfway down, she looked up to see John standing with his brother waiting for her. The look of love on his face was so powerful that her eyes filled with tears of joy. Looking up at the altar, she silently thanked God once again for bringing her to this day, this special day in her life.

As they reached the second pew where Susan was seated with Cathy and Dave, in all her excitement and innocence, Carrie heard Susan cry out, "Oh Mommy, you look so pretty!" That just made her tears flow heavier and by the time she took John's arm and stood at the altar, she felt as if she must have streaks of mascara running down her face onto her wedding dress.

The day after the dinner dance at the Hotel Del last July, Betty had come over for coffee when she brought Susan back home from taking care of her overnight.

"Well, how was it? Any bells?" she asked.

"Heavens no. John is just a friend but we did have a terrific time. I was so relaxed, probably because I don't really care about him. Oh, I care about him but you know what I mean. We danced our legs off, went for a long walk on the beach and than sat here talking after we got home."

"Sounds like a great guy. Don't brush him off too early, you never know."

Betty was so right. Her love for John grew slowly but it never receded for one day. The growth was always forward as though she was peeling of another layer of a beautiful mysterious flower. The quality that attracted her to him the most was his air of self assurance and his generosity in helping her believe more in herself. After he found a small apartment in Coronado, he asked her to help him decorate and shop for it. He was quite content with his new job and shared many of his work experiences with her. He really valued her opinion.

In the fall, he stopped by most Saturdays suggesting a ride to the mountains or a quick trip to the beach. He was wonderful with Susan and always assumed their trips would include her. Susan's response to him was open and loving, always looking for a hug.

During the week, Carrie usually had him to dinner one night and then they would play Scrabble or just sit out in the yard and talk. By the end of October, they had become close friends and Carrie was so grateful for his company. He had unwrapped a part of her that had been buried for seven years, the part of her that she liked best and missed most.

The Ellingtons invited her to Thanksgiving dinner that year and in their usual style, presented a lovely day. After dinner, John asked his mother if she would mind watching Susan, that he wanted to talk with Carrie. Carrie looked surprised but went along wondering what he had up his sleeve.

When they started on their walk, she asked, "What are you up to John?"

"You'll see, it's something that couldn't wait, had to be done tonight."

They walked along the same route they had taken to the fireworks the previous Fourth of July. The evening was cool but the millions of stars above glowed in romantic sparkle with their steps. When they arrived at the Glorietta Bay, they sat on a park bench.

"Carrie, everyday I drive by here on the way to work and everyday I think of you and Susan and our walk on the Fourth of July, that's everyday for the past four and a half months. I can't believe how happy you have made me and the reason I wanted to bring you down here tonight was because I wanted to sit here with you in this same spot and tell you that I have fallen deeply in love with you."

Carrie was dumbfounded.

"I don't know what to say, I had no idea."

"You don't have to say anything. I know we have been more friends than lovers and I'm glad about that. We have gotten to know each other so well without the confusion of an intimate relationship before we were ready. I've gone slow because I didn't want to repeat a mistake I made in Groton. I wanted to be sure this time."

Carrie sat quietly just listening to him try to explain his love. Everything he said was so sincere but she didn't know if she loved him. The last person she loved had been Pete and that was so exciting and romantic and filled with daring and new experiences. With John, it was just a gradual deepening of getting to know him and see him live his everyday life. She was no longer the naive innocent Navy nurse. She was scarred and she was a mother now.

"This is one of those times I wish I hadn't given up smoking," she laughed. "Oh, for a cigarette."

"I didn't tell you this so that you would tell me back. I told you because this is how I feel and I want you to know it. Nothing has to change between us. We can still go out and you can have all the time you want to think about what I've said."

Carrie put her hand in John's.

"This is really different for me and you mean so much to me. I don't know if I love you but I do know I could not bear to stop seeing you. I'm glad you told me."

She stopped talking and looked into his eyes, the reflection of the lights on the boats in the bay looking back at her. John reached his arm behind her and holding her, kissed her lovingly and passionately, their first, a break from hello and goodbye pecks and hugs at the front door. In his embrace, Carrie finally allowed herself to let go and to feel feelings for John, she had, up to now, denied. Snuggling her head into his shoulder, she looked up at him and told him, "You are a very classy man, John Ellington."

"I might add that I am with a classy woman."

The walk back to the Ellingtons was slow and gentle. Holding hands, they talked about their past four months together and with each step, Carrie knew more and more that she loved him, but she had been so hurt she didn't dare even admit it to herself until John put his own heart on the line. She had built a wall around her. She never wanted to be hurt again.

On Christmas Eve, Carrie invited John to attend Midnight Mass with her. John was raised a Lutheran but admitted that he had fallen away from the practice of organized religion. When they returned to Carrie's house, they decided to wait and open their gifts with Susan the next day. John promised to set his alarm early and come over and share Susan's Christmas morning joy with Carrie.

"I wouldn't miss her wondrous morning for all the world. Being part of a child's Christmas doesn't happen that often to us bachelors."

Still wrapped in the warmth of Midnight Mass, Carrie lay in John's arms on the sofa listening to the soft Christmas music on the FM station. She was so comfortable and they had become closer than ever since Thanksgiving. He made her feel beautiful and precious, like a treasure.

She got up to refill John's brandy glass. When she returned to the living room, he took the glass from her and set it on the coffee table. Holding her at arms length, he stood up, looked into her face and asked her to marry him.

Carrie was agog. He had caught her off guard, but she was sure of her love for him.

"Yes, John, I will," she told him, looking at him and at that moment bursting with love for him.

John wasn't Pete. There was no one like Pete but, she thought to herself, there is no one like John either. In the few months she had spent with him, she regained her serenity, her self assurance and her ability to love again. It wasn't the wild passionate love she'd known with Pete but the day by day quiet building of friendship, trust and caring that she had no cause to doubt. John was so open and honest in his love for her, she knew she was truly blessed to have him. She knew John's was a love she would never have to question.

"You can take your time. You don't have to tell me tonight."

"I don't need any more time. The answer is yes, again."

She put her arms around him and told him she loved him and at that moment, she thought she was the luckiest person in the world. She never thought it would happen. After seven years she had resigned herself to raising Susan alone.

"Well, as long as you said yes, I have a little something for you that can't wait until tomorrow." He reached into his pocket and presented her with a beautiful diamond ring.

"Here, let me put it on you. I've always seen this done in the movies and I don't want to miss my only chance. He gently placed the ring on her finger. She looked down at it, looked up at John and the thought crossed her mind that this is how it should be, just the two of them, in the quiet of her home with Susan sleeping soundly in the next room.

"I can't believe you bought this. What if I said no?"

"I worked it out with the jeweler. He assured me there would be no trouble returning it and I assured him, he had nothing to worry about. When John Ellington goes after a wife he means business."

"I'm full of so many feelings. There's so much to say, to tell you, so much I've held back."

"We have the rest of our lives, Carrie."

"No, I don't mean that, I mean about Susan. I've never told you who......"

"Shhh," said John, covering her lips with his fingers. "It doesn't matter. If you are at peace with it, I am at peace with you. We are both over thirty and we are not the first date each other has had. I love you exactly as you are, and how you were. It's our life together that I want to talk about and how soon I can change your name and Susan's to Ellington. You will let me adopt her, won't you? It's probably the only way we'll ever get a girl into the Ellington family, we're so boy prone."

"Of course.

"What about religion? Mine means a lot to me and I know you can take it or leave it."

"Whatever you want. I want you to be happy and if that means my kids are Catholic, fine. It's just not a big deal to me one way or the other. How do you feel about another child?"

"I'd love it. It'll be great for Susan and you've already shown me what a terrific Dad you'll be from watching you with her."

"When do you think we should get married?"

"Tomorrow, while the poinsettias are still fresh in the church, save on the florist bill."

"John, you nut. No, when?"

"I was thinking about the weekend after Easter. Don't you Catholics have something about not getting married during Lent?"

"Yes. That sounds okay with me, that is if the boss lets me off. Do they know about this yet, John?"

"Nope, just thee and me. We'll lay it on them tomorrow."

Christmas Day at the Ellingtons was magical. When Carrie and John told them of their engagement, they discovered that they were the only ones who didn't know.

"We saw it coming last summer," said Dr. Ellington, as he proposed a Christmas toast to their happiness and to the joy of the Ellingtons in gaining two new treasures in their family.

Standing at the altar, Carrie lovingly recited her wedding vows to John. At the end of the service, they turned and faced the small group and received a round of applause. Susan could not contain herself, ran out into the aisle and walked back down the aisle holding Carrie's hand.

They had a garden reception at the Ellingtons' and the only damper on the day was the absence of the Craigs. Carrie had mended her fences with her parents and had even taken Susan back home last year to visit them. Two months ago, her Dad suffered a heart attack and was now recuperating from heart surgery.

Betty ended up as her only attendant as Cathy was seven months pregnant and Candy had been transferred to Tokyo in a supervisor's position for the airlines and they were hosting the International Convention this weekend.

In a way Carrie was glad Betty was her lone attendant. Starting with the morning after the dance last summer at the Hotel Del, Betty had been her confidant through the entire courtship and engagement to John. Having Betty also got her off the hook of having to choose between Cathy and Candace.

The reception at the Ellingtons' was everything Carrie dreamt about. Dr. Ellington and Katie forgot nothing, even going as far as to have a three piece combo and small portable dance floor. Shortly after the band started to play, Dr. Ellington approached Carrie.

"May I have the first dance with my new daughter-in-law?"

He led her to the ten by ten floor and lovingly danced with her proudly displaying his new relative.

"I hope we will always be as happy as we are today." he said, whispering in her ear. "I am fiercely proud of John and proud of you, and for me to have you both in the family makes and old man burst with glee."

"You're not old, Dr. Ellington."

"It would give me great pleasure if you would call me Dad. I don't know what the traditions are in your family, but we Ellingtons make everyone part of the family once they cross that altar railing."

"I'd be glad to call you Dad, although it may take awhile to get used to it. I do want Susan to call you Grandma and Grandpa though."

"Oh, Susan. That'll be no trouble. I've already thought of her as my granddaughter. I have big plans for her. She's the closest thing I'll ever get to raising a little girl."

The music stopped and the best man proposed a toast to the happy couple. There were many tears of joy brimming in eyes, especially among long time friends who knew about the long journey that had brought Carrie to this day. She sent invitations to both

Annie and Paula from Japan days and was delighted Paula was able to come. Still single and still in the Navy, she was in graduate school in Denver. It was a strained visit because the memories that they had in common and held so dear together had little to do with Carrie's wedding day but Carrie was flattered that Paula made the effort to come.

"Does Pete's family know about Susan?" she'd asked the night before.

Carrie's face went ashen. That was the first question on the subject she'd ever been asked. Her new friends had long ago accepted the fact that she was a widow whose husband had been killed in Vietnam.

"No, they don't. I saw no reason to upset his family. Right from the beginning, I decided that Susan was mine and it was up to me to take responsibility and made the decisions effecting her life."

"If I remember him, she doesn't look anything like him. I think she looks a lot like you, except for her strawberry blonde hair. She sure is a little doll."

"It was very difficult in the beginning. I had betrayed my own values. I didn't want to leave the Navy and was really on my own. Remember, we weren't so broad minded as we are today. Now, everything is therapy; EST, Transcendental Meditation, everyone doing their own thing and having their own space. But, if you remember back in Yokosuka, we would have died before we would have ever let it be known that we thought we needed to talk with a psychiatrist. Life has been very kind to me. I have a daughter whom I adore and tomorrow, I shall marry the most wonderful man in the world."

"I'm happy for you Carrie. I wonder if marriage is ever going to happen for me. I came really close last year but when I was honest with myself, I had to admit I was more in love with the trappings than the man.

He was a physician, a widower. At first it looked made to order but as time went on, I knew I could not be happy with him. He was just too rigid and traditional and I started to feel stifled."

"Be patient. Work hard in graduate school. Someone will come along who will see what an unclaimed treasure you are. I'm so glad you are going to be here tomorrow. The two years we shared are precious to me. Susan will always be a part of that and so will you. Now, let's get some sleep. I don't want to have bags under my eyes in my wedding pictures."

"You look great, beautiful in fact. I wish the whole Yokosuka gang was here to cheer you up the aisle. Remember how husband hunting crazy we were? It's a shame we didn't keep up better. Oh! I forgot to tell you. Last year I saw Father Paige's orders in the Navy Times. He was assigned to some special task force at Quantico. Did you keep up with him at all?"

"No, I'm so bad. I didn't keep up with anyone. As I said, in the beginning, I was so confused and then I just got too busy and really got into my life here."

"Well, I guess that's sort of the same story with all of us."

Paula walked across the room and gave Carrie a goodnight hug.

"I'm happy for you friend, really happy for you. I've never told you this but I really do love you, love you as much as any of my sisters."

"Me too, me too."

The Hawaiian music spun through Carrie's head, and sunlight streamed through the branches of the quivering palms on Kalakaua Avenue. Walking along, her hand in John's, she was lost in the waft of perfume rising from the plumeria lei. Her eyes opened slowly and it was the sun peaking through the slats of the venetian blinds in their bedroom that awakened her. Blinking her eyes, she realized that she had been dreaming, back three weeks ago to their honeymoon in Waikiki.

It had been a perfect honeymoon. The Carsons kept Susan while they were gone for just six days. Neither she nor John had spent any real time there. She had stopped for one day on the ship on her way to Japan eight year ago and John had changed planes there both on the way over and back from Vietnam, so Hawaii was their first choice when they planned the trip.

Waikiki surely showed the effects of millions of R and R dollars that had been left there by married couples stealing away for five days of love in the middle of the war. High rises replaced huts and traffic was as dense as any big mainland city. The R and R stories of married couples were as notorious as the single R and R stories she had heard from her young Marine patients in Japan. Hotel clerks and maids told of couples who never left the room for five days, ordering room service and filling the hallways with cast off half eaten trays of food.

Carrie and John stayed at the Hawaiian Village and did all the typical tourist activities. It the morning, they went sight seeing and in the afternoon spent their time on the beach and in the water. They visited both the USS Arizona Memorial and Punchbowl National Cemetery, holding each others hands tightly as their memories of still another war filled their thoughts.

"I wonder if there will ever be a memorial to the casualties from Vietnam here someday?" asked Carrie.

At night, they had dinner around eight and visited the different clubs, one night seeing Don Ho at the International Market Place and another, enjoying Hilo Hattie at the Hilton. Happy and dreamy, they returned to their hotel each night where they made gentle and sweet love. John was a tender and caring lover and Carrie now, for the first time, understood that the really important part of love making was total trust and commitment. She was John's and John was hers and that giving brought them together spiritually as well as physically. She loved John more and more each day as she lived with him and could feel his love for her make her a stronger and more confident person. In turn, she returned it in her passion to him. They were not only in love, they were each other's best friend and confidant. She was filled with joy in the arms of her new husband.

Stirring in the bed, she put her hand out, John's side of the bed was empty. She smelled the coffee and looked at the clock. She could not believe it was nine o'clock. She always woke up at seven. Stretching, she sat up, her feet searching the floor for her slippers. She reached down for her robe when a sick feeling came over her. She stepped quickly into the bathroom and just reached it in time to vomit into the sink. Gosh, she thought, that came over me quickly. The retching continued and when it finally subsided, John was beside her.

"Good morning, sleepy. What's up Hon, except last night's supper, that is?"

"I don't know. What did we have? Oh, yeah, roast chicken. That shouldn't be any problem. Oh, look out."

Pushing John aside, she went to the bedroom and lay back on the bed.

John rinsed out a wash cloth and took it in placing it on her forehead.

"Mind if I sing you a song, Hon?"

Carrie looked at him through eyelids that felt green. Softly and sweetly, John started singing "Rock-A-Bye Baby".

Startled, Carrie looked at him.

"No, it can't be."

"Why not? Have they changed the formula in the past few years, something I didn't know about?"

"No, dummy, I just never thought, so soon."

"Fine by me. I'd love it but if this morning is any indication of the next nine months I can see why you wouldn't be so thrilled."

"You know, now that I think of it, I haven't had a period since the wedding. I bet you're right. I was such a basket case when I got pregnant with Susan, I don't remember any of the day by day early details of the pregnancy. I guess I was sick then, too, but I tried so hard to deny the pregnancy, somehow, I blocked the memories of morning sickness.

"Let's see, I'll even tell you when this one will be born. We have a formula for that you know. My last period was April tenth, the week before the wedding, so if I am pregnant, our child will join us around January seventeenth."

"Great! Right on superbowl Sunday, we'll have a party."

John slipped off his shoes and climbed up on the bed next to his wife.

"I'm sorry you feel so badly, Carrie, but I want you to know once again that I adore you and if you are pregnant, I am the happiest man in the world. I want you to understand something very clearly. I do not consider this my first child. This is my second child. Susan is my first child and on Monday, I am going to start to fill out the adoption papers. It would work out so well if her name is changed and we are all Ellingtons by the time the new baby comes."

Carrie just looked into her husband's eyes.
"Thank you, darling, thank you."
John returned her look adoringly.
"Grow old along with me, the best is yet to be." He whispered the words of Robert Browning in his wife's ear.

Susan was adopted by John in Superior Court in San Diego in November. They let her make all the transitions slowly. During their courtship, she had called John, "John." After the wedding, she called him "Daddy John" and then slowly, it just shortened to "Daddy." They had a beautiful relationship and it was impossible to figure out who thought they had gotten the better deal.

Christmas that year was joyous for them all. They were a new family with new traditions. Carrie was huge with her pregnancy so they did not attend Midnight Mass but went as a family to the ten o'clock Mass on Christmas Day and then to the Ellingtons for dinner. This was Carrie and Susan's second Christmas with them and it only proved to her more so that she had married into a loving family. The senior Ellingtons were beside themselves in anticipation of the new baby.

Carrie and John tried hard to make Susan a part of the pregnancy as they looked forward to the arrival of their child. She was seven now and very excited about a baby coming.

John and Carrie talked for hours about names. One night, John told her if it was a boy, he would like to use an English name like Percival, Alistair or Nigel. Carrie almost died. How could I know and love him and not know this part of him she asked herself and was about to protest when she caught the grin on his face.

"Don't worry, hon, I'm not that crazy. I want our son to have a nice boy's name. What about you?"

"Do you want him to be named for you?"

"No, I think everyone is entitled to their own names."

After looking through name books, they decided that if their child was a boy, they would name him Stephen John and if it was a girl, they would call her Sissy. Carrie loved the name and her favorite Aunt was Aunt Sissy. If she were a Southern girl or a Texan, she would name her Sissy, but being a New England Catholic, she would give her a Christian name and use the nickname Sissy.

January dragged by and Carrie was becoming impatient and short tempered. Around noon time, the second Saturday, John came in from working on the car and said, "Why don't you go next door and get Susan and I'll take us all to the movies."

"Jaws" was at the local theater and John felt it would help, at least, pass one afternoon for Carrie.

"I do feel like it and I don't feel like it."

"I know you're a mess. Let me make the decision. Let's just go."

It turned out to be a good idea. Five minutes into the film, Carrie was glad she had come and Susan was totally absorbed by it. Suddenly, Carrie shifted in her seat and then shifted again.

"Oh! no," she thought. "Oh! no, not here, I don't believe it."

She nudged John. "I think my water broke."

"Your what, shhh, they are about to cut the shark open."

"My water, the sac the baby is in. It means I'm going into labor."

"Now, before they get the shark?"

"John, the baby doesn't care about the shark. See, it really was a great idea to come to the movies."

Carrie looked up to see the two people in front of her glaring at her for talking.

"John, we have to leave."

The three of them got up and the whole theater turned their way. No one could believe that anyone would leave "Jaws" at that point in the story.

"Shall I drive right to the hospital?"

"Heavens no. I don't want to lie around there all night, besides, I want to take a shower, shave my legs and pack my own suitcase."

"Then why the rush to leave the movie?"

"John, I was dripping a puddle under my seat. I promise, after your child is born, we'll go back and see it."

Susan was listening to all of this in the back seat.

"Mommy, what are you talking about? Did you wet your pants?"

"No, darling, but something happened that told me the baby is probably going to be born today or tomorrow. Isn't that exciting? We're finally going to have our baby."

"Do I get to go stay at Betty's again?"

"You sure do, but only 'til I come home. Then I want my little girl with me with our new baby."

Carrie's labor lasted just three hours, and with John at her side, they watched their second daughter enter the world with a loud and lusty cry. Both had tears streaming down their cheeks as the nurse placed the infant in Carrie's arms and then they both laughed because she looked exactly like John, balding and all.

"What's her name?" asked the nurse.

Carrie and John looked at each other. They explained to the nurse that they planned to call their daughter Sissy, but had not decided on her Christian name.

"I bet you think people like us are nuts. We have nine months to get ready and then we act like it's a big surprise when the baby comes and we have no names."

After talking if over for an hour, they decided to stick with a traditional and old fashioned name. They named their daughter, Mary Elizabeth Ellington, knowing full well she would hardly ever use the name.

5

Coronado, California
April, 1979

Carrie took advantage of Sissy's nap time to catch up on her ironing. She had always enjoyed ironing for it was a quiet time and she got some of her best thinking done standing at her ironing board. Suddenly, the quiet of her mind was shattered by the voices of two little girls in the back yard.

"He is not."
"He is too."
"He is not."
"He is too."
"He is not. I heard my mother and father talking. He's Sissy's but he's not yours."

A chill broke Carrie's serenity as the back screen door opened and Susan came in visibly upset and headed for her bedroom.

"Susan, honey, come here. What is going on?"

Susan ignored her mother and went to her room slamming the door. Carrie knocked and went into her daughter's room. She sat on Susan's bed and just rubbed her back, at the same time fighting back her own nausea. How could I have denied that this would ever happen? How could I be so stupid?

Susan rolled over and looked up at her mother.

"Debbie says that Daddy isn't my real daddy, that he's only Sissy's real daddy. That's not true, is it Mommy?"

Susan was nearly twelve. Up until now, it had been a lovely day. The schools were on Easter break and Susan had invited Debbie over for the day.

The Ellingtons had been in their new home nearly a year. Cathy and Dave had received orders back to San Diego and naturally, wanted to move back into their home. Although Carrie and John knew that day would come, when it happened, it caused an upheaval in their lives. Coronado was so expensive and they dearly loved it. They looked at other areas of San Diego but nothing pleased them. Then, one Sunday last year, they found the perfect house but as they suspected, it was a bit above their means. After much debate, they agreed to accept a generous gift from Dr. Ellington. His explanation was that he had paid for Burt, Jr to go to medical school but that John had paid for law school himself between his savings from his time in Vietnam and the GI Bill. Dr. Ellington really pressed the issue until John and Carrie agreed to graciously take a check for the amount of Burt's medical school education, enabling them to buy their home in Coronado.

Betty Carlson was no longer Carrie's next door neighbor but the relationship thrived and Susan and Debbie often spent the day at each other's house. In the meantime, Fred Carson had received two sets of orders but by switching back and forth from shore duty to sea duty he had managed to stay home ported in the San Diego area. They still lived in the same house.

Carrie knew she had to answer Susan's question. She wished she could run to the phone and find out just what it was that Debbie had overheard in her parent's conversation.

"Honey, that's not anything knew. You know that Daddy adopted you. Remember, before mommy's wedding, there was just you and I? Daddy has always loved you and the day he adopted you and your name became Ellington, he was the happiest daddy in San Diego."

"Did I have another name before that?"

Carrie couldn't believe that Susan had forgotten all of that.

"Yes, Sweetheart, your name was the same as mine. It was Craig."

"Oh."

There was silence in the room.

"Did I have a daddy before my daddy now, a real daddy?"

"Yes, but he did not know about you. He was killed in the war. Now Daddy is your real daddy."

Carrie knew she was taking advantage of Susan's innocence and evading the real answers but her short answers seemed to appease her daughter and the crisis passed. She knew the lid had been let off a pot and the rest was only a matter of time. Adolescent girls were so curious about how and why everyone got here. The worse curse to befall any adolescent was to be different. More questions would surely follow.

Carrie hugged her daughter.

"Let's get Debbie and have some lemonade."

Carrie had a hard time finding Debbie who was hiding on the side porch knowing she had caused quite a stir. In spite of the fact that she herself was upset, Carrie decided she had to say something to smooth the situation out between the two girls.

"Debbie, didn't you know that Mr. Ellington was Susan's adopted daddy?"

Debbie just looked down.

"Don't be embarrassed honey. Susan's daddy loves her to death and is very proud of her. Her first daddy was killed in the war."

Carrie left it at that and after a few minutes of cookies and lemonade the afternoon was back together. By now, Sissy had awakened from her nap and they all walked over to the park and then to the library.

But no amount of activity or involvement with the girls could erase the smudge on Carrie's heart. Her life with John had been nearly perfect, their only sorrow being two miscarriages in two years after Sissy was born. They were a happy family and John had been promoted to the head of the legal department at General Dynamics. As such, he assigned all the necessary trips to his staff each year. On at least two company trips, Carrie had gone with him.

With so many women in the work force, Dr. Ellington decided to open his office one night a week to accommodate them. He asked Carrie how she felt about coming back to work that one evening. Carrie jumped at the chance. She missed her professional role and one night was just enough. John encouraged her to return and he looked forward each week to his night alone with the girls.

Carrie got up to count the library books she had placed on the check out desk. They had to have a system or they could never remember how many they had out at a time. How she wished tonight was her work night but it was only Tuesday. She worked on Thursday evenings. She had to get out and think tonight without telling John. She had to do this by herself. She thought back to the night of their engagement when she started to tell him and he silenced her with his total acceptance and approval of having her exactly as she was.

Church! Oh thank God. Her old Irish Catholic practices came to her rescue. Nearly every church, for years had devotions to St. Anthony on Tuesday evenings. Most, over the years had discontinued them but Saint Mark's still held the services. She'd tell John she wanted to go to church. He never interfered in the practice of her religion.

At dinner, John looked a little surprised but gave his whole hearted approval and as she walked to the car, added the proverbial, "Say one for me."

Carried entered the darkened church. The only light was the red lamp over the tabernacle. She sunk into the back pew, and tears streamed down her face. She prayed in a conversation of rapid and disjointed thoughts.

"Oh, dear God, please tell me what to do. You are the only one Who really knows the whole story, the one Who knew what was in my heart. I've tried to do the best I could with our lives and thank you so much for John but I know she is going to want to know his name, I know that is going to be one of the next questions, it's only a matter of time. I don't want to hurt anyone, least of all my own daughter. Please let her stop asking, just give me some more time to think about all of this. How could I have been so dumb to think she would not want to know and it would never come up? Everyone wants to know who their parents are. What am I to do? Help me."

Carrie felt emptied, drained, but only slightly relieved. Her relief came from her belief that the crisis today was over for awhile. She dipped her finger into the holy water font, made the Sign of the Cross and left just as the worshippers were arriving for the eight o'clock services.

On the way home, she stopped at Baskin Robbins and bought a quart of ice cream. Ice cream always made her feel better and would be a nice family treat to end this terrible day.

The family sat around the table with chocolate sauce and whipped cream and made sundaes. John knew his wife was upset when she left for church and was relieved that she seemed at peace now. He looked around the table at his girls, all three of them. How he loved them all.

When Sissy started kindergarten at Saint Mark's School, Carrie was alone at home. At first, she was elated at the free time but before long, she became bored. She thought of going back to work a few days a week at the office with Dr. Ellington but remembered how demanding and draining the job was when she did it right. She did not want to deprive her family of her care and love.

When it came time for eye exams at school, Sissy brought home a note asking for any mothers who were nurses to volunteer with the health program. Starting with a simple afternoon of volunteering, before long, Carrie was at the school two or three mornings a week. She had spoken to Sister Rachel, the principal and slowly, together, they prepared a health course of sorts for the children. Carrie adored the work. She started with safety and nutrition and gradually added other areas until her program received acclaim from many parents.

"You are such a help to us Mrs. Ellington," said Sister in her Irish brogue.

"Oh, Sister. I get so much more out of it than I put into it. I have a real nursing job you know, one night a week."

"Now, we're not tiring you out are we?"

"Well, I have to admit I do tire more easily than I used to but I so enjoy getting caught up in the excitement of the children."

"We feel badly that we are not able to pay you, you are such an asset to the school."

"Sister, my husband and I are very blessed and we consider this as part of giving back what we have received."

"A lovely man, your husband. He's not Catholic is he?"

"No Sister, he isn't. The Ellingtons are Lutherans."

"Well, you better run along or Sissy will be home before you. Thanks again, Mrs. Ellington.

John brought home several brochures about cruises. He was dying to take one. The idea held great appeal for Carrie also but she had reservations about leaving the girls.

"Why don't we take a Christmas cruise, then they can go with us?"

"Are you serious?"

"Sure. All the good lines have children's program directors aboard for the holidays."

"I'm not worried about Sissy but Susan is nearly fourteen and you know how she can be."

"Why don't we give her a choice? If she doesn't want to go, she can stay with Mom and Dad."

"What about them? How do you think they will like not having us here for Christmas?"

"My parents have never been selfish people. They will be happy for us and will do just fine with their own Christmas."

"You're right there. I don't think either of them has a selfish bone in their body."

"I told you a long time ago that I lucked out in the parents department."

As it turned out, Susan opted to go and the family had a terrific time. They flew across country and cruised in the Caribbean. There were just enough interesting teenage boys on board to keep Susan in a flutter and Sissy was kept busy with other children in arts, crafts, games and every imaginable activity. They went ashore in San Juan and St. Thomas.

The morning they docked in St. Thomas, Susan asked if she could go in town with the friends she had made instead of with the family. Carrie said that she didn't think that was a very good idea but John took her aside and gave her a little talk.

"You've seen these young people all week. You've met their parents and the kids want to strike out on their own. They are only going to walk up and down the main street out there anyway. Come on Mama, your little girl is growing up."

John was right. Susan was blossoming into a beautiful young lady. She was in the eighth grade and in her swimsuit, was shaped more like Carrie than like Sissy. Her thick strawberry bond hair was cut into a wedge, the latest style. She adored her little sister and was generous in giving her time in everything from playing games to curling and braiding her pale blonde hair. Seven years was a big difference in age and Carrie saddened a moment when she thought of the two babies she lost and how different the family would be. She was thankful she had John's perspective on raising her daughter. Susan needed room to grow and stretch and John would make sure she had that.

Susan returned from her trip ashore with her new friends and Carrie was so glad that she had listened to John. She'd had a wonderful day, told them everything, showed them her purchases which included small gifts for each of them and thanked them for letting her go. I guess that's how you do it Carrie thought, one positive experience at a time.

At the end of the trip they returned to San Diego full of tales of the joys about cruising, making the senior Ellingtons promise to go on one themselves.

The New Year arrived and the family all got back into their routines, Susan in eighth grade, Sissy in second grade, John busy running the legal department and Carrie working one night a week with Dr. Ellington and helping out at Saint Mark's school two or three mornings a week. She was happy, fulfilled and adored her husband and two daughters. As she and John joked in bed one night, about getting near the big four 0, John held her close and said the world would be a great place if every guy was as happy as he was. Carrie kissed her husband and clung to him. He was truly her treasure.

6

Coronado, California
April, 1984

Carrie sat on the edge of Susan's bed gazing in awe at her daughter. Tonight was her junior prom, a night that so far had gone perfectly. After walking the stores of San Diego, Susan had finally found the dress of her dreams. It was aquamarine, in three layers of cotton gauze cloth, trimmed along the edge of each layer with a quarter inch of aqua satin. The color against her strawberry blond hair was breathtaking.

She was a junior at Coronado high school. At first, Carrie and John had enrolled her in one of the parochial academies, across the bay in San Diego, but on further reflection, decided to keep her in Coronado. All her friends were here and they felt that between home and Saint Mark's grammar school, she had been given a good foundation in her faith.

Susan blossomed in high school. She was a cheerleader, a class officer and at a time when many of America's teens were driving their parents crazy, caused hers not a bit of trouble. In spite of her qualities, she had the same insecurities of all teens and was sure she would not be invited to the junior prom.

"Mom, I just know no one will ask me. What am I going to do? I've been active in everything and now I won't even get to go to my own prom."

Carrie was relieved when three weeks ago, Brian O'Neill called and asked Susan to go with him. Susan left the ground that day and hadn't touched it since.

Brian, whose father was a Navy pilot had only transferred to the school this past year and Carrie had heard lots of details about him all year long, enough to know that Susan was madly in love with him, but from afar like many teens.

"Mom, I don't think these pearls look quite right. Can I look in your jewelry box for something else?"

"Sure, I agree. They're a little old lady looking for the trendiness of your dress."

Susan came back into the room, hands empty.

"Mom, that's it. That'd be perfect. Can I wear that? Can I wear the diamond cross and chain you have on?"

Carrie's heart jumped in her chest.

"This. I don't know. I've never let anyone borrow it. It's very special."

"Oh Mom, I'll be careful, I promise. Let me try it on."

The diamond cross and chain lay upon Susan's neck like a lily on a pond. It was the perfect accessory but Carrie felt wrenched, like she was losing her last tie to Pete.

"Anyone home?"

John came in the front door out of breath.

"I was so afraid I would be late. Here Princess, Wow! you look gorgeous." John stopped and gazed at his daughter. "It's a little something from your old dad for tonight. I can't have Brian thinking that he's the only man in your life."

Susan opened the gift wrapped box. In it was a delicate sterling silver bracelet with two tiny diamonds set in a flower welded on a disc.

"Oh Daddy, thank you," she said and gave John a hug and kiss.

"I feel so rich tonight with all these diamonds," she said pointing to her mother's necklace.

"Nothing's too good for our pride and joy," beamed John.

Brian arrived for Susan. Carrie and John took pictures and praised them. All four were full of selfconscious quips and remarks. At last, Susan and Brian left, Susan proudly adding a corsage of white carnations to her dress.

As Carrie watched her daughter leave the house, she couldn't believe how fast she had grown up and what a beauty she had become. She thought of the necklace around her neck and when she did, she unconsciously put her hand to the empty place on her own neck where the necklace had lain. A chill shot through her body as she groped the spot again. She rubbed and rubbed and could not believe what she was feeling. How can this be? It couldn't have popped up overnight. How did it get so big? Her fingers were resting on a large firm mass, an immovable lump lying just under the muscle in her neck.

"How about a glass of wine, hon? Let's savor this evening out on the porch and wait for Sissy to come home."

Sissy was at Cathy and Dave's. Having them back here was great and their two little girls were Sissy's best friends as well as her first cousins. Robin was the baby that Cathy was carrying at Carrie and John's wedding and Sharon was born the next year, six months after Sissy. All together in a row, they could be mistaken for triplets, they shared so many of the same features, blond hair, freckles and big new second teeth!

"Didn't she look beautiful?" asked John. "We are so lucky when I look at the problems of other parents."

Carrie didn't answer

"Carrie? Are you okay? Come on. Tonight's not a night to be sad."

With that, Sissy came bursting through the side door.

"Guess what? Uncle Dave took us to the ship for dinner. It was neat. We had hot dogs and french fries and we made our own sundaes. One of the sailors let me sit in an airplane."

Dave was now the oral surgeon on the USS Ranger, home ported at North Island, and the girls liked nothing better than to go on board with him and roam the huge ship.

John looked at his joyful daughter, so full of life. She was nine years old and he cherished each remaining day before she had to enter the trauma of her teens. She had her hair in two side ponytails like Dagwood Bumstead and she was an Ellington through and through; bright, independent and full of motion and activity. In a way she was like Susan but in other ways, she was far more independent. As hard as Susan tried to hide it, she was fiercely dependent on Carrie, where he often had the feeling that Sissy could walk out the door, turn around and wave, and never look back. The relationship between the girls was loving and caring. Susan was the perfect older sister and Sissy adored her. In his heart, John had to admit that Sissy would never be the looker that Susan was but laughed to himself as he acknowledged the fact that he wasn't the looker that Carrie was either.

After Carrie settled Sissy in bed, she returned to the porch and John, once again, saw the worry on her face.

"Honey, you're not worried about Susan are you? She'll be fine. They're not even going to leave Coronado tonight."

Carrie put her hand up to her neck and told her husband what she had found just an hour before.

"What does it mean to have you this upset?"

"I don't know, but I'm scared. You're not supposed to have lymph nodes in your neck unless you've been sick with an infection in that area. I feel fine. Here, feel it."

"Honey, you know I don't know a thing about medicine. You've got the wrong brother."

Carrie unburdened her anxiety to John. She rattled off the signs of bad lymph nodes and hers fit all of them. It was matted, firm, painless, and all the things lymph nodes should not be. She thought of all the Hodgkins disease and lymphoma patients she had cared for when she first came in the Navy. It seemed to be a young person's disease.

"Tell you what. Let's get some sleep and we'll have Dad take a look tomorrow. It's probably nothing. John put his arms around his wife and led her to their bedroom trying with all his heart to reassure her knowing full well that there could never be anything seriously wrong with someone so full of life as Carrie.

At one o'clock, Carrie heard a car door slam and she pulled the bedroom curtain aside to see Brian walking Susan up the front walk. When they reached the steps there was an awkward pause and then Brian took her in his arms and kissed her. Carrie felt all tingly and a little naughty spying on her daughter from the window. Here is my Susan, she thought, already feeling the wonderful feelings of young love. She put her hand to her neck. The loving sight of Susan and the cold, harsh touch of her neck clashed like alien planets in her head.

Carrie drove with John to the hospital where Dr. Ellington was monitoring a woman in labor. They told him the story and he asked lots of questions and then examined Carrie's neck. John did not like the look on his father's face.

"I can't really say Carrie. You know how it is with lumps. They really have to be biopsied to get any definite answers. Let me call Al Brock. He's the best at what he does and I'm sure he can give us some answers. I know you've thought the worse but it could be just a node from a scratch you had in your head and didn't even know about. It could also be one of those crazy California viruses like Valley fever or toxoplasmosis from cats."

7

John stood up from his desk and looked out the window at the beautiful San Diego Bay before him. It just didn't get much better than this he thought to himself. Sensing motion in the room, he turned to see his father standing in the doorway of his office.

"Dad! What brings you here? I thought you doctors hated lawyers."

"Son, I'd give a million dollars to be anyplace else right now but here is where I belong. You don't keep a bottle stashed anywhere here do you?"

"Geez, Dad, what's wrong? You wanting a nip in the middle of the day?"

"I've come to talk to you about Carrie, the news isn't good, in fact, it's terrible."

John was stunned. Carrie's biopsy report was not due out until tomorrow and truthfully, he hadn't given it much thought. She was so alive, so healthy that he was sure it would turn out to be something insignificant.

"I've just come from Al Brock's clinic. He is shocked at what he found." John sat down at his desk, his heart racing in his chest, his palms gathering moistness.

"When I examined Carrie on Saturday, there was little doubt in my mind that she had a malignancy, I was sure of that. The characteristics of the lymph node were too classical. My guess at that time was she either had Hodgkins disease or lymphoma. Both are serious illnesses but are treatable. But, that is not the case. When she saw Al, he took a chest x-ray and was astounded. Her entire mediastinum had nodal tumors wrapped around it like concertina wire on a prision yard fence.

"Here media what?"

"The mediastinum, the center of the chest where the heart, major blood vessels, trachea and esophagus all meet. When he examined the tissue from the neck node, the cells were those of bronchogenic carcinoma, a fancy name for lung cancer."

John just stared at his father in disbelief.

"I'm at a loss for words or explanation. First of all, the disease is much more prevalent in men and in smokers. Carrie hasn't had a cigarette in over ten years not to mention her lack of symptoms. At her stage in the disease, she should be coughing her head off and raising blood."

"Come to think of it, she has had a cough but nothing she thought much about, just figured it was something she picked up from Sissy or the kids at school."

John picked at his fingernails.

"Dad, what are we talking about here in terms of treatment and time?"

Dr. Ellington sighed looking at his son compassionately.

"Al thinks surgery is out of the question because of the vital location of the tumors. The latest treatment is a combination of chemotherapy and radiation. If those are successful, it'll buy her some time. They are coming out with new drugs everyday."

"Come on, Dad, this is me you're talking to, not some kindergarten kid. What are we talking about in terms of time?"

"Give or take a few months, not more than a year."

John pounded his fists on his desk in anger and frustration.

"Damn, damn, damn."

Carrie, beautiful Carrie, his loving wife. No. His mind could not accept it. He'd try anything, take her anywhere. Some of these genius doctors must have a cure. Dr. Ellington kept silent and let his son vent his anger. Finally he spoke.

"Al wants to see Carrie tomorrow and I thought I would see how you wanted to break the news to her. That's really the reason I came by. We've got a few hours before the kids come home from school if you want to go home now."

"I don't think we have any choice. Let's go."

Carrie finished the lunch dishes and patted the bandaid on her neck. The stitches were itchy from the biopsy and she was dying to scratch them. In the past three days, she felt she had earned a master's degree in lymph nodes. She dragged out all her nursing and medical books from school and after reading everything she could, was pretty sure that she had Hodgkins disease. Seeing as she only had one node, she figured she was in stage one, and from all she read, she knew her chances were excellent for a cure.

Her thoughts were interrupted by the sound of a car door shutting out in front of the house. Looking up, she saw John and Dad Ellington coming up the front walk. Those bums, she thought, I bet they are taking the afternoon off to go play tennis.

"Come in, come in, you two, goldbricking it again?"

They each gave her a hug standing like two statues, eyes roaming the room for a place to lite.

"How are you feeling?" asked Dad Ellington.

"Oh, fine, except I'm being driven mad by the itching. I'd like to rip this dressing off. You know how we nurses are, Dad. I've practically read the print off my medical books. I hate to be morbid but I'd lay odds that this thing is Hodgkins. I'm not happy about having cancer but if I have to have it, it's probably the best one to have because from what I figure, I'm in stage one and it's probably curable."

Dr. Ellington just looked down at his lap.

"Carrie, there's no easy way to say this, I spent the morning with Al Brock. You don't have Hodgkins disease, you have lung cancer."

"Lung cancer, are you sure?"

"Yes, he showed me the slides, it's bronchogenic carcinoma and the chest x-ray pretty well confirms it."

The room screamed with silence.

Finally Carrie spoke.

"A thorocotomy, chest surgery, that's heavy duty stuff."

Dr. Ellington decided right then to bow out as her physician and recapture his role as father-in-law. He chose not to tell her that she wasn't a candidate for surgery. She was seeing Al tomorrow and he would leave all of that to him. His role now was to be kind, compassionate and a loving family member. He knew the year ahead was going to be a sad one for the Ellingtons. He wanted to establish his most useful role right now before the news spread and everyone slipped into their various reactions of shock, horror and denial.

"How about an ice cream?" asked John as they returned to Coronado over the bridge. They were both drained after their visit with Al Brock who, kindly, gently, but honestly told Carrie her diagnosis and what lay ahead in terms of treatment and care.

There would be more tests, a CAT scan, and they would design a program of radiation or chemotherapy or both. He predicted that the tumors would respond well and shrink, relieving pressure on vital organs. She could probably expect to feel quite well after completing the therapy.

"But I feel well, now," she said.

"I know, but, Dad told me that it won't be long before the nodes get big and started raising hell."

Carrie didn't ask any more questions. She just wanted to get home to her medical books again and read all about lung cancer now that her new found knowledge of Hodgkins disease was worthless.

Lung cancer. Damm all those cigarettes she had smoked for twelve years, from eighteen to thirty. It was so long ago. On top of everything else, she did not want to accept the guilt for causing this herself.

They got their ice cream and John stopped at the park on Orange Avenue. He looked at his wife and tears steamed down his cheeks. Carrie took his hand.

"We're in this together," he sobbed. "Whatever you want, what ever you do, I'm with you."

Her eyes filled.

"Our beautiful life, our beautiful family. I have to lick this even if I have to go for experimental drugs."

After a time, John asked, "What about the girls, what should we tell them?"

Carrie didn't answer right away. Finally, she said, "Time is different for teens and kids that it is for us. Susan will have to know that I am sick because when I get chemotherapy, there will be no way to hide it, but for now I'd like to avoid the word cancer until you and I have come to terms with it ourselves. I feel quite well and I think we should be a little more used to it before we try to introduce the girls to it. Right now, we don't have any idea of really what's ahead so it would be difficult to answer questions."

"Good thinking, as usual. You're something else, wife, my special something else."

Carrie knew that she was entering a new phase of her life, one from which every action and thought would be forever referred to as before or after cancer. For years, she thought of her life as before or after Susan and then it was before or after John. Now, she had a new benchmark that was indelible, that completely overpowered all other events in her life.

She threw her ice cream cone out the car window. She thought to herself, I haven't littered the street in ten years and I know for sure that this is the first time in my life that I have ever thrown away ice cream.

The Ellingtons made it through the summer, each dealing with the changes in their own way. Susan worked at the Navy Exchange at the North Island Naval Air Station and loved her job. She was a natural at sales and the setting provided her with an opportunity to meet and make new friends. Special among them was Doug Hauser, a midshipman from the Naval Academy who was assigned to the USS Ranger for the summer to gain experience at sea. A husky, tall blond, he had that clean cut Naval Academy look like the plebe on the Navy poster outside the Coronado post office. He had come into the exchange to buy a gift for his mother and Susan had helped him select some perfume. After stopping by several times that week, he finally got up the courage to invite her to a movie.

At first, John and Carrie were reluctant to let her go out with Doug but on thinking it over, they decided that he really was a fine young man, part teenager, part Naval officer. He was young enough to provide fun but his experience with the Navy forced a certain maturity upon him. The whole family was under great stress, and perhaps the addition of a boyfriend to Susan's life was just what she needed right now. He had just completed his first year at Annapolis so there was really only two years between them.

"You're so mature and serious." Doug said to Susan as they headed toward the tennis courts one evening.

"It's hard for me to believe that you're only sixteen, well almost seventeen, actually."

Susan paused in their walk and looked at Doug. Up until now, she kept their family business private but her fear and sadness were increasing each day and she had to have someone to talk with outside the family.

"There is something I haven't told you, that I haven't told anyone. I'm not usually this way, in fact, most of the time, you can't shut me up."

"Is there anything I can help you with?"

"No, there's nothing anyone can do, that's the bad part."

"It can't be that bad, Susan. You've got a great family, a fun job and you live in the best place in the country. Why the sad face?"

Arriving at the courts, they sat on a bench. The evening was cool with the breeze coming off Point Loma adding to the chill that Susan felt within her.

"I'd like to tell you if it's all right, Doug. I've got to tell someone."

He took her hand and gave it a squeeze. She sure liked him. Being with him was entirely different from being with Brian. She enjoyed Brian and would probably date him again when he returned from visiting his family in the East. Life was going by so fast for her and she felt like she had to run full speed just to stay in place.

"I have just about the greatest parents and family anyone could have. I hear my friends complain about their folks and it's just not like that for me. My folks love each other and they love us. My little sister is a doll and I have everything I could ever want. But, in May, we found out that my mom is very sick. She has cancer and it has been a terrible summer for her. She has to have radiation and chemotherapy and gets so sick that she sends Sissy off to her sister's for two days so Sissy won't see it. I see it, of course, and Mom tries to put on such a good act but it tears me up to watch her. Worse than that, it tears me up to see my dad. He loves her so much and I know he feels helpless."

"I am so sorry, Susan. I didn't have any idea."

"How could you have? I didn't tell you and Mom always looks great when you come by the house."

Susan looked off over the ocean and the sinking sun.

"I know I'm afraid to say it but what I'm really afraid of is that my mother is going to die."

As soon as she said the words, she started to cry and Doug gently held her in his arms, in silence. It was the first time she had voiced her fear to anyone. When John and Carrie decided to tell her the truth about Carrie's illness and treatment, they had sugarcoated the whole thing, really just telling her only as an explanation for the violent treatments. But, on her own, her fear had grown until the tension within her was nearly unbearable.

"Thank you for listening. You're the first person I've dared to tell how scared I am."

"Your mom looks so great, it's so hard to believe that she could be that sick."

"I know. I look at her and I forget too, but you should see her when she gets her treatments."

"Gosh, what a time for me to be going to sea."

The Ranger was heading out tomorrow for two weeks of maneuvers.

"What good am I? Now that you've finally found someone to talk with, I'm taking off. Please write me.

Write it all and I'll try to answer you and hold up my end of it for you."

By now, the lights came on the tennis courts but the playing spirit had left Susan.

"Let's go get some ice cream and walk home," she said. "I want to see my mom."

The summer for John was a whirlwind of activity created to block the horror of his wife's illness from his mind. Although he had been told the truth about her chances, he refused to believe it and he and Carrie faced her illness like two soldiers facing a battle at sunrise. He accompanied her to all her treatments and sat up with she while she vomited for hours afterward. Some nights he would just get on top of the bed and hold her while she wretched and heaved with spasms of pain and nausea.

In the third week of her treatment, her hair fell out and rather than have her embarrassed in the store, he talked the salesgirl into letting him take four different wigs home. Carried tried them on in the privacy of her bedroom and they laughed together because two of them looked ridiculous but were happy that the frosted one looked very much like her own hair. Many days he arrived home with a gift, a piece of jewelry or a scarf or a best selling book hot off the press. Carrie loved to read and could lose herself for hours in a good book. Her heart broke as she watched her husband try to keep her alive by boosting her spirits with presents.

After the first course of therapy was completed, her x-ray was practically normal and her blood work was a match for Charles Atlas. She felt terrific and as fall ended, she entered the Christmas season full of thanks and joy that in spite of the horrors of her treatment, it had worked. Maybe she would be one of the lucky ones and be cured.

Susan was a senior now and was busy looking through college catalogs to select the right one for her. She wasn't quite sure what she wanted to do but she was leaning towards becoming a nursery school teacher. Her experience with Sissy and her little cousins showed her how much she loved being with children. She knew one thing for sure. After seeing what her mother went through, she did not want to be a nurse.

Sissy was nine and in the fourth grade at Saint Mark's school. The nuns knew about Carrie's illness and were gentle and sensitive with Sissy on days that she seemed sad and upset. She knew her mother was sick and had to have treatments to make her better but she had no idea of the severity of the disease.

Christmas was beautiful for them all. Carrie felt well and everyone was optimistic. Maybe it really had all been a nightmare. This was the tenth year of their marriage and John presented her with an anniversary ring, a gold band with four quarter carat diamonds. he had considered a necklace but he knew without ever asking that her diamond cross and chain that she wore so often had special meaning to her and he did not want her to feel she had to make a choice.

After dinner at the Ellingtons' on Christmas Day, he and his dad took a walk.

"How are you doing son?"

"Fine, couldn't be better, Dad. Doesn't Carrie look great? She's so excited about her hair growing back."

"Yes, she looks great and I'd give a million to have half her attitude. The girls seem to be doing well too."

"I was a little worried about Susan for awhile. It's pretty heavy stuff for a sixteen year old even though she's quite mature for her age."

"How about being heavy stuff for a forty two year old?"

John looked at his dad and cast his eyes down.

"Son, you've been dealt a bad hand, no doubt about it. I'd give all that I have to see Carrie stay as she is but you know, that is not going to happen. I don't mean to be the bearer of sad tales but I think part of my job as your old dad is to keep you reality oriented. The girls will deny it and go on their way and Carrie will cope in whatever way she has to, but in the end, you're the guy who's going to be left holding the bag. Oh, I don't mean for you not to be cheerful and to do anything you want to for your wife. That's your right and your duty, and, I might add, your joy, right now. But at best, this hiatus in her health is only temporary. The whole mess could start all over quite suddenly, in fact, it probably will."

They had reached the benches around Glorietta Bay, a fact not lost on John as this is the spot where he had first told Carrie that her loved her. He was dying for a cigarette although he had not smoked in fifteen years.

"Thanks, Dad. I needed that and it couldn't have been easy for you to do. I want to make whatever time we have left together perfect and in doing so I just blocked out the fact that that might not be very long. I can't talk about it to anyone at work. It just makes them uncomfortable."

"I'm always here, son. I'm always here and I mean that on good days and bad."

John put his arm around his father.

"Thanks, Dad. Carrie and I always said that I lucked out in the parents department. If I can be half as good with Susan and Sissy, I'll consider myself a success as a father."

"We love her just as much as you do and the family is all in this together."

"Thanks, again, Dad. Thanks."

Carrie answered the phone to hear the breathless voice of Betty Carson on the other end.

"Carrie, Fred's orders came in. You'll never guess where we're going. We're going to Japan, to Yokosuka. Isn't that where you were when you were a Navy nurse?"

"Betty, that's great, yes it is, but I'm sure it's an entirely different place now. That was eighteen years ago for heaven sake. Oh, Betty, what am I going to do without you? When do you go?"

"In June, as soon as the kids get out of school. I have so many questions. I guess we'll have a sponsor who will write to us. Do you remember anything about where we'll live?"

"What is Fred's job?"

"His is going to be Chief of Staff for the Admiral."

"Oh, then you'll go into the VIP housing. Actually, they are quite nice. I went to a cocktail party at the Commanding Officer of the hospital's house. They are part of a row of cottages set back from the street going up a long hill. If I remember, they had nice Japanese gardens and three or four bedrooms."

"It would be great if you would feel well enough to come over for a visit."

Carrie felt something wrench within her. That was a long time ago. Over the years, she had managed to repress the bad and enlarge the good and her whole Japan experience was now categorized in her mind like some romantic fairy tale.

"I don't know, Betty. The flight might be too tiring for me. I'm really happy for you."

Carrie put the phone down and her thoughts drifted back to Yokosuka, to her friends there, to Pete, to Paula and Annie, to Father Paige. She was sorry she had not kept up with them but when she married John, she was so happy that she threw herself into her life with him and really, had no regrets. For a second, she allowed herself to think about her illness and Susan but quickly banished the thought from her mind. She was in remission and there was no need to dwell on morbid thoughts.

8

Coronado, California
April, 1985

As Susan walked toward her home, she could see Sissy skipping rope from the opposite direction. This was the most important part of Susan's day lately, checking the mailbox for a letter from Doug. He was back at the Naval Academy and she was in love. When Brian had returned from the East, she went out with him but could only now think of him as a friend.

"Did you have a fun day, Sissy?" she asked her bouncy little sister.

"Yeah, we had an Easter Bunny party and it turned out that it was Sister Rachel in the Easter Bunny costume. She looked so funny."

Pushing through the front door together, Susan was surprised to see Aunt Cathy and Candy both sitting on the sofa.

"Aunt Candy," she screamed, giving her seldom seen Aunt a hug. Candy had been transferred to New York three years ago and the girls didn't see her often but when she could, she gave them great treats with airline trips. In the past year, she had taken them both to San Francisco and Chicago and the girls idolized her.

"Where's Mom?"

"Your dad has taken her to the hospital, she isn't feeling well."

"But she was fine this morning, what happened?"

Hesitating until Sissy left the room, Cathy told Susan that her mother had coughed up blood and then hemorrhaged and had to be admitted for a blood transfusion.

"Is she okay? Can I go see her?"

"Why don't you wait until we hear from your dad. I'm sure it'll be alright. How about coming home with us now?"

"Aunt Cathy, if you don't mind, I'd like to stay here by myself for awhile. I'm okay and I have two letters from Doug to read. I'll walk on over later."

Susan became lost in the love of Doug's letters. He wrote of their getting married when he graduated and of children and it was all so romantic and exciting to the young high school senior. When she finished, she thought of her mother. How she wished Doug was here right now. She was scared to death, scared her mother would die. She wanted to talk with him and she had to talk with her mother, to touch her, to make sure she was still here. She took the two letters and added them to the collection in her pink lace box and locked it. Her letters from Doug were her only tangible piece of hope right now. Everyone else seemed far away, out of touch.

At first, Carrie did very well. After four units of blood, the bleeding stopped. Her x-ray showed marked extension of her disease so Dr. Brock scheduled her for another course of radiation. She went into a depression. She just didn't think she could go through it all again but when her family came to visit, she knew she had to try. She was not ready to leave them.

The night before she was to be discharged, she awakened with an excruciating pain in her chest. She called the nurse who in turn called Dr. Brock. After another x-ray, they learned that she had both pneumonia and fluid in her chest cavity.

"Looks like we'll have to keep you here a little longer, Carrie," said Dr. Brock sympathetically.

"Your counts are still a little low and now with this infection and fever, I want to keep a real close eye on you. We'll give you something for the chest pain and I'll get you started on antibiotics. In forty eight hours, you should start to feel a little better. I'll call John and tell him that you won't be going home."

John and Susan were disappointed but by now, they had both learned to live with a little uncertainty in their lives. Susan now had her driver's license so she visited Carrie each day right after school. It was a treasured time because she was usually the only visitor at that hour.

"Hi honey," said Carrie, as Susan entered her room the day she was supposed to have been discharged.

"Hi Mom, how do you feel?"

Susan was frightened by the return of the IV and oxygen to her mother's assorted array of hospital paraphernalia.

"I'm a little uncomfortable but more disappointed at having to stay here. How are your graduation plans coming?"

"Great, I'm on the prom committee but I just can't get too excited about it because, of course, I can't go with Doug."

"Can't you go with someone else?"

"Sure, but I don't think you realize how much I love Doug, Mom. I wouldn't miss my prom for anything, I'm just saying I can't get that excited about it."

Suddenly, their was a bustle at the door and Dr. Brock asked that Susan step outside.

"Carrie, I just saw your x-ray and reviewed your blood gases. We haven't begun to get on top of this thing. I think the best thing to do right now is to move you to intensive care?"

"For Heaven's sake, why?"

"Your lungs are terribly compromised and I'm afraid it's going to be a strain on your heart. Also, there's always the possibility of another hemorrhage."

Carrie was frightened. She had no illusions of licking her illness but she thought she would have a long time and that certainly, nothing so rapid as this would happen. She started to cry.

Dr. Brock sat on the edge of the bed.

"It's not all that bad, Carrie. I just don't want to take any chances, you've done so well."

That night, John called Carrie's parents and told them that he felt they should come. It was a time for the family to gather.

The next day, when Susan visited Carrie in intensive care, she knew that her mother was dying. Carrie told her she had received the Sacrament of the Sick that morning and that frightened Susan.

"You mean last rites?"

"No, honey, they don't call it that anymore. It's a Sacrament to help the sick and dying."

Susan lowered her eyes and thought of Doug and looked at her mother. She had something she wanted to talk with her about but her mother looked so sick.

"Mom, there's something I want to talk about with you."

"You look so scared, honey. Are you in trouble?"

"No, no, nothing like that."

"Well, you can talk with me, you know that."

"Mom, remember a few years back one afternoon when I was playing with Debbie in the yard and she made a big deal about Daddy not being my real father?"

Carrie knew what was coming and suddenly found herself gasping for air in spite of the assistance of her oxygen.

"I thought you'd forgotten all about that, that we had explained it that day."

"I've never forgotten about it. I just never brought it up again because I somehow knew it would cause problems."

Carrie felt terrible. Her wise beautiful daughter had been protecting her these past years at her own expense.

"Mom, I really love Doug and I know we are young but I think he is the man I am going to marry. Someday we will have children and I want to know who my father was so I'll know who is part of my children."

"But Daddy, he'll be your children's grandfather. He adores you."

"Daddy has nothing to do with it. I love Daddy and he'll always be my dad, but there's someone else I wonder about, someone else who is a part of me. Won't you please tell me Mom? It's really no different from all the stories we read in the paper about the adopted kids wanting to know who their real parents are."

Carrie closed her eyes and whispered a silent prayer for guidance.

"I've never told anyone, Susan, I mean no one, not even Daddy. I was happy with you and I was afraid people would be hurt if I told."

"That's what I mean, Mom. You're the only one who knows and if you....." Tears welled in Susan eyes.

Carrie placed her hand over her daughter's on the sheet.

"Honey, I am going to die, maybe not now, but I am very sick and I'm not really going to get much better."

Mother and daughter looked at each other and both just let their tears flow down their faces. It was a cleansing cry and opened doors between them that had been shut throughout Carrie's illness.

"Oh Mom, I can't imagine being here without you. Are you scared?"

"No darling. I'm not scared. I'm sad because I won't get to see you and Sissy grow up but where I'm going, I'll be happy. I've always tried to do the right thing and I know everything is going to be fine."

Susan sensed that her mother had already started to leave them, that part of her was already someplace else.

"I'll take care of Sissy for you."

"That's what I'm afraid of. You have your own life to live. I want you to go to college like you are planning and let Daddy worry about Sissy."

"Poor Daddy. What's going to happen to him?"

"Daddy will do fine. He's a strong and courageous man."

"Mom, we're getting off the subject."

Carrie closed her eyes.

"Let me sleep on it tonight and pray on it. When you come tomorrow, maybe I can tell you."

Carrie asked the nurse for a pain shot. Slowly she felt it take hold of her. As she drifted off to sleep, she thought of Susan's question and the last sound she heard was that of pelting rain on the roof and bamboo branches slapping against the rice paper windows.

Susan stopped in the hospital chapel on the way out. Dear God, she prayed. I know my mother is going to die soon but please let her tell me who my father is.

I love the dad you sent me but I want to know about that other part of me without hurting anyone else. She wiped her eyes and drove home so she could take care of Sissy while John came to the hospital.

At four-thirty that morning, John was awakened by the bedside phone.

"John, it's Al Brock. I think you better come to the hospital. Carrie has taken a turn for the worse."

John hung up the phone, threw on a jogging suit and sped to the hospital. ICU was a bedlam of machines, tubes and people. When Dr. Brock finally spotted John in the doorway, he came out to talk with him.

"Well, we pulled her through, John, but she's in a coma. The pneumonia is just overwhelming her and she has so little to fight with. I'm afraid her heart is just not going to be strong enough. We've put an endotracheal tube in her to help her breath and we're using all the drugs we can. I'm afraid it's just a wait and see situation now."

"Can I see her?"

"Sure, but let me warn you, it isn't pretty."

John stood by his wife's bedside and could not believe that the person on this bed was his beautiful Carrie. Soaked with perspiration, her short hair was matted to her scalp. The respirator was breathing for her and her hands looked like wax. He looked at the cross and rosary on her pillow and said a silent prayer.

"Lord, if this is what she is going to be like, please take her."

After eleven years of marriage, John was ready to give his wife back. He knew he was licked and he could no longer stand to see her suffer. He leaned over and kissed Carrie on the forehead and then left to prepare breakfast for his daughters.

The girls were both up when he arrived home.

"Where have you been?" asked Susan.

"I'm just coming from the hospital. Your mother has taken a turn for the worse."

"Daddy is Mommy going to die?"

Sissy shocked John with the blunt question. Somehow, in all of this, John knew he had been unfair with Sissy but he always counted on the fact that Carrie would get better one more time. Now he knew his time had run out.

"Yes, sweetheart, Mommy is going to die and go to heaven."

Sissy look at John and then at Susan.

"Who's going to take care of me?"

"I'm going to be here, and Susan and Aunt Cathy and Grandma and Grandpa. We're all going to take care of each other."

John picked up his ten year old daughter and held her in his lap at the kitchen table.

"We all feel very sad that Mommy is going to die and I know it's not fair to not have a mommy when you're only ten years old."

"I don't want Mommy to die."

"I know, Sissy, I know."

Susan left school at noon that day. She was too upset to study and she had to get to the hospital. She had to talk with her mother about her father.

As she approached her mother's bed, the nurse came over and put her arm around Susan.

"How's my mom?"

"She's very sick, Susan. She not conscious."

"You mean she can't talk."

"That's right."

Susan sunk into the chair in disappointment. She looked at her mother through her tears. I'll never know, she thought. I'll never know. The only thing that soothed her sadness and defeat was the serene look of peace and joy on her mother's silent face.

Carrie died the next day at noon without ever regaining consciousness. She was buried the following Monday, the day after Easter Sunday. She was forty two years old.

BOOK THREE

SUSAN

1

Bremerton, Washington
July, 1985

Father Paige called the last couple on the list and then closed the manual before him. This was to be his last Marriage Encounter Weekend here in the Northwest. He silently thanked the Lord for his involvement with the organization. After being with military troops so long, he had started to feel disconnected with the families of the church, the everyday people. At a discussion after a dinner party in a parish home on evening, all the new changes of the church, good and bad were batted around like a volley ball. The discussion was heated with passion, anger and disappointment at the lack of real change following Vatican II. Finally, one couple looked at Father Paige and said, "We are the Church, all of us here and it's up to us to make a difference. Through that night, he became involved with the Marriage Encounter Movement and it had reconnected him a very personal way to the people of God.

He looked up from his desk to see a nurse in her dress blues with four gold stripes on her sleeve.

"Hi, good lookin', remember me?"

Tom looked at the name tag, BRANDON, and drew a blank.

"Don't bother with the name tag, Father. Where would an Italian girl get a name like Brandon?"

"Paula? Paula Ferrara?" He bounded out his chair and threw his arms around her.

"What are you doing here, and a Captain, no less?"

"I'm the new chief nurse. Can you believe it? Old hell raising Paula from Yokosuka, now a chief nurse."

"That's right. I heard the new chief nurse was Captain Paula Brandon, but, of course, the name didn't mean a thing. Tell me about Mr. Brandon."

"Nothing like you'd ever pick for me, Tom. Quiet, laid back, sure of himself, a junior high school teacher. We've been married three years. Marrying him was the best thing that ever happened to me."

Looking around the office, she added. "I'm so glad you're here."

"Not for long, I'm afraid. I'm heading out in two weeks, back to Japan, to Yokosuka, of all places, to be the senior chaplain. It's a job I've wanted ever since we were all together eighteen years ago. I can't wait.

"You're going to love it here. In a way, it's very much like the old days in Japan. The people are good people and they lead a simple life, lots of camping, fishing and family activities.

How about some coffee?"

"Sure, love some."

"You know, I always felt badly that all of us didn't do a better job of keeping up from those days, but I guess the intensity of the war and the difficult time we all had coming back just scattered us all over the place. I do still hear from the Gleasons at Christmas. He's at Boston Children's Hospital and Betsy's busy with their six kids."

Paula waited for a sign that he knew. When it didn't come, she said, "I have some sad news, Father, that I just learned myself about two weeks ago. Perhaps you've heard it too. It's still hard for me to believe but Carrie died in April. She had lung cancer and was sick on and off for a year.

"You know, I was in graduate school in Denver when she got married and I went to her wedding. It was a beautiful wedding and all but things just weren't the same. We had gone our separate ways and there wasn't enough of our old Japan life to hold us together."

Tom was shocked.

"I can't believe it. She couldn't have been much over forty."

"She was forty two and she left two darling daughters."

"How did you hear about it?"

"Well, quite directly, as a matter of fact. When it came time to leave Charleston, I had fifty days leave on the books, and, of course, Dan was out of school for the summer. We decided to drive leisurely across the country, taking the southern route and driving up the west coast. We knew it would be unbearably hot but we have a new luxury car with an excellent air conditioning system. When we arrived in Phoenix, Dan suggested I call Carrie in San Diego. She was the only reason we were going there, and, if for some reason they were going to be away, we'd headed out on Highway Ten to Los Angeles, instead of Eight to San Diego."

Paula rolled her eyes giving a clue to the horror she was about to relate.

"John answered and somewhere in the first few minutes, he said, 'I guess you don't know,' and proceeded to tell me about her death. He begged us to come anyway so we did and I'm glad. Everyone seems to be doing well and we had a nice visit."

Tom was slowly overcome by his feelings of sadness and sheer hopelessness. His thoughts were thrown back to Carrie's love affair with her Marine and the wonderful trips they had to the orphanage in Gotemba.

"On our last trip to Gotemba, to the orphanage, we talked about our dreamsheet, and I projected my whole career for her. I distinctly remember ending up with a tour in the West, back to Japan, and then retiring in San Diego. Whoever would have thought I could be so accurate?"

"How about you? Where have you been?"

"I, too, have been lucky. I've been to Great Lakes, Oakland, to graduate school in nursing administration at the University of Colorado, Naples, for a taste of the old country, a tour in Washington, DC, nursing administration at Charleston, and now, out here as chief nurse. As of now, I plan to retire from this job."

"Was overseas in Naples anything like overseas Japan?"

"Not a thing. No war, we lived off base and you just can't substitute for the Oriental mystique. I enjoyed it because I'm Italian and it also gave me a chance to see Europe. No, Tom, I'm afraid Yokosuka was a once in a lifetime experience."

She stopped and lit a cigarette.

"I promised Dan I'd quit these this year and I'm really serious about it now since hearing about Carrie.

"Guess who else I heard about? Remember Ed Walker, the officer that got us the free airplane ride to Hong Kong. We were all dying to date him but he never dated anyone more than once or twice. Well, he went into the seminary and is now a priest, back in the Navy in the chaplain corps."

"Oh, I knew that, of course, from the chaplain corps, in fact, I'll be stopping to see him for a few days in Hawaii on my way to Japan. He's stationed at

Kaneohe Marine Corps Air Station. I knew about his seminary plans in Yokosuka because he counseled with me about them, but, of course, I couldn't break his confidence and tell anyone. We had a lot in common because we were both late vocations."

Pausing, he looked at Paula.

"I can't believe that Carrie is dead. She was so full of life. Was she happy in her marriage?"

"Very much so. She married a wonderful salt of the earth type guy, an attorney and they lived their entire life in Coronado.

"You know, Tom, I often thanked God none of us married those jerks we partied with over there. Most of them were all flash, or should I say all flesh, and no substance, although I have to say, Carrie met a gem in Pete. She didn't talk about Japan much. I often thought that Pete's death was just so painful for her that she repressed the whole two years. Who knows, Father. None of us were operating with a full deck in those days. We were young, full of hell, worked like dogs and then partied like fools when all those jet jockeys would come in. It's probably the same thing over there now. I'll bet nothing has changed."

"Yeah, you're probably right, but with no war on, I'm sure there are not that many people in and out as there were then."

"I know you're probably busy this being your last weekend, but I'd love for you to meet my husband, Dan. Can you come for dinner?"

"I'm sorry, I'd love to but I can't, but thank you. I've gotten involved in Marriage Encounter and this will be my last one up here. By the way, I strongly advise you and your husband to participate in one while you're here. It's a great experience and so enriching for your marriage."

"I'm glad I got to see you, even though it was brief, Tom. I feel that we who served together over there in the sixties are forever bonded by some invisible ties of friendship and love even though we all haven't been the greatest at keeping up."

"No doubt about it, Paula. I can close my eyes and still see every person in the group, what they wore, who they dated, who they cried over. It was a special time under special circumstances."

They hugged each other again both with tears in their eyes and Paula was back off to her office.

Tom put his head in his hands. He prayed for Carrie. He felt terrible. His mind flooded with memories of her, activities with the group, listening to her tears and her guilt after Pete left and their final trip to the orphanage. He looked at the clock. It was time to head to the chapel for noon time Mass. "Thank God I have a place to go and something to do. I can't just sit here", he thought.

Coronado, California
July, 1985

As bad as John thought life without Carrie would be during the last year, when she was ill, it was a hundred times worse. He had survived May and June by throwing himself into Susan's high school graduation. Cathy and Dave were so generous about taking care of Sissy and it afforded her a place to go where she felt so at home before Carrie's death so there was no transition requiring a new adjustment for her now. He returned to work on May first and was home every night. He knew the girls had suffered a devastating loss and he never, for one minute, wanted them to have to question whether or not he was going to be around.

"I'd like to go back to my job at the Exchange," Susan said to John one night at dinner.

"Sissy will be cared for and Doug is spending the summer with the Marine Corps at Quantico, Virginia. He won't be coming out 'til the end of August."

"I think that sounds like a good idea." replied John.

At the end of June, the Carsons moved to Japan and before she left, Betty had a discussion with John regarding Susan's coming over to visit in the fall. Susan had already told her dad that she did not want to start college in the fall but to wait until January. She just felt that she had been through too much and that she really wanted to be close to her family the next six months. She had been accepted at Stanford, John's Alma Mater, and there was no problem with the college delaying matriculation until January of the following year. John had no problem with her request, in fact, he thought it would be good for all of them.

When Betty asked Susan how she felt about a visit with them in Japan in the fall, she was ecstatic. Debbie was also going to delay college entrance a semester so she could experience their first six months over there.

"Oh thank you, Aunt Betty, that'll really give me something to look forward to. Mom had such a great time there. I've always wanted to visit and see the places she talked about."

Widowhood brought John face to face with myriads of paperwork, unpleasant decisions of what to do with Carrie's clothes, jewelry and books, but the thing that threw him for a loop was the behavior of other women. He was literally hounded and pursued by young woman especially divorced single parents. He could not believe the aggressiveness and the lack of decency and sensitivity to his loss that these women displayed in their quest to capture him.

The first incident occurred when one of the employees, an executive secretary asked him to her home for dinner. He was flattered and happy for a get together when something she said made him realize that the girls were not included. Although not happy about it, he went. They had cocktails and dinner and gradually through the conversation of the evening, he could tell that, in her mind, she had planned a whole summer of activities for them together. Suddenly, he felt smothered and wanted to scream out for Carrie.

During the summer, this experience was repeated by other women. Whether it was for a drink, a picnic or tennis match, the story was always the same. It was set up to appear casual but as the date wore on, the women almost took on an air of desperation. Finally, he stopped accepting all invitations unless it was a company party that included the girls. He was, in no way, ready to be with another woman on a dating basis and at this point wasn't sure he would ever be. Theirs had been as close to a perfect marriage as he could ever have dreamed and he planned to live wrapped in the warmth of both those dreams and his daughters for a long time.

He was thrilled for Susan and her chance to visit Japan, especially in the company of the Carsons.

But, he was beginning to see signs of stress in Sissy. Ten years old was awfully young to lose a mother. It wasn't that she didn't get enough attention but he wasn't sure it was the right kind. He thought about it a long time and one day he made a decision. That night when he arrived home, he presented Sissy with an eight week old cocker spaniel. He checked with

Cathy to be sure she wouldn't mind the dog as well as Sissy for awhile.

He knew he'd made the right decision when he saw the look on Sissy's face. She was delighted and immediately referred to the puppy several times as "my" dog. That's what she needed thought John, something that is totally hers.

Sissy named her puppy "Sunshine", and that evening, John saw joy return to his sad little daughter's face.

2

Japan Air Lines
Flight 061

Susan was lucky. She had a window seat and the middle seat was unoccupied. She lifted the armrest, thus allowing her a wide, comfortable space in which to spread out for the long flight.

She watched as the beautiful Japanese flight attendant came down the aisle of the huge 747 towards her. Clad in a white silk brocade kimono with a pale blue sash, the obi, she was the epitome of graciousness and femininity.

"Would you like a cup of tea?"

"Yes, thank you. That would be nice."

The lovely lady bowed and Susan felt honored. It was John's travel agent that had suggested to him and Susan that she travel on Japan Air Lines. She always recommended to her clients when they were visiting a foreign country that they travel on that country's airline. She said it subtly helped them to prepare for some of the country's culture before arrival. Susan now saw what she meant.

The flight was nearly eleven hours long. To break it up, there were two meals served and two movies. Now, after eating her lunch, Susan felt sleepy. Looking at her watch, she noted that they were exactly halfway there.

When she awakened, she was amazed to find that she had slept two and a half hours. The remaining time passed quickly and she loved it when the flight attendants passed out hot oshiburi, the steaming small white cloths to wash her hands and face with before landing.

Because the new Narita Airport was four hours from Yokosuka by car, they all agreed that she would take the express bus from the airport to YCAT, the Yokohama Central Air Terminal and the Carsons would pick her up there.

She could not believe the efficiency of the Japanese airport. When she arrived at the luggage carousel, her luggage was already there with plenty of free luggage carts. She was through customs and exchanged some dollars for yen in ten minutes. She then wheeled her bags to the front door only to find the first bus in line said YCAT.

"There she is, there she is," she heard but could not see Debbie in the crowd until she felt arms clasp around her in a hug that felt great.

"How was your flight?" asked Aunt Betty.

"Oh, it was fine. I really enjoyed it. The scenery was beautiful as we flew over just before we landed."

"This is why we wanted you to come in the fall. Japan is brilliant with color like back home in New England."

"Well, it worked out to be a good time in many ways. Sissy is back in school, dad's doing great and I needed to get away for a little while. The only state occasion I'll miss is my eighteenth birthday." she said giggling.

"Don't worry honey, we'll do it up big for you here, your first Japanese birthday."

After she recovered from jet lag, Susan and Debbie spent everyday sightseeing and Susan fell in love with Japan and the Japanese. They went to Tokyo to shop, to Kamakura to see the Great Buddha, and to Mount Fuji for a view of scenery that was breathtaking. The snow capped Fuji overlooking the red and gold leaves of fall, reflecting from the lake, made every view it's own postcard. Susan's favorite activity was just milling around the large department stores. They were packed with gadgets and trinkets and the salespeople were so friendly and helpful. On Friday night, they went to the Officers' Club. There was one aircraft carrier in port so the place was hopping with pilots celebrating one of their shore leaves before heading out for the Indian Ocean for six months to keep an eye on Iran.

"They're making these Navy nurses younger and better looking everyday," said a voice approaching their table in the cocktail lounge. Susan and Debbie decided to play along and loved every minute of it. It was this part of Japan that Susan felt her mother must have also loved. They had so much fun that night, genuine true fun but nothing to sway her love away from Doug Hauser.

Betty Carson dialed the phone at the same time she was writing down a menu that she and Nobuko, their Japanese maid, could prepare for the party.

When the phone was answered on the other end, she greeted the listener with, "Hello, Father, this is Betty Carson, Fred's wife."

"How are you Betty? What can I do for you?"

"You can come to dinner. I've sincerely meant to have you over sooner than this but now I have a good excuse. We have a young friend visiting from San Diego and Thursday is her birthday so we are having a few friends in for dinner."

"I'd love to come, Betty. Thanks. Can I bring anything?"

"As a matter of fact, I usually say 'No', but I would like you to bring a birthday present so we can do it up big. Nothing expensive but just something that will be fun to open up and serve as a memory of her visit here. She's eighteen."

"I'll be glad to. See you Thursday evening."

Father Paige put the phone down and was happy about the call. Time had started to hang heavy on his hands and he was grateful for evening invitations to dinner in the homes of the families. He started thinking about a gift and even looked forward to his search for the perfect one.

Thursday night, October eighth, arrived accompanied by wind and pelting rain. As far as Susan was concerned, that only created atmosphere. Seated around Betty's dinner table, the group was full of merriment and she loved the sound of the rain beating on the roof and slamming against the windows. The mixture of the sounds of nature added to the warmth she felt in her heart. There were the three Carsons, herself, Father Paige, Dr. Taft and his wife and Donna Bently, one of the nurses.

"Father Paige was stationed here during the Vietnam War." said Betty.

"I bet you find a lot of differences, Father," chimed in Donna.

"I certainly do. First of all, there is no war being fought now and there's a lot less people stationed both here and coming in and out all the time. Secondly, nurses are now allowed to live off base so after work they head home. In those days, they would resurface after an hour or two rest, in one of the clubs and you could always find somebody to eat with or just kill a few hours with in the club. Thirdly, none of the nurses was married then but since the influx of male nurses and dual careers, one third of the nursing staff is married."

Pausing to take a sip of his wine, he continued.

"We went through a tough anti-military time in our country that has just recently been resolved to some extent so the people here are somewhat different than then. They are no longer naive and blindly obedient. They question everything and I hate to say this but they seem to be more for themselves instead of for each other."

Doctor Taft nodded his head in agreement.

"I've been in the Navy twenty two years and I couldn't agree more. It's not that the Navy has changed all by itself, society has changed and the Navy along with it. I remember when a nurse would do anything to help out a busy ward or clinic but now, I'm almost afraid to ask for extra help because I know I am going to have to justify my request."

When Father Paige finished talking, Susan looked at him.

"Did you know my mother?" She assumed that Aunt Betty had told him about her.

"What did you say your last name was?"

"Ellington, it's Ellington, but that was not her name. Her name was Craig. Caroline Craig."

Father Paige felt the color drain from his face.

"Yes, I knew Carrie quite well. She was one of the old fashioned nurses Dr. Taft was just describing."

Tom took a gulp of his wine and said, "I'm not only shocked at the amazing coincidence of meeting you, Carrie's daughter, here, but somehow I had it all wrong. I knew your mother died and I'm very sorry and extend my sympathy. I found out about her death when her old friend, Paula Ferrara Brandon arrived in Bremerton. She told me Carrie had two daughters but somehow I assumed they were little girls like ten or eleven."

"I do have a ten year old sister and yeah, Paula and her husband, Dan, stopped by for two days this summer on their way to Bremerton."

Suddenly the lights dimmed and Betty, signing and leading the group in "Happy Birthday to You", entered from the kitchen with a huge cake ringed with lighted candles. The festive air reappeared and they all had lots of fun watching and sharing with Susan as she opened up her crazy gifts. There was a yukata from Debbie, a placemat, napkin, chopsticks and one place setting of every conceivable dish from Father Paige. The Tafts gave her two MaMa-San aprons, Donna, a Japanese doll and Betty and Fred, a watchman TV. Susan was delighted. The evening was perfect for her. She would never forget her eighteenth birthday. It had been a perfect evening.

As the group started to leave, bustling into raincoats, and searching for umbrellas, Susan quietly approached Father Paige.

"Father, may I meet with you tomorrow. I'd like to talk with you about my mother."

"Sure, so would I. Why don't you come to twelve o'clock Mass and I'll take you to lunch out at the Marina in Hayama. Then we can walk along the beach and talk."

"Great, I'll see you at Mass, and thank you for the dishes. That was a neat idea."

Tom did not sleep well that night. The excitement of the party plus meeting Susan was just too much. He tossed and turned and when he awakened in the morning, he remembered having seen the clock glow three-thirty.

Before he started Mass, Tom came down the aisle in the small chapel and told Susan that he would offer the Mass for her mother.

"Thank you, Father. She'd love that. She was so religious."

He winked and returned to the altar, and making the Sign of the Cross began the ancient rite passed down over the years from Christ at the Last Supper.

During the thirty minute drive to Hayama, the conversation stayed with generalities. When they were finally seated and had both ordered tempura, Tom asked what was on her mind, adding that he was willing to answer any questions she had but that she understood, of course that he could not tell her anything he'd heard in confession or that he'd been told in confidence, even if it was eighteen years ago.

"I know that and I would never expect you to compromise you honor."

The tempura was delicious and Susan commented on how the States tried to copy foods from other countries, but that you just couldn't beat the real thing.

Searching for words, she looked up at Father Paige.

"Father, what I really wanted to know and I hope you have some information that will help, is who is my father?

"When I realized that my mother was dying, I asked her, begged her to tell me. She told me over the years that he was killed in the war and that she had never told anyone who he was because too many people would be hurt. She would then quickly switch the conversation to my dad, John, and emphasize how much he loved me. He legally adopted me and I'm crazy about him. She told me he didn't even know my father's real name, that he said it was her business and all he wanted was to be married to her and be a dad to me."

"Sounds like a fine person."

"The best," replied Susan.

"I knew that with her death, I'd lose all hope of finding out. She was hesitant and promised to think it over and pray about it and probably tell me the next day. During the night, she went into a coma and died at noon the next day."

"How frustrating. I think I can help you a little. During her second year here, Carrie met and fell in love with a patient, a Marine Captain. His first name was Pete and I'll try to recall his last name. It was an ethnic name, Polish I think. You mentioned at Mass how religious she was. Well, she was religious back then, too, and carried tremendous guilt over falling in love and seeing Pete. You see, he was married. He was here about eight weeks and a few days after he returned to Vietnam, I called to check up on how she was doing. I even went over to visit her on a Saturday afternoon. It was one of the saddest pastoral calls I've ever made in my priesthood. Not only was she sorrow filled about his departure but she was guilt ridden about his marriage. She also knew they had no future together."

"Gosh, it gives me chills just listening to it. Pete, hugh? Somehow, it helps just knowing his name."

"I'm not through," continued Father Paige. "In January, I had to go to Sasebo, that's in Southern Japan, to fill in for a priest there for two weeks, and then I left immediately to meet my family in Hawaii for a two week vacation. While I was gone, Pete was killed in Vietnam and Carrie had received an emergency transfer to San Diego because her father had suffered a heart attack. I wrote her at the San Diego Naval Hospital but the letter came back stamped, "Not stationed here". I know I should have pursued it more but I let it go. I was transferred to the Naval Academy at Annapolis and did not hear anything else about her until Paula walked into my office this past summer. If I can scout up Pete's last name you can write to the Headquarters Marine Corps and we can use my Marine connections to find out more information. But I must warn you. Somewhere out there is a wife and children who know nothing about this so we want to be discrete."

"Oh, I would never want anyone hurt by this but I'm so excited because I really thought all doors to any further information were sealed shut."

Susan proceeded to tell Tom about her boyfriend, Doug, her dad, John and her sister, Sissy. Tom shared with her the fact that he was going to retire in two years in San Diego and they talked about different areas of town where he might consider buying a home. By the end of lunch, each felt they had found and made a new friend. Susan was leaving in two days, on Sunday, and they promised to continue their new friendship and search, through the mail. When they reached the Carsons' home they hugged each other with genuine warmth and new found love. Each had found a key that opened up a treasure from the past.

3

Coronado, California
October, 1985

The night after Susan returned from Japan, she invited Aunt Cathy, Uncle Dave, Sharon and Robin to dinner. She had brought back gifts for them and wanted to present them all together.

"Do I have to wait 'til tomorrow for my present?" asked Sissy.

"No, of course not," and gave her little sister a Japanese doll and a porcelain figurine that looked just like Sunshine. Sissy was so excited.

"Thank you Susan, these are neat!"

During the long plane ride home, Susan gave a lot of thought to whether or not to tell John about meeting Father Paige and their conversation. She finally decided to tell him about meeting him, that he had been there with her mother but to keep the topic of their conversation a secret.

On Tuesday night, the Peterson clan arrived. The kids were so excited, there was no way they could wait until after dinner to open their gifts so they all sat on the floor in a circle and Susan passed them out.

"The first gift goes to the man who made the whole trip possible with his wallet. Here Daddy, thank you again."

John was genuinely pleased with his gift, an excellent pair of binoculars.

"I can stand at my office window now and spy on all the sidewalk traffic," he joked.

For everyone else she bought yukatas.

"Let's put them on for dinner and make it a real Japanese scene."

Out of the corner of her eye, she could see that Sissy felt a little left out, not receiving a gift in the middle of everyone's joy. Getting her gifts last night paled in the party atmosphere of tonight. Susan reached behind her.

"Here, Sissy, someone must of snuck this into my suitcase."

A smile glistened across Sissy's face. She tore the wrapping from her gift and, sure enough, there was a yukata for her. When the three little girls put theirs on, they were just adorable taking little straight steps like the Japanese and bowing every ten seconds.

They gathered at the dinner table for a feast of tacos, and Aunt Cathy burst out laughing.

"I can't help it, Susan, All this Japanese atmosphere and we sit down to Mexican tacos."

Susan began to laugh too.

"I wouldn't begin to try and make some of those Japanese concoctions and I knew we all loved tacos, so let's just call it International Night at the Ellingtons'"

In spite of the fun last night, when she woke up the next morning, Susan stayed in bed.

I can hear Dad and Sissy out there, she thought, but I feel sad and confused and I don't want to get up until they leave. I sure would love to talk with my mom today. That's the trouble. No one ever talks about her. She always had a way of making things better for me just by listening. If only I had someone to listen to me like she did.

She pulled the covers tighter around her. I think I'll call Aunt Cathy and go over and talk with her. In lots of ways, she is like Mom.

She threw on a robe and dialed the phone.

"Aunt Cathy, this is Susan."

"Susan, thank you for the great party last night. It was so much fun and we all loved our presents."

"You're welcome. Can I come over this morning. I really need someone to talk to."

"Any big problem?"

"No, I don't think so, but I need to get some things out in the open and maybe get some advice."

"Sure," she said breathing a sigh of relief, "come anytime."

"Thanks, I'll be there in half an hour."

Watching Susan leave the car and walk up to the front door, Cathy looked at her slim, tall niece. Wearing the uniform of the new age, she had on a stone washed jeans jacket and mini skirt. Seeing Susan's once long, lovely strawberry blonde hair, now curled into millions of corkscrews, the result of a curly perm, she winced as she struggled to accept the hair which seemed to be heading in five different directions from atop her head. At the bottom of her legs were ankle socks and two inch high heel shoes. She is eighteen years old, thought Cathy. This little baby whose arrival brought out the best and worse in all of us. Where has the time gone? Carrie would be so proud of her now, just as she was at every other phase of her growth. It saddened Cathy to see the happy light hearted girl, now, apparently immersed in sorrow and confusion.

Susan came in and got settled in the living room, while Cathy served her a cup of tea.

"I'm so glad you came over. With the kids here all the time, we never get a chance to talk between ourselves. Now, what's on your mind, pretty niece?"

"I'm so confused these days and I really miss mom and talking with her, in fact, one thing that bothers me is that no one talks about her or ever mentions her name. Dad is great but he's not the same as Mom. My life seems to have become so serious all of sudden. I guess after she died, I was busy pitching in to help the family adjust to our new life, especially helping making it easier for Sissy. Now, I miss her something terrible.

Cathy looked down at her teacup.

"Susan, I miss her terribly too, and I know we don't ever mention her name probably because it hurts too much. That would really hurt her if she knew it, but oh, she would be so proud of you. You are so much like her. I see so many things in your character and personality.

"Like most teens' mothers, she'd probably fuss about the way you wear your hair and way you dress but she'd understand that it was really important to you. I think you look great. You are really a mixture of our generation and your own. I think that's because you were raised in such a traditional, loving home but you fit right in with your friends, too."

"Something is bothering me but I can't put my finger on it. I feel confused, sad, even angry at times."

"Honey, maybe you are having a delayed reaction to Carrie's death. Some people cry and mourn right away but maybe, you didn't do that and a lot of feelings are floating to the top now."

"It might be, I miss her, that's for sure. But, so much happened to me. I was a happy high school teenager, then I got a boyfriend, Doug. Then, Mom died and on top of everything, overnight I became a new mom to Sissy. Next, there was the trip to Japan and now, I'm getting ready for college." She chose not to mention her visit with Father Paige and even wondered if her quest to find her father was one more thing confusing her.

"Anyway, thanks for listening. It helps just to know that I have someone to talk with about all of this."

"I've always been here, Susan but I must admit, I should have been more open about letting you know I was ready to listen. I'll try to pitch in more with Sissy and give you a break. You're too young to be thrown into the mother role."

On the way back, Susan drove to Coronado beach and parked the car facing the ocean. "I don't really feel better", she thought. "I guess I expect too much, like an instant magic solution. It's so hard to be patient. I can't fix it until I know the problem. We were such a loving family and it seemed okay for the first few months Mom was dead but now it's different and I don't really know why. I wish Doug were here. I can always talk to him".

At three o'clock the following morning, she sat up in bed with a jolt. That's it. I found it. It's Stanford. I don't want to go there. I don't want to go that far away. She felt an enormous weight lift from her mind and heart. That's it. But, the weight was immediately replaced by another. Dad. He was so proud that I was accepted to his Alma Mater. He'll be so disappointed. But, I know it's the right thing for me to do. I wonder why it took me so long to zero in on the problem.

I'll go to USD, the University of San Diego, and live in the dorm. That way I can have a full college life and come home for visits on weekends or even during the week. With her problem identified and brought to the surface, she lay back in bed and fell asleep.

After Sissy was in bed on Thursday, Susan fixed some tea for her dad and herself.

"Dad, I've changed my mind about college."

There was a look of alarm on John's face.

"Oh, don't worry, I'm still going to go but I don't think I want to go all the way to Stanford. I just don't want to be that far away from you and Sissy. We have only each other now and I think it would be particularly hard on her. She's lost Mom and then to lose me is a lot for an eleven year old."

"But, honey if you're home here every night, there's no way you can experience a full college life."

"I won't be here every night. What I'd really like to do is to go to the University of San Diego and live in the dorm. That way I can come home on weekends even if it's just for an afternoon or you could drop Sissy off once in awhile to spend some time with me. That way I would have everything. I would be on campus for all meetings, clubs and sports events but I'd be close enough to remain a part of the family's daily life."

John shut his eyes in thought and Susan held her breath.

"You never cease to amaze me. I think you have come up with a marvelous plan and if you're happy with it, I fully support you. I have to admit that part of it is selfish. I'll just love having you close by rather than in Palo Alto. Five hundred miles isn't exactly around the corner."

"Gee Dad, thanks for understanding. I'm sure this will be much better."

The Sunday before second semester started, the three of them packed John's car and over the bridge they went to USD. The University was easily spotted by the huge blue dome atop the church on campus, overlooking Mission Valley.

Susan was a little anxious as to who her roommate would be, but was quickly relieved to meet Nancy Downey, a transfer from the University of

Arizona in Tucson. She reminded Susan of Debbie and right away they started to become friends.

Sissy enjoyed her informal tour of the dorm and seemed to take the parting okay. Susan felt her eyes fill with tears as she watched Sissy and her dad, holding hands, leave the dorm for their car. She didn't in any way want Sissy to think of this as any kind of a goodbye. As she stood watching them leave, John turned around, threw her a kiss and winked.

Susan loved college and quickly became involved in many social activities. One weekend, when she came home, she asked John about something that was bothering her.

"Dad, I'm really in a dilemma. I love Doug very much and I know you think I'm kind of young, but I really think we are going to get married."

"So, what's the problem?"

"It's about school. I love school and I've made so many great friends. A lot of the guys have asked me for dates, to the movies or the games and just small campus parties. So far, I've said 'No', but I'd really like to go to some of them with a date. But, somehow I feel I'd be cheating on Doug or worse, what if I messed up things with him by going out with someone else? Do you think I should do it and do you think I should tell Doug?"

"Let's see how old Dad should answer this one," said John, rising to refill his sherry glass.

"More wine?"

"Just a little, thanks."

"Let's take this one step at a time. Should you do it? I know that young love is just about the most intense feeling in the world. Trust me, I went through it many times and it's good because it helps you get to know yourself and a variety of young men. You say you love Doug and I don't doubt that for a minute.

Both your mother and I were very fond of him. But, you are not married to him or even engaged for that matter. Sure, you want to be and in your heart you've perhaps even made that leap in time, but that's just an effort on your part to keep those great feelings going.

"To deny yourself dating at this stage of life would be foolish. If you're that sure of your feelings for Doug, you don't have a thing to worry about. You'll enjoy your dates at school and nothing will change with Doug.

"Now, for the second question, that's a little stickier. Doug is holed up there, back in Bancroft Hall with thousands of other lonely midshipmen, thinking of you as more beautiful, sexier, and every other quality than you really are. If you tell him, his imagination is going to go wild. But, if you don't tell him, you have to get over the fact that you're cheating. You are not cheating. You are doing what is your right, enjoying all aspects of school. So, I guess my advice would be to go out with anyone you wish but don't tell Doug."

Susan hesitated, trying to absorb all that John had said.

"Gosh, Dad, you break it down so analytically but what you say makes sense. Right now, I don't know what I'll do but it's great having your blessing, so to speak. Thanks."

"Susan, honey, as long as you are honest with yourself about your feelings, you'll be fine. Remember, you're not going to feel about these guys the way you feel about Doug."

"You're right. I was so upset because I imagined getting caught in a situation where I had to decide among four or five guys that I had the same strong feelings for."

"You should be so lucky."

John looked at his daughter across the room. She's so much like her mother, although I'm sure Carrie would have a hard time swallowing that hairdo, but both of us always dressed in the "costume" of our day. Her thoughtfulness, her sensitivity, right out of Carrie's mold. How I miss her especially tonight. Watching Susan is a living memorial of Carrie.

Susan did well in school making the Dean's List the first semester. She accepted several dates, had a wonderful time but never for a moment did any of them pose a threat to her feelings for Doug.

She took two courses in summer school and planned to do so each summer so she would eventually make up that first semester and graduate with her class.

At Christmas time, Doug was on leave from the Naval Academy. He went to his home in Chicago to be with his family and the day after Christmas flew to San Diego. He couldn't wait to see Susan and to bask in the California sunshine after the chill of Annapolis and Chicago. He was short of money, so John, knowing how much it meant to Susan, paid for part of the ticket.

Their visit was dreamy. Susan took him up to school and proudly showed him around. Being on the campus, in the atmosphere where she had lived and dated the past year, did nothing to shake her love for Doug.

"I'm glad you didn't go to Stanford. You've got the best of both worlds right here."

On the last day of the year, while walking in Balboa Park, they sat down to rest on a park bench. The Christmas decorations were still up and people were strolling slowly enjoying the holiday atmosphere.

"I've made a big decision. I'm not going to stay with the Navy. Instead, I'm going into the Marine

Corps. I've given it a lot of thought and I really liked the whole organization the summer I was with them."

"How will it be different after graduation?" asked Susan, squeezing up against him as the late afternoon coolness started to engulf them. She smiled to herself remembering that Father Paige said her father was a Marine.

"After graduation, I'll have a few weeks leave and then I'll report to Quantico, Virginia for training as a Platoon Leader. There'll be a leave period again, depending on how many days I have on the books and then I think the chances are quite good, that I'll be assigned to one of the large Marine Divisions. That means Camp Lajuene, Camp Pendleton out here or even Okinawa. Everyone goes someplace. The guys who choose aviation go to Pensacola, Florida, the sub guys to Groton, Connecticut the various surface warfare specialties to Newport, Rhode Island for Destroyer School. Some even come way out here for Amphibious Warfare School."

"Gee. After living close as clams for four years at school, you'll be scattered across the country like birdseed. I'm glad you're enthusiastic about it. I think people usually do well in fields that they are excited about."

"I'm sure excited about this so if you're right, I'll do great."

Doug sat straight up toward the edge of the bench and took Susan's two hands in his. Looking directly in her eyes, he squeezed her hands tighter, holding them close to his chest.

"Let's get engaged."

He really took Susan by surprise. I can't believe it, she thought, not now.

"You really have surprised me. I'd love to become engaged to you but I never thought it would be this early. I'm only in my second semester at school and I'm young but, you know, we have been going together for two and a half years. I don't know about you but I'm finding it harder and harder to be apart."

"Harder doesn't even come close for me. I just can't stand it anymore. I think about you all the time and paint pictures in my mind of how it will be when we are married. In my rush to pop the question, I guess I didn't think much about your school and I'm sorry. Of course, you'll finish school. You can come with me when we get married and enroll in college regardless of where we are."

The two sweethearts wrapped themselves in each other's arms and Doug kissed Susan as though they were on a deserted island rather than amid hundreds of holiday strollers.

"I love you Susan and I want to spend the rest of my life with you as your husband."

"I love you, Doug and I think I have since the day I meet you in the exchange that first summer."

They grinned and hugged each other tightly.

Walking back to the car, Susan asked, "How soon do you think we should get married?"

"I have a gigantic piece of business to take care of first and that is to ask your father for his permission and his blessing. If he gives it, I'd like to get married after my training at Quantico, which will be in the fall. That way, you could take two more courses this summer and that would give you two semesters and two summers completed. That's just shy of two years and you might be able to transfer as a junior.

That evening after dinner with John and Sissy, Doug asked John if they could have a private talk. Susan took Sissy out for an ice cream.

"Mr. Ellington, this may come as a shock to you but Susan I would like to become engaged."

"You're right it is a shock for a guy who didn't get married until his thirties."

"I know but we've been dating over three years and it's getting harder and harder to be apart."

"Tell me more. If I give my permission, when do you plan to be married and what about Susan's finishing college?"

"We haven't talked about a date because we wanted your blessing first. I will graduate in June and because I have chosen the Marine Corps, I'll be sent to Quantico for Platoon Leader training. After that I'll be sent to one of the big Marine Divisions to put into practice what I've learned at Quantico. Susan says she will finish her education by transferring to a college near the base."

"I'm very fond of you Doug. You're a bright and honorable young man and I know you'll take good care of my daughter. You are young but you're right, it is hard to be apart when you're in love. As long as you understand that I do have some reluctance, that I'm putting my faith in you and Susan, you have my blessing to make your plans as you wish."

Pausing, he looked at Doug and with a quick wink, he said, "Just send me the bill."

"Thank you Mr. Ellington. I promise I won't let you down."

"How come Doug didn't come with us?" asked Sissy, as they enjoyed their ice cream at a little table and chair at Baskin Robins.

"He wanted to talk with Daddy, to ask him something."

"Do you know what about?"

"Ahuh. He wants to marry me and he's asking daddy if it's okay."

"Susan, that's neat," but suddenly, a look of fear came over Sissy's face.

"Does this mean that you'll move away?"

"I think so."

Susan looked at her little sister, her charge that she had grown to love even more since her mother's death and picked her words carefully.

"I'll really miss you, but I'll come to visit and you can come visit us. If daddy says it's okay, that Doug and I can get married, I want you to be my maid of honor, and Sharon and Robin to be bridesmaids."

Knowing she would play a starring role in the wedding helped ease Sissy's feelings.

"By the time of the wedding, you'll be twelve and a half already to jump into your teens and junior high school. Don't worry beautiful, everything will be fine."

They returned from their ice cream safari. As they entered the house, John said, "Congratulations, daughter. You've caught yourself a good man."

Rushing across the room, she threw her arms around her father.

"Oh Daddy, thank you! We'll make you proud of us. I promise."

"You already have."

The next day, Susan and Doug could talk about nothing else but the wedding.

"I've always thought those Naval Academy weddings with the swords were so beautiful and romantic. Can we get married there?"

"Sure, if you really have your heart set on it, but after seeing several, I'd rather not. You only have about twenty minutes a wedding and it always feels like a formula for military action to me with all the rules. I'd rather get married here at St. Mark's or at my home in St. Lucy's."

"Well, if you've seen them and don't like them, then I guess you know best."

"You can still have a military wedding, dress white uniforms, crossed swords, the whole works, anything you want."

"I'm so excited just thinking about it."

"So am I, but we have plenty of time to plan so that everything will be just as you always wanted it."

4

September 5, 1987
Coronado, California

The guests seated in the church for the wedding all turned to sneak a peak when they heard the commotion at the back of the church. Susan looked each girl over and was pleased with how darling they all looked. Like her mom, she selected pale blue as the accent color for her wedding. The three girls had matching dresses with lots of satin and ribbon trim. A ring of white flowers on their heads held fragile eight inch lite blue ribbons flowing gently over their faces and the back of their heads.

John looked at his daughter, offered his arm, kissed her and said, "Let's go make you a wife."

As she walked up the long aisle to the traditional wedding march, she was radiant. Up ahead, she could see Doug waiting for her with his brother as his best man. How she loved him.

Her love of the three little girls, now all grown up at eleven, twelve and twelve and a half glowed in her eyes as they proceeded her up the aisle. At the altar, she kissed John and her only tears were shed as she thought of her mother. How she wished she was sitting in the front row with her dad.

The words of the ceremony were tender and beautiful to her and she was happy she had chosen a traditional wedding. Coming back down the aisle at the recessional, she was filled with joy. As the reached the front door of the church, the newly wed couple passed under the crossed swords of Naval and Marine Corps Officers in their dress white uniforms.

In the same elegant fashion, that they had hosted Carrie and John's wedding reception in 1974, the Ellingtons' again hosted Susan's reception. There was a hugh candy stripped tent in the back yard, a combo, even a small dance floor. Their wedding gift to them was their honeymoon, a trip to Hawaii.

Like many honeymoon couples, they experienced Hawaii for the first time and fell in love with the islands. This is the most perfect place in the world thought Susan, and for her and Doug, it was. Their honeymoon love cast a rose colored glow over all the island.

After a week of sun, surf and sightseeing, they returned to San Diego to bid their farewells and then cramming Doug's car with all of Susan's earthly goods, they started out on their long cross country trip to Camp Lejeune in Jacksonville, North Carolina.

Washington, DC
August, 1988

Flying up to Washington from Camp Lejuene, Susan looked out the airplane window and into her heart. They were just about to celebrate their first wedding anniversary.

She loved married life, and all their dreams, so far, had come true. "Doug was happy with his duty with the Marines and I love my courses at school", she thought. By the end of this semester, I'll have already made up all the credits for the semester I entered late.

She shifted her weight to try and get more comfortable. The big surprise in their lives had been her pregnancy. Laughing, she thought of the past February when she couldn't understand why she missed her period. They learned that the most obvious reason is one no one thinks of. Well, she thought, we got used to it and now we are really excited about it. I'm so glad we are taking this trip. It'll be the last one we will be able to take worry free. I've never seen Washington, DC, and I can't wait to go home to California and see everyone, to actually get to hold them all in my arms. I'll even get a chance to see Father Paige. She had recently received a letter from him telling her about his retirement from the Navy and about buying a home in Pacific Beach.

She loved Washington with all the monuments, statues, and white buildings. They stayed in Georgetown and in the evening when it cooled off a little, they walked the historic streets there, drinking in the history. They toured Georgetown University and late at night stopped in a coffee house where Roberta Flack had started her career.

In the daytime, the heat was so oppressive, that walking was unbearable especially in her advanced stage of pregnancy. They took a city tour on a bus with comfortable seats that was air conditioned. They were able to clear the tour lines at the various stops quickly through some prearranged system with the tour company.

"One place I am getting out, in fact, we might as well leave the tour there because it is the next to the last stop, is the Vietnam Memorial. I'd like to spend some time there. We can take our own taxi back to Georgetown."

This pregnancy has brought up all the feelings of curiosity about my father, she thought. My genes and heritage are passing to a new generation. Somehow, I think if I go and walk the length of the wall, I'll receive some sign when I come to his name.

"I'm so disappointed and feel even a little foolish. Did I think his name was going to light up in neon lights?" said Susan, holding her husband's arm.

"I'm sorry. I know how disappointed you are."

Suddenly, she was struck by a thought that so far, had never occurred to her. Maybe his name wasn't even on the wall. Maybe he wasn't even dead but still alive, the victim of a communication mishap in the middle of a chaotic time of war. She could not rid her mind of this new thought.

Because of the heat and having seen all they wanted to see, the next day they cut their visit short and flew out of Dulles Airport for San Diego. As the plane lifted off, Doug held her hand.

"We're going back home, honey, we're going back home."

5

Coronado, California
August, 1988

As the plane made it's descent into San Diego, Susan was filled with awe as they passed over the Naval vessels in the bay, the Coronado bridge, downtown and onto the runway. As soon as she and Doug entered the passenger waiting area, they were engulfed by all the relatives. At the front of the group were Sharon and Robin who trapped Sissy in their arms surrounded by a bouquet of balloons. Susan's tears began to flow as she hugged Cathy, Dave, John and the senior Ellingtons. I hope my baby can feel all this love, she smiled to herself.

"How wonderful to have you here!" said John shaking Doug's hand, "you and your beautiful wife."

"Not too beautiful now, Dad," Susan said pointing to her immense abdomen.

"You're wrong. You're more beautiful than ever," replied John.

Driving out of the parking lot, John said, "We are just going to have a quiet dinner at home tonight. We know that a travel day is exhausting. Tomorrow, Burt and Kate are hosting a dinner party and inviting several of your friends."

"That sounds perfect, I could use a quiet night tonight."

Weaving their way onto the freeway that would take them across the bridge to Coronado, Susan did not want to miss either a tree or a new building. It's so good to be back here, she said to herself as she gave Sissy a squeeze. She hadn't seen her in a year, but the year from twelve to thirteen was one of many changes. She had braces on her teeth, her long blonde hair had a big hunk of it coming out of the top with a barrette holding it high and she tried so hard to add an air of sophistication to her mannerisms. The timed rolling of her eyes and the flicking of her hair with her hands did not miss Susan's notice.

Both dinners were perfect. The one that John hosted was for Cathy, Dave, their girls, and Sissy, Susan, Doug and himself.

"How's the life of a grunt officer?"

"I love it. I know exactly what's expected of me and I made it clear to my troops what I expect of them. We live near the base so I don't spend hours commuting. Susan and I are usually back together again at night by seven at the latest."

He looked over at Susan and saw that her eyelids were drooping.

"Excuse me please. I think I'll tuck my wife in. It's been a long day for her."

"For us all," said Dave. "Just the anticipation of everyone waiting for you was tiring, then the airport, then waiting for more conversation with you at dinner. We're so happy you're here."

The next evening at the Ellingtons was as elegant as any other party they hosted. There were twenty people for a beef barbecue, casual but casual in the Ellington way. The yard was strung with lights, there was music and the crowd was divided around the patio into little conversational pods. Susan was so grateful to Kate for bringing everyone together for them. Her pregnancy was slowing her down and this way, by seeing them all at the party, it cut down on the number of separate lunches and visits she would have to make.

On her fourth day in Coronado, she decided to try and find Father Paige and set up a visit. Since he had only arrived from Japan in late June, she knew he would not be listed in the telephone book so she dialed directory assistance and asked if they had a listing for Father Thomas Paige or Captain Thomas Paige. The operator gave her the number immediately.

The phone rang three times before she heard Tom's voice.

"Hi! guess who?"

"Susan! How are you? Where are you?"

"I'm here in San Diego. We left Washington a day early because of the dreadful heat. With my big bump in front, I was just too uncomfortable."

"Everything going all right?"

"Great, but I'm ready for it to be over. Pregnancy should be seven months. That's when I decided I'd had enough."

Tom laughed. I've heard that before he said to himself.

"What are you doing now that you're retired?"

"A little of this and a little of that. Two days a week, I work for the Bishop here in the marriage tribunal trying to help married couples find a way to annul their first marriage so they can be married to their present mates in the church. On Sundays, I say Mass in parishes that are short of priests. It's just enough to keep me busy and current on the latest in the church."

"When am I going to see you and finally meet that husband of yours?"

"I'd like to come alone, Tom. Maybe if we have time for a second visit, we'll include Doug? Are you free for lunch tomorrow?"

"Sure. Why don't you come here. I want you to see my condo and we can sit on the balcony. It's out here in Pacific Beach and has a great view of the ocean."

Susan took directions down and then she, Doug and Sissy headed for Balboa Park to find their bench and bask in the sun. They wanted to give Sissy lots of attention in addition to getting to know her better at thirteen and a half. It had been three and a half years since Carrie's death and Susan wanted to see how Sissy had coped over this time. The park provided a casual atmosphere in which to observe her and have a good talk without being obvious about it. Tonight they were taking her and a girlfriend to dinner and a movie.

As Susan drove along Mission Boulevard, she unknowingly passed the block where Mission Boulevard became Pacific Beach. On the left was a new shopping center and tiny homes had been razed for condos that were going up in their place. Most of these had access by narrow alleys. Susan finally found Seabreeze Way, a big name for a small street and when she located Tom's condo, found that rare of rares in the beach area, a parking spot.

As she stepped out of the car, she was cooled by the breeze from the ocean, a free refreshment on a hot day. She had to search for the number so she could be sure she was at the right door. Finding the building was always one challenge with condos. Finding the unit within the building was another.

Tom answered the bell right away and they hugged each other, so happy to meet again.

"Be careful of my bump," said Susan.

"Don't worry I have no desire to turn my new condo into a delivery room. Here let me show you my new pride and joy."

They toured through the house and Susan loved it, especially the decor, a combination of Japanese and beachcomber that Tom had created.

"You're so lucky to be near the beach."

"I know and I don't forget it for a minute. Let me get you settled on the balcony with some iced tea while I finish putting together our salad."

"What a beautiful spot," thought Susan,"but I don't think it would be a great place to raise a child, too confining. In the summer, there's all the tourists to contend with also, but it's great for Tom".

"Tom, this is lovely."

"Glad you like it. I'll join you and finish my beer then we'll have lunch. By the way, how was Washington?"

"Oh, I enjoyed it but it was beastly hot, in fact, we left early. We saw most of it by tour bus except the Vietnam Memorial. I'm such a jerk. I don't know why but I sort of had talked myself into this illusion that if I went there that my father's name would sort of jump out at me. Of course, nothing happened. I was ready to give up when another thought appeared to me. Maybe the reason his name was not on the wall was that he was never killed, that he survived and his death notice was just another snag in communications out of Vietnam. From what I have read now, that was a very busy time there and anything is possible."

Tom put his beer down. He looked at Susan and was saddened by her look of loss, and frustration. Closing his eyes, he realized that she was about to embark on a whole new search for a living father. He had to stop it.

"Susan, it's getting hot out here in the sun. Let's go on inside."

When they got to the living room, Tom positioned himself so he was across from Susan and could look into her face and eyes. Searching for the right words, he looked over at her.

"When I met you in Japan, three years ago at your birthday party, there was something about you that bothered me. Don't get me wrong, I thought you were great and so much like Carrie, your mother, but there was something I could not identify, that I could not put my finger on. After you left Japan, it took a little while but I put it all together. What I'm going to tell you Susan is not easy for me and it won't be easy for you but I think it is the right thing to do now.

"After Pete, the Marine, left in early November, your mom was devastated. One of the things I did to try and help was to invite her into our group that went down to Gotemba, a town about two hours south of the base, to an orphanage. We always had a wonderful time and the group was such fun and supportive friends. Carrie did come along even though at the time, she had not spirit for it. She was still depressed about Pete's going back to Vietnam.

"We all planned big projects for Christmas gifts and parties for the kids but neither she nor I could go because we both had duty Christmas eve and Christmas day. We planned to go on New Year's day though because we would both be off and we didn't want the holidays to pass without going down there.

"More iced tea?"

"Yes, please, it really hits the spot."

"We got down there about noon and had a marvelous day with the sisters and children. We saw what a great job the sailors from the ships had done in our absence in setting up two deluxe swing sets. Before we knew it, it was five o'clock so we left hastily because it was already dark and sprinkling, two terrifying conditions for driving in Japan!"

Susan laughed. "Yeah, I remember."

"By the time we got off the hill, and through Gotemba, the rain was pouring down and I, literally, could not see five feet in front of the car. I was terrified and so was your mom. Although we were self-conscious about it, we agreed to try and find an inn and stay overnight, planning to leave early in the morning. That did not prove an easy task so we turned around and retraced our way back to Gotemba, stopping at the first Japanese inn we saw. I was never so glad to get out of a car. Just going from the car to the inn, we both got soaked, all the time laughing and joking. I guess we both felt a little funny about it and that was our way of hiding those feelings."

Tom got up and got another beer.

"In typical Japanese fashion, the innkeeper was only concerned with comfort. I told him we would like two rooms and before he registered us, he insisted that Carrie go to her room, get out of her wet clothes, put on a yukata and head for the hot bath. When she was through, I did the same. Afterward, we felt a lot better, but looked like two drowned rats.

"The innkeeper came by and asked which room we would like to have dinner in, that the maid would be cooking on a hibachi in our room. It didn't matter to either of us so she set it up in my room, along with two tiny bottles of hot sake.

"The dinner was delicious and she brought two more bottles of sake. As we relaxed and were less selfconscious, your mother really poured her heart out to me and I, in turn told her some of my frustrations. It was a wonderful evening and as it continued the level of the conversation became more meaningful, maybe, even more intimate with each of us telling a little more and more.

"It's so hard to talk about this Susan."

"That's okay. I think I know what's coming next."

"You're probably right on.

"After denying it for two months, I finally admitted to myself that I was in love with your mother, that I had been struggling with it since spending time with her and Pete.

"Believe me, I'm not trying to make excuses or to blame anyone but myself, but the combination of the intimacy of the room and conversation, the sake, and pelting rain on the rice paper walls and bamboo roof was intoxicating. Suddenly we were in each other's arms and in an instant, wrapped around each other on the futon. I was blinded by my love with a passion that overcame any sense of judgement. I think your mother just craved to be close to someone. She was so badly damaged by Pete's leaving and returning to Vietnam.

"In the morning, I woke up first and felt terribly guilty. I had betrayed my vows and was no longer protected by the blind passion of the night before. When your mother awakened, she wouldn't even look at me. She felt so guilty, she was inconsolable. 'But a priest,' she kept saying over and over.

"How are you doing? I know this has to be difficult for you."

Tom needed a break but he needed more to finish his story.

"I'm fine. I really want to hear it."

"Well, we left for home and the ride was horrible. There was silence most of the way. Regardless of how I tried, she was so hard on herself that I knew I was getting nowhere, so finally I just let her be. I also did a lot of thinking and praying. I decided if I could help penitents trust in the love and forgiveness of God, then the same rules applied to me. I could not put myself above the forgiveness of God. I tried to explain this to Carrie but she wouldn't hear it.

"I was never so glad to see the main gate of the base in my life. Before she got out of the car, I tried to talk with her one more time and all she said was, 'As soon as I can, I'm going to Tokyo and go to confession at the Franciscan Chapel.' As she left the car, I said the only thing I could at the time, I told her to call me anytime.

"Two days later, I left for Sasebo, to a base on the Southern island of Japan, for two and a half weeks to fill in for a chaplain who had to be away and then went from there to Hawaii to meet my family for a vacation. When I finally got back to Yokosuka the end of the second week in February, I could not believe she was gone. Your grandfather had suffered a heart attack and because she was so close to her rotation date anyway, they let her stay and just report to San Diego Naval Hospital."

"Gosh, Tom, what did you do?"

"The only thing I could do, I wrote to her. I lied about that to people, even you I think. I said the letters were stamped, "NOT HERE". But I didn't send them to the hospital, I got her address from Miss Mullaney and wrote her there three times. She just never answered me. So finally, I decided to let her be if that's what she wanted. I didn't hear a word about her until Paula Ferrara, I mean Brandon, walked into my office at Bremerton, and then, your visit a few months later to Japan.

"I went through my own hell back there, but time, prayer and involvement in helping others helped me get on with my life and my calling as a priest. I prayed every day that Carrie found the same peace."

"Oh, Tom, I can assure you she did. I don't ever remember my mother being anything but a happy person and she was really active in our church. I think, she too, must have worked it out."

"Do you feel better now that you've told me?" she asked.

"I'm not through."

Standing up, Susan excused herself for the bathroom.

"I'm really starved. I'll listen all afternoon but I have to do it over some food."

"Oh gosh, I'm sorry. I got carried away, I forgot you came for lunch. Sure."

Tom watched her walk into the bathroom and thought that she didn't seem to be the least bit shocked or scandalized. I guess these kids have been brought up in a world where married priests and sexual openness is a much more frequent occurrence than in my day. She can't relate to a time when both were never considered or discussed.

Alone in the bathroom, Susan thought how wonderful they were having this talk, how helpful to Tom after carrying this burden of secrecy for over twenty years. "Actually, I don't know what the big deal is anyway. Two people who cared a lot about each other got caught in circumstances where they gave into overwhelming temptation. Probably happens everyday".

Returning to the living room, Tom set up two TV trays and they started their lunch.

"Um, delicious, I was starving."

"Eating for two," said Tom.

"No, that's how we rationalize our overeating. I am only supposed to be eating for one. I'm ready to listen some more if you still need to talk."

"What an up front, honest young lady. A lot like Carrie but with none of the scruples that kept Carrie's life so full of fear and self condemnation".

"Two weeks after you left Japan in 1985, I was just finishing up hearing confessions on a Saturday afternoon, when the whole thing stuck me like a bolt of lightning. Suddenly, the missing link, the inner scratch that was annoying me about you became crystal clear. I brought your face and hair to my mind and there it was. You look so much like my sister, Meg Ann; facial features, hair and all. Our family has produced, for four generations, a person with strawberry blonde hair. First, my grandmother Bartlett, next, my mother's sister, my aunt Roseanna, then, my sister, Meg Ann. That stimulated another set of data that took me awhile to figure out. I'd like to tell you but it is confusing. Let me get you a pencil and paper and you can jot down some notes at I speak."

Susan had no idea what Tom was talking about, but she decided to go along with him, giving him another chance to get it all out.

"Susan, the day after Pete left Japan, I went to see your mom who was so distraught. I told you about that. She was sad, guilty, depressed, the whole bit. I felt so badly for her and that's when I invited her into the group that visited the orphanage. It was around November twelfth or so because I distinctly remember that one of the last things that she and Pete did was attend the Marine Corps Birthday Ball which is always held on the Marine Corps Birthday, November tenth.

"At the dinner in Japan at the Carsons, when we celebrated your birthday, I told you before, the first shock was when I discovered how old you were because I thought Carrie's girls were a lot younger. All of these thoughts swirled around in my mind and got me thinking about New Year's in Gotemba with Carrie.

"More salad?"

"No, thanks, this was great, really hit the spot."

"Now, I'm no gynecologist but I do know a few basics like it takes nine months to bring a pregnancy to term. When I returned to my room from the church, I took my calendar off the wall and started working with dates."

Tom could tell Susan still was not following where he was heading. She was just being a good listener.

"I can't believe he is carrying this so far", she thought, looking at his distraught face.

"Finally, it all came together. If Pete had been your father, you mom would have to have been pregnant nearly eleven months. No, way. Then I reworked the pregnancy using January first as the day of conception with your October eighth birthday. Bingo! That along with your beautiful strawberry blonde hair left no doubt in my mind who your father is."

"Wait a minute, I guess I was just listening half heartedly, like you said, it's confusing. What does January first have to do with it?"

Tom got up, walked across the room, took her hand and with guilt and shyness in his voice spoke softly to her. "That's the night we stayed in Gotemba in the storm. Susan, I am your father."

She gasped and withdrew into the sofa in disbelief, still holding his hand.

Tom went on.

"From January first to your birthday in October is just the right amount of time for a pregnancy."

Letting go of Tom's hand, Susan said, "I'd be lying if I said I'm not shocked but I can't argue with you. It all makes sense. You'll have to give me a minute or two to absorb this. How long did you say you've known?"

"Since two weeks after you left Japan after your visit with the Carsons."

A faint hint of anger sounded in her voice. "You mean for two and a half years you've written me and held this secret while I went on for my search for Pete?"

"Yes. I didn't want to deal with it through the mail. I often wondered why you didn't come down on me harder for not contacting my buddies in high places in the Marine Corps. Of course, the reason for that was that I knew I was your father and it would be worthless information on Pete, but when you came in here today and announced that you were going to start a new search for a living Pete, I decided now was the time, that I had to put an end to your search. I had to stop it before you contacted Pete's wife in an effort to establish your soon to be born child's heritage lines. I never counted on you being so persistent. I can tell you all you want or need to know about your baby's genetic lines now. We Irish never forget a thing."

Susan got up off the chair and walked around the room, stopping to look at the view out the window toward the Pacific.

"All sorts of things are running through my head, for instance, I don't think I look a thing like you."

"I don't think so either but wait, if ever, 'til you meet my sister."

"One thing that does make sense is the story Mom held to all those years. She said that she was the only one who knew and she wouldn't tell because too many people would be hurt. Of course, I assumed it was because Pete was married and she was talking about his wife and kids. Now, I realize what she meant when said 'other people', especially since she was so ashamed."

"Did your dad know?"

"No, she told me she tried to tell him when they got engaged and he put his finger to her lips and said that it was all in the past and if she was at peace with it, then he was at peace with her."

"Must be quite a guy."

"Oh!, he is, the best," smiled Susan.

"I wish we could leave some of this for later, not have to cram it all in one visit but with you getting ready to fly back to Camp Lejeune and have your baby, it'll be awhile before we are together again."

"That's okay, I want to know everything, all the details and then we can catch up by mail."

"That's all there really is to tell. The only other thing we might do is decide what we are going to do about it, how we are going to act with each other, what effect we are going to let today have on our lives."

"I know. It's going to take awhile to get Pete out of my head. After all, for seven or eight years, I've thought my father was a dead Marine Captain. I've created such an image of him that I felt I could pick him out of a crowd. I have to erase all of that now and replace it with you."

"Susan, I think that's all you should do, think of me. John is and always will be your dad and the grandfather of your children. You can do what you like but remember, you said you wanted information so you would know the heritage of your children. Now you have that."

"Surely, you don't expect me to forget you now."

"No, not at all. I think we should keep our friendship just like it has been the past two and a half years. I think if you want, you should tell you husband Doug, but no one else, especially John. If he didn't care about hearing if from Carrie, we should respect that and at this stage not force him to hear if from us."

Susan closed her eyes and thought a minute.

"I think you are absolutely right and very wise. I do want Doug to know. We always said we would keep no secrets from each other."

Tom looked at her and for the first time actually looked with the thought that she was his daughter. "Where did I get the courage?" he thought. "I never thought I would see this day". He looked up and took a minute to thank his Maker. He knew the courage had come from someplace outside himself. It was the intimate grace of God, a gift freely given in a moment to help him through a tough time.

"Can you forgive me for the past two years when I knew and didn't tell you?"

"I don't think there's anything to forgive, but if it will make you feel better, of course I forgive you."

Flight 769
San Diego to Atlanta
September, 1988

After they were airborne for an hour, Susan decided this was the time to tell Doug. She didn't dare mention it in San Diego because she was afraid she would get carried away and tell her dad or even worse, Aunt Cathy and then everyone. Her mom would never want that.

Starting by reviewing what she had told him in the past, she took Doug through the entire afternoon with Father Paige. When she finished, Doug held her hand tightly.

"Well, what do you think?"

"I'm happy for you, love, because I know how much you wanted to know, but I would be lying if I didn't say that I'm shocked. When I think about it, they were just two human beings who cared about each other, but the whole thing about your father being a priest is heavy. It really shows me what a great lady your mom was to have kept that secret all those years and protect him."

"I'm not so sure she did it for that reason or to hide her own shame, but you're right, she was a great lady. In any event, I'd like this to be our secret. The important thing is that we know the background of the missing grandparent of our child. Outside of that, I am still an Ellington and my family is still my family."

"Fine, I agree. Just think, the baby will be here in just about a month. Do you realize we haven't even discussed names?"

"I know. I like so many, it's hard to decide. Let's play a game up here. We might get an answer and it'll help pass the time." She stopped the flight attendant and asked for some scrap paper.

"Here, let's work on boys' names first. Let's just list three boys' names and write down if your naming them after someone."

Doug laughed, "Susan, the organizer. Okay, I'll give it a try."

Each didn't take much time. Although they hadn't discussed it, obviously each had thought about it themselves.

"Now what?" asked Doug.

"We switch and discuss. If we are still speaking to each other after the discussion, we'll do girls' names."

Susan looked at Doug's choices. Not bad she thought. She could live with any of them. She read Kurt Douglas, John Martin and Martin John.

"Tell me how you decided on these?" she asked.

"Easy, Kurt, because it's a nice German name and Douglas for me, John Martin for your dad and my dad, Martin John, the reverse, in case we wanted to use Marty as a name for everyday instead of John."

Doug looked again at the list Susan had written. First, she had John Ellington Hauser, after her dad, next, she had John Douglas, after her dad and Doug, and lastly, she had Craig Ellington, her mother's maiden name and her maiden name.

"I like all the names we've chosen," said Doug. "Let's just hold them in our heads and eventually I think one will float to the top as the winner. That was fun. Now, let's do the girls."

That took a little longer but they got the job done and switched lists. Susan read Doug's choices. Susan Maria, he explained was for her and his mother. Next, Mary Caroline, because he liked traditional names and of course, Caroline for Carrie and lastly, Caroline Elizabeth, for Carrie and a traditional name he had always loved. Susan liked them all. She couldn't believe how each chose names the other liked.

Doug read her list. The first name was Catherine Craig, to be called Kate, after Mrs. Ellington and Carrie's maiden name. Catherine was also her own middle name. Next, was Anna Maria, after Doug's mother and lastly, Caroline Ellington, after Carrie and John. The project lasted an hour. They had great fun and learned they'd have no problem when the time came to pick a name for their child. They both liked all the names.

The four remaining weeks of her pregnancy seemed to just drag for Susan. The heat and humidity this time of year in North Carolina was unbearable. On October eighth, she celebrated her twenty first birthday and was so glad the baby was not born on that day, but woke up on the ninth and decided 'anytime, now baby, anytime'.

It felt funny not to be going to school. For all her life, except the semester after her mother died, she had started school in September. This year she worked on getting the baby's room ready and tried to think ahead to stock everything in the house that she would need to care for her infant.

At four o'clock in the morning, on October sixteenth, she awoke lying in wet sheets. Nudging her husband awake, she said, "Doug, wake up, my water broke. I think we have to go to the base hospital."

"Your what?"

"Come on Doug, this is no time to play dumb. We talked all about this in the parenting classes only they called it by its proper name, "ruptured membranes."

Protecting her clothing and the car with a big towel, they drove to the hospital. Susan was examined by the doctor on call and admitted to the labor room.

It was a long Sunday, but finally at ten o'clock that evening, she looked up in the delivery room to see the doctor hold aloft her first born screaming red child. She looked at Doug who leaned down and kissed her. "Thanks, honey, just what I always wanted."

By the time Doug got back home, it was eleven o'clock. Realizing it was only eight in California, he called John to deliver the great news.

"I'm too bushed to call everyone, would you do the California calling for me, please?"

"Sure," said John. "I'm always delighted to spread good news. There's not enough of it these days, and Doug, congratulations again, and thanks for your part in making me a grandfather."

Pacific Beach, California
October twentieth, 1988

Tom Paige had been waiting everyday hoping for a small note in the mail. He knew the time was near.

Today, he was not disappointed. He opened the mailbox to see a tiny four by five inch envelope.

He waited until he was back inside for he wanted to open the envelope with a letter opener to avoid creating raged edges on it. He knew he would save this one. He took his letter opener, the one with the Japanese characters for "long life" on the end and slit it open as perfectly as a trained executive secretary. From all the pink on the front of the card, it was obvious that the child was a girl. He opened the card and gasped. Through tearful eyes, he read:

Name: Paige Caroline Hauser

Date: October 16, 1988

Weight: 7 lbs. 7 ounces

What beautiful people he thought. They had found a way to include him without anyone ever guessing how and of course, no explanation was ever needed for the name Caroline. He lifted his heart to God and whispered silently, "Thank you Lord for little Paige Caroline and for being able to share in the joy in heaven today on Carrie's face, Carrie the grandmother!

He closed the card and turning it slightly to slide it back into the envelope, he saw some tiny words, printed on the back. Looking closer, he read in Susan's fine handwriting, "She has strawberry blonde hair!"